TABLE OF CONTENTS

Cover illustration by Robert Hand

SPECULATIVE AND SCIENCE FICTION

Welcome to GLIESE, BIG PULP's magazine of science fiction!

GLIESE (pronounced GLEE-zhuh) is named after the planet Gliese 581 d, the fourth planet in distance from the red dwarf star Gliese 581, and is an indirect tip of the hat to Wilhelm Gliese (1915-1993), a German astronomer who specialized in studying and cataloging nearby stars. Discovered in April 2007, Gliese 581 has at least 6 planets, one of which—Gliese 581 d—is believed to be within the star's habitable zone. Around the office, we call it Earth 2, and consider it a likely setting for the speculative and science fiction that appears here.

Leading off our science fiction section is our cover story, James R. Stratton's "On the Road From Galilee," a time travel tale with a twist. Then, find out what it feels like to be "Built for the Kill" with Malon Edwards, and join WC Roberts on a "Nether-Air Ambush." Take a rocket to "Luna Springs" on Patrick Hurley's dime and kill time at "My Dumb Summer Job" with Jamie Mason.

Enjoy the trip!

BIG PULP

fantasy | mystery | adventure
horror | science fiction | romance

Welcome to **BIG PULP** Fall 2011!

BIG PULP is a modern amalgam of the classic newsstand of the Golden Age of pulp and popular fiction. In this issue, you'll find science fiction and horror, romance and mystery—sometimes in the same story!—just as you would have on a street corner in the 1930s, when publishers offered dozens of magazines catering to all kinds of reading tastes.

Our cover story this issue is James Stratton's "On the Road From Galilee," a time travel tale in which a modern scientist discovers the means to rid history of its greatest evil. But can she pull the trigger?

In the rest of this issue, take a rocket to "Luna Springs" with Patrick Hurley; learn what melts "Sensitive Ice" in Keyan Bowes' romance; spend "One Night in Manhattan" with Edward Morris; hear what "Blood Tells" in Conda Douglas's Irish fantasy/horror tale; fight a mysterious "Virus" with Paul Von Hippel; ride along with Jennifer Povey "Aboard the Lady Maria"; and then treat yourself to more tales of aliens, cheating spouses, goblins, super-heroes, pirates and pop art serial killers.

Visit us online at www.bigpulp.com, where you can find even more great fiction and poetry, as well as links to novels, story & poetry collections, blogs and other publications by our contributors.

Thank you for purchasing this issue of **BIG PULP**. We hope you enjoy it and will help spread the word! Look for the Winter 2011 edition in December!

Bill Olver
Publisher

BIG PULP

fantasy | mystery | adventure
horror | science fiction | romance

BILL OLVER Publisher
contact: editors@bigpulp.com

*Visit us online at **www.bigpulp.com***
Follow us on Facebook and Twitter (twitter.com/BigPulp)

Submission guidelines are listed in the back of this publication
and posted online at http://bigpulp.com/submissions.html

BIG PULP is available for single-issue purchase online and at
selected retail outlets. To order, or for a current list of stores, please
visit http://bigpulp.com/store.html.

Big Pulp is distributed by Ingram Periodicals.

BIG PULP Volume 2, Number 1, September 2011

ISBN # 978-0-9836449-0-3

Published quarterly in March, June, September and December by Exter
Press. All credited material is copyright by the author(s). All other
material © 2011 Exter Press. *M, Gliese, Vice for the Lovelorn, Lore, the Chill of
Night*, and the *Fellow Traveler* © 2011 Exter Press.

James R. Stratton is a chameleon: by day, a mild-mannered government lawyer specializing in child abuse prosecutions, living with his wife and children in Delaware. But in recent years he's been forging a dark alter ego of genre fiction author through publication in venues like *Dragons, Knights & Angels Magazine, Ennea & Nth Degree Magazine.* The appearance of his first foray into poetry in *The Broadkill Review* is but another step in his master plan. Soon he will step into the light as his stories appear in 2010 & 2011 in *Tower of Light Online Magazine,* **Big Pulp**, and *Paper Blossoms, Sharpened Steel,* an upcoming anthology of Oriental fantasy. His final reveal, the novel *Loki's Gambit,* is under review for possible publication in 2011, when he will finally step into the brilliant light of day, triumphant.

ON THE ROAD FROM GALILEE

Out of the corner of her eye, Sarah Green saw Professor Johnson bustling into the computer room waving a sheath of computer printouts. Sarah grinned as she ignored her superior.

"Sarah, I need you to run these figures for me. If my math is right, I may have an answer to why time is directional."

The young graduate assistant sat oblivious at the computer with Beethoven's ninth blaring in her headphones. Growling, the Professor tapped her on the shoulder. Sarah slapped at the offending hand and spun around. "Hey, don't paw the goods! I heard you. I'll be with you in a sec." Sarah turned back to the keyboard and tapped in the last line of data. She smiled as old man Johnson fumed behind her. *Let him wait. I'm the best darn programmer in the department.*

Turning to the Professor, Sarah said, "Okay, gimme!" and snatched the sheath of printouts. After a moment, Sarah frowned. "This data is from a particle beam run on the minicyclotron. When did you get funding for that?"

The Professor just shrugged. "I didn't. Professor Hardcourt agreed to modify his runs to give me some experimental data."

"Oh. And what did you give him?"

"He'll get half the credit for the discovery if this data proves my theory."

"Lord!" Sarah snapped. "Do you have any idea how lame that is? He's done nothing, and gets half the glory if this pans out."

Professor John flushed and looked away. "Yes, that's true. But I've never been funded for this. It's the only way I can."

Sarah turned away. The old man was obsessed with this. "The arrow of time," he called it. Chuckling, Sarah began punching in the data. Professor Johnson walked away when Sarah didn't turn back.

Sarah first met Professor Johnson at the Physics Department faculty mixer.

"Why is it that time moves in one direction only? At the level of subatomic particles, either direction is fine. The math works in either direction," were the first words out of his mouth. *Oh lord*, Sarah thought as she smiled.

"How could the universe exist if all reactions ran from beginning to end and back again?" Sarah replied.

"I'm not saying that time moves in both directions at once. Hobson's work with proton/antiproton reactions proved that. But there must be some force that causes time to have directionality. Time moves in one direction because something is pushing it in that direction."

Sarah laughed. "Pushed? By who, fairies?"

Professor Johnson laughed, and launched into an incomprehensible monologue. Sarah grunted and nodded at regular intervals until she was able to slip away.

Sarah recalled this conversation as she glanced back and forth from the computer screen and the Professor's printouts. There was a small but consistent amount of extra energy in the reactions. Small enough that most experimenters would ignore it if they weren't looking for it. But this was the amount of energy predicted by the Professor's equations, enough to justify the existence of a force-carrying time particle. Sarah's heart thumped as she ran to find Professor Johnson.

◇◇◇◇◇

Professor Hardcourt's team spent three months trying to detect the time particle (or chronon, as Professor Johnson named it) before succeeding. After that, more were found once the particle team knew what to look for. Shortly, Professor Hardcourt found the antichronon and the department chairwoman talked of research grants and awards. Membership on the Hardcourt/Johnson team became the most envied post on campus.

One Friday night, Bill Jacobs, the team leader, took Sarah back to the particle beam lab after pizza and beer. "This will freak you out," he said as they climbed the stairs to the lab. "We just got enough control over the chronon stream to try this." Giggling, he set a pencil on the revolving stage where the chronon detector normally sat. "I'm going to give it a 10 second burst," he said. The lights dimmed and an almost subliminal hum filled the room. In the chamber, the space over the stage wavered like the air in a furnace, and the pencil was gone. Sarah blinked, and found two pencils on the stage now. The second disappeared as soon as Bill cut power. Sarah gripped the edge of the consol, panting.

"From what we've got so far, you have to apply a set amount of chronon energy to an object to break it loose from the time-space continuum," Bill said. "After that, the more particles that interact with the object, the further it moves along the time-space continuum. That was about a three second displacement. Things get really wild when we bombard a target with antichronons. The target appeared on the stage before we started the run. That really scared Hardcourt."

Sarah just nodded. *Jerk. He's got no idea what he's got here!*

Sarah felt a glow in her chest as she considered events. It all made sense. She always knew she was meant for something special. *This is why I'm here, what I was born to do! So, what should I try for? Riches? Too easy. The first event has to be something historic.*

At the next beer and pizza session with the team, Sarah asked the question, "If you wanted to go back in time and stop the Holocaust, what would you do?"

The other grad students hooted and laughed. Bill Jacobs slurred,

"Get Hitler! Drop a bomb in his Reichstag!"

"No! No!" another shouted. "Hitler didn't start the persecution of the Jews. It goes way back. Queen Isabella ejected all the Jews from Spain in 1492. They lost everything, and most died on the road. A couple of Popes ordered inquisitions against them before that. Real nasty stuff with dungeons and torture, all sanctioned by the Roman Church. You'd waste your time with Adolf."

"Hey!" Jacobs said. "Why go halfway? Get the man himself! Go for J.C. in Galilee. Without him, there can't be no Catholic Church, no Pope, no harangues against the Christ-killers."

"But what would take its place?" Bill asked as he filled his glass. The discussion took off on a tangent without Sarah. Her head throbbed as she considered. *Why not? It only involved one man at a well-known place and time.* Even as she considered it, she could see the math in her head.

◊ ◊ ◊ ◊ ◊

Sarah stepped onto her makeshift stage in the particle lab as chills ran up her spine. She'd spent six months brushing up on her high school Latin and gathering supplies. *So should I do this?*, she wondered as she looked about the lab.

Sarah was still debating when a sound like the rushing wind filled the chamber as her computer program took control of the equipment and the platform spun. A flash blinded her, and then she fell onto bare ground. Standing slowly in darkness, Sarah looked across a quiet, moonlit hillside and dark buildings below.

"Okay, I went somewhere," Sarah muttered. "Where?" There was no light or movement visible.

Sarah jerked around at the voice calling from behind her. A heavy-set man wearing a tunic, leather breastplate and metal helm stood there, hand rested on the pommel of a short sword.

In Latin, Sarah said, "I am sorry. I don't understand."

The fellow grunted and rubbed his chin. "I asked if you were lighting a fire a moment ago. I saw a flare up here."

Sarah smiled. "No, that wasn't me. I just arrived myself. Could I ask who I'm addressing?"

The soldier scowled. "I'm Septemus Lucius, Legionnaire third class, in the Fifth Legion under the procuratorship of Governor Pontius Pilate. And I'll ask the questions."

Bingo! Sarah clasped her hands and bowed.

The soldier nodded. "Who are you? What's your business here?"

"My name is Sarah Green. I'm traveling from the west to visit the holy city during Passover. I am afraid I'm turned around. Is that Jerusalem? Am I in time for the holy day?"

The soldier laughed. "You're on course. That's the west gate down there, and your Jewish feast is still six days off. But, you can't enter Jerusalem at this hour, the gates are closed. Settle down here until dawn. The gates open at first light."

Sarah nodded. As the soldier was turning to leave, Sarah called out, "Do you know if Jesus, the Prophet of Galilee, is in town? I was hoping to hear him preach."

The soldier turned and glared. "You aren't one of his followers, are you?" Sarah shook her head.

"Good!" the soldier said. "We almost had a riot when he arrived yesterday. You'd be well advised to stay away from him. Every time he speaks, people get all stirred up. If he keeps causing trouble, the Governor will find some excuse to cut his stay real short." The soldier drew a thick forefinger across his throat.

"I didn't know he was a trouble maker. I'll keep that in mind." The soldier nodded and walked off. Sarah sat with her back against a tree and chuckled.

"*En garde,* Jesus of Nazareth. I've come."

◊◊◊◊◊

Sarah entered the city the next day with the other visitors to Jerusalem swirling around her. Nobody paid her any attention. Jerusalem was the seat of the local government of the puppet ruler Herod Antipas, the center of the Jewish priesthood and the military headquarters of the Roman occupational forces. Foreigners were common.

Sarah spent her first day looking into the movements of the Nazarene. According to a wine seller at the temple square, the

5

preacher entered the city the day before surrounded by his followers and spent the day with the other rabbis at the temple preaching.

Later that day, Sarah cautiously followed the crowd into the temple square. *This is it, my first contact with the Christ.* Leaning against the wall, Sarah breathed deep to calm her thoughts as she drank in the chaos. It reminded her of a smelly flea market. The odor of animal waste and unwashed bodies assailed her. Merchants shouted and waved their goods. Stalls and tables were jammed so close together that narrow lanes just wide enough for one were the only walkways. Grimacing, Sarah pushed into the crowd and inched down an aisle. She tried ignoring the wheedling merchants until one thrust a scroll under her nose. "Blessed by the High Priest himself! Take one home for luck!" Sarah waved him off.

The aisle grew wider and the stalls plusher as she approached the the temple entrance, which formed the rear of the square. A number of speakers already held forth on the stone steps before the temple, surrounded by crowds. Most wore the purple-and-gold robes of the priesthood. But one at the far end of the steps was different. He wore a threadbare robe of undyed cloth and sandals. His listeners were even shabbier, many bearing crippling injuries. Sarah strolled closer, feigning indifference. *Is this my quarry?* Pausing at the edge of the beggars, Sarah strained to hear, then sighed. *Damn! He's speaking Aramaic. I'd love to know what he's saying.* She edged into the crowd.

He looked ordinary enough, tall and dark-haired like most men here, his arms and chest knotted with muscle from hard labor as he gestured. Then he looked up, right into Sarah's eyes. She thought her heart would stop. His eyes grasped Sarah and held her so she felt naked and alone in the middle of this clot of people. *Does he know who I am? Why I'm here?* The moment passed and the preacher looked away. *What was that!* Sarah gasped for air. The people around her stared. Sweating and panting, Sarah lurched out of the square.

Sarah later confirmed this was the Nazarene and shadowed Jesus over the following days, but he was always surrounded by crowds of disciples. When Sarah tried to follow Jesus and his entourage out of the city at the end of the third day, she was confronted by two burly disciples at the east gate. "Sister, the preacher goes for food and rest.

He will return to the temple tomorrow. Is there something we can do for you?" Sarah smiled and walked away.

So how do I get at him? He's always in the middle of a crowd. Joseph Caiaphas and the priests will move against him soon. Passover's coming, and history tells us the priests will have Jesus eliminated before that high holy day arrives. Perhaps once they have him?

Sarah wandered the route the Gospel described, from the temple to the Roman headquarters to Herod's palace and back, without inspiration. The narrow lanes were all on main thoroughfares where there would be crowds. The days rolled by without an answer. Sarah began to feel like a ghost at the feast, always hovering at the edge of the disciples as they sang, chanted or listened raptly to Jesus. Their joy and peace was a tangible thing, but Sarah wasn't able to join in it.

Worse, she could see events hurtling forward despite her efforts. Temple officials appeared when the Nazarene spoke, their numbers growing as they stood frowning and grumbling. Temple guards soon appeared at the edge of the crowd as well, armed and armored. That night as she lay in the stable where she'd been staying, Sarah could feel the weight of history towering over this place. *No! I can't fail this close.*

And then Sarah overheard a conversation in the temple square. "Do you know if Lord Herod plans to attend temple services on Passover?" a merchant asked a priest as he served him a cup of wine.

"No, thank heaven!" the priest replied. "Ever since John's execution, he stays away from the city. The priests threatened to riot the last time he tried to enter the Temple. I heard our mighty King is staying at his estate near the river for the holy season."

Sarah grinned. *There's nothing in the Gospels about this!* Sarah got directions to Herod's estate north of the city. And that was it.

◊◊◊◊◊

Sarah's weapons gleamed in the hot sun as she watched the road. She'd hiked out of Jerusalem just ahead of the priests and their prisoner after they'd left Pilate's Hall of Justice. *And they have to come this way.* Sarah loosened the .38 on her belt and glanced to the air gun and anesthetic darts on the ground.

Overnight, everything had gone as written. The city was aflame with wild rumors about the Carpenter of Nazareth; that Jesus and his disciples had stormed Herod's palace and claimed the throne, that Jesus had assassinated Ciaphas and declared himself high priest, or that he and his men had been slaughtered attacking the Roman barracks. Sitting with a group of pilgrims at the temple square, Sarah laughed as each new rumor circulated. At dawn, a priest strode out the main door to the temple steps and proclaimed, "Jesus of Nazareth, son of Mary and Joseph of the House of David, the so-called prophet of Galilee, was examined by the Counsel of Priests and admitted to the sin of blasphemy, to the High Priest himself. A sentence of death shall be requested of the Proctor-Governor."

◊◊◊◊◊

Sarah jerked alert at the sound of a horse's whinny and snatched up the dart gun. Pushing aside a branch, Sarah stared up the road. Riders cantered around the bend. In the lead was a priest sweating under the blazing sun in his formal robes. Behind him, Jesus rode on a donkey with his hands tied to the saddle horn, swaying with the motion of the animal. Bringing up the rear was a temple guard in full armor. Sarah raised the dart gun as they passed.

The gun coughed and a dart slapped into the guard's thick neck. He yelped and snatched the dart out. Clutching the feathered missile in his fist, the guard swept the heavy brush with his gaze.

"What ails you, man!" the priest shouted. The guard just shook his head. By the time the priest rode back, the guard was swaying in his saddle.

"This thing stung me," he slurred and fell off his horse. The priest glanced around as he dismounted, then bent over the fallen man. Sarah slid another dart into the gun, aimed and fired.

"Aiiee!" the priest screamed when the dart thunked into his left buttock. He yanked it out with one hand and yanked out a short sword from under his robe. "Where are you?" he shouted. "Come out and face me, coward." Sarah sat still, patient. Still glaring into the bushes, the priest collapsed with a sigh.

Sarah threw the dart gun into her pack and stood. Down the road,

8

the horses whinnied, staring. Nearby Jesus sat on the donkey gazing at her with a puzzled frown on his face.

Sarah pulled the cloth from her face and smiled. "Rabbi, I've come to rescue you. Wait there and I'll free you."

Jesus' frown deepened as she approached. "And who are you that comes to me unasked?" She freed his hands with her knife.

Sarah shouted over her shoulder as she walked up the road to catch the horses. "I'm Sarah Green. I heard about your dilemma and decided to save you. Now, help me corral those horses, we'll need them if we're going to get away."

Jesus slid off his little mount, but walked up the road toward the guard and priest. "I would that you had not harmed these men in my name. Such violence grieves me."

Sarah turned when she saw Jesus wasn't following. *What is he doing? We need to be gone!*

"Rabbi, don't concern yourself about them. They'll wake up tonight. Now, please help me. We've got to get moving before someone comes along. This is the main road from the city to Herod's palace. Someone'll be along sooner or later."

Jesus was kneeling beside the fallen priest as Sarah ran up and grabbed his arm. "I don't think you understand. These people were going to kill you. They still will if they recapture you. Now please, we must go!"

Jesus pulled free and glared. "You obviously do not know my teachings if you can say that about these men. I intend to move them out of the sun. I then will go seek aid in the city for them. I would recommend you take one of the horses and leave. The Temple guards will arrest you otherwise."

Sarah stared as Jesus dragged the priest off the road into the shade of a tree. "Are you insane? I've gone to incredible lengths to save your life, and you don't want to go because you disapprove of my methods? I've been planning this for months and I'm not going to let you screw it up."

Jesus glanced at her before turning to the guard. "You should consult with those for whom you are planning before you decide their fate. I am well aware of the risk involved in my mission. Your plans do not interest me. I have been following the path laid out for me for years. How can I turn aside now? Please, go away! I do not need your help."

Sarah jumped in front of him, blocking his path. "Look, Rabbi, I've seen the future. They're going to flog you until your skin is stripped away, torture you with thorns, and then drive spikes through your hands and feet so they can hang you on a big piece of wood. You don't want to stay."

Jesus brushed past her. "Sarah, I have long ago decided I will do what needs to be done. I have come to Jerusalem for that purpose and I will not be driven away. These things I must do, whether I will it or not. Truly, I have no choices available to me." Jesus grunted as he dragged the guard toward the shade.

Sarah drew the .38 and fired, shattering a branch next to Jesus' head. "Enough! You'll come with me. I'll do whatever it takes to make you."

Sarah saw only surprise in the man's eyes when he turned. Slowly, Jesus stood and walked toward her. "I have told you what I intend to do. If you mean to kill me in order to save me, then do so." Jesus stopped a few paces away and waited. Sarah could see no sign of fear in his face.

One shot! That's all it'll take. One bullet and the architect of Christianity will be gone. There'll be no showy execution, no symbol of sacrifice to drive the Christ-lovers to madness and murder down the centuries. He'll disappear, just another of the would-be messiahs that came and went during this era.

They stood face to face, frozen. Sarah found she could not pull he trigger, confronted the image of herself standing over this man as his blood ran into the sand, and her hands began to shake. *Can I kill him like this? Watch him fall and die right now? Will I be any different from the Nazi butchers if I do?*

After a moment, Jesus pulled the gun from her hand. He turned it over several times frowning, then hurled it into the bushes behind her.

"Rabbi, you don't understand," Sarah said. "The image of you dying on the cross will drive people to kill millions in your name. All because of what happens today."

Jesus put his hands on her shoulders and leaned close. "I do not understand this vision of yours. I can tell you this. Anyone who performs such acts in my name does not understand who I am. There will always be those who use others for their own purposes. That does not mean I am in error. The people need me badly. I cannot ignore that. Go home, Sarah Green. I cannot give you what you seek."

Jesus climbed onto one of the horses and galloped away toward Jerusalem. Sarah stared until he disappeared. *What do I do now?* She watched the other horse cropping grass on the side of the road. *Maybe I should write a book for the Bible. The Gospel according to Sarah! At least it'll be accurate.* Sarah ran to catch the horse before it got away.

◊ ◊ ◊ ◊ ◊

For the third time, Pontius Pilate read the report from the tax collector of Northeastern Judea. He could see that the numbers were wrong, but couldn't find the error. A soldier rapped on the open door and saluted.

"Well, what is it, Lucius?"

"Sir, the Jewish prisoner you sent to Herod Antipas is back."

"Damn it! What do I care if he's back? Can't you see I'm busy? Did Herod sign the death warrant those bloody-minded priests wanted?"

"No, sir, he didn't. But, you don't understand. The prisoner never reached Herod. He rode in on his own after the third hour claiming his party was waylaid on the road. The squad I sent out managed to capture one of the bandits."

"Wait! Wait!" Pilate set down the scroll and glared at the soldier. "This carpenter fellow just rode in after escaping his guards to report an attack? Is that what you're telling me?" The soldier nodded. Pilate sighed and shook his head. "Lucius, I will never understand these Jews, not if I live a thousand years. I'll bet he even has some high minded reason for coming in on his own."

Pilate rubbed his bald scalp as he stared at the ceiling. "Well, I'll be happy to oblige him if he wants a taste of Roman justice. Frogmarch his butt down to the cells and lock him up. If Herod won't sign the death warrant, I will. I don't need any more trouble with these priests. What about this other prisoner?"

"I can't get much sense from her. She speaks gibberish mostly. She's a foreigner from the western lands. The squad caught her near the ambush site riding a horse stolen from the temple guard."

Pilate nodded. "A foreigner? Okay, that means she's mine to deal with. I don't have to turn her over to the temple for judgment. And she was riding a stolen horse? That makes her a thief, so I don't need proof of her being part of the ambush." Pilate frowned and pulled gently on his ear. "Fine! Lock her in the cell with that other thief. We'll take care of both them with that carpenter fellow after the sixth hour today. That'll put a kink in the priests' guts. A woman nailed up with their two prisoners. Draft the proclamations and bring them for my signature. Now get out and see to it that I'm not disturbed until then."

Lucius saluted and strode from the room, as Pilate began rereading the tax records for the fourth time.

Malon Edwards was born and raised on the South Side of Chicago, but now lives in the Greater Toronto Area. Much of his speculative fiction is set in a near-future Chicago. He serves as a Grants Administrator for the Speculative Literature Foundation's Older Writers and Gulliver Travel Research Grants, which provide $750 and $800, respectively, for writers of speculative literature.

BUILT FOR THE KILL

Snouts low, golden eyes hard and focused on the lectern, they loped up the aisle. There were seven of them. Fabien had gotten as far as:

"When I was a student here at the Pritzker School of Medicine—"

before he noticed them. By then it was too late. Not as if there was anywhere to run, but four hundred and fifty people tried anyway. Fabien went down in a flurry of grey-black fur as torn robes flashed across my field of vision. Never saw the alpha male hit me. I shrugged him off, easy like, and then the other five hit me. Two on my arms. Two on my legs. One at my throat. My collar exploded open. My Dolce & Gabbana tie bit into the back of my fat ass neck, then burst into silk ribbons of tamarisk and obsidian. My favorite tie. Cost me seven hundred.

I'm guessing you want to know who the fuck I am and what the fuck I'm talking about. Not much to tell. My name is Levi Rucker, but everybody just calls me Ruck. Bodyguard for Fabien Desjardins. Was bodyguard for Fabien Desjardins. Should have known Stanford Sutton and the People Against the Transformation of Humans would do some shit like that. Fucking wolves. But then Fabien had only been my first gig, and Big Cat Smooth doesn't give out three hundred page dossiers with his merc assignments.

Not that any of this is Big Cat Smooth's fault. Fabien's death is all on me. But I don't need to be indebted to Big Cat Smooth anymore than I already am. From what I hear, I'm lucky to be alive in the first place. When I was in college, I bounced at the Soul Spot over on 87th and Stony Island to put some scratch in my pocket. That was how Big Cat Smooth found me.

The Soul Spot is this little throwback juke joint for grown folk. I was there to make sure young cats like me who wanted to step with the grown folk didn't try to shoot up the place. Three weeks after I started bouncing, Big Cat Smooth came up in there flanked by two of his mercs, looking for me. I was naïve. I had thought I could just walk into a club off the street and they'd make me door muscle.

Back then I had been six-foot-eight, three hundred and seventy-five pounds. What club wouldn't want me on their door? But things don't work like that in Chicago. No bodyguard, bouncer, security guard or bounty hunter could get work in this city without going through Big Cat Smooth first. Even the mayor handpicked his security detail from Big Cat Smooth's Mercenary Guild.

Miss Laurie knew that, but she needed door muscle in a bad way. When she hired me, she never asked to see a guildcard, and since I was just nineteen she would pay me under the table. From what I hear, Big Cat Smooth went easy on me that night. Not many people who freelanced merc were given a choice, let alone the choice I had been given: guild or broken legs. But then it wasn't everyday Big Cat Smooth came across a big motherfucker like me who can do what I do and move like I move.

Those wolves never had a fucking chance. Seven more closer to extinction. After the one at my throat ripped off my tie, I hit the floor and rolled. Heard a yelp and felt bones split and crush and snap beneath me. It felt fucking orgasmic. So I rolled again. Heard another yelp. Just a foreleg this time. Saw the wolf whimper and hobble away on three legs down the right ambulatory. Saw the alpha female tearing out Fabien's throat.

Every year for the past three years, Fabien had the University Of Chicago Pritzker School Of Medicine jack him off when he spoke at Winter Convocation, the beloved son he was. And each year I warned Fabien about being predictable. The commencement ceremony was always held in the Rockefeller Memorial Chapel on the corner of 59th and Woodlawn. It was straightforward when it came to security, but that didn't mean one of PATH's bullets couldn't find him. And they had every reason to put one through his head.

Five years ago, the Chicago Council of Guilds sold Fabien land to build an estate and a small, private medical center. The Council didn't give a fuck about the Lincoln Square residents who were against the deal. The Council also didn't give a fuck about the land itself: California Park and Horner Park, side-by-side public green spaces used by families for recreational activities. All that mattered to the Council were the free organ upgrades Fabien gave them whenever their dicks fell off or their tits reached their bellybuttons.

Which, of course, pissed off PATH. Not that they could prove anything shady was going on in Fabien's medical suites, but if there was one thing that made ex-wives, ex-husbands and hentai girls talk, it was scratch. But no amount of scratch could overcome the power and influence of the Council. Roma Russo, an investigative reporter with the *Sun Times*, found that out when her editor dismissed her sources as bitter and disgruntled.

So, with the Council in his back pocket and no threat of exposure for his illegal non-guild sanctioned activities, Fabien hired me, a live-in bodyguard with bison muscle and bone grafts, as a big fuck-you to Stanford Sutton and PATH.

But if it were up to Big Cat Smooth and Ignacio, I would be a much more complex moddy. Originally, I was supposed to be agha, like Big Cat Smooth, who I'm not ashamed at all to say, is fucking beautiful. That night he came into the Soul Spot I couldn't help but be transfixed by his slitted yellow eyes doing that weird reflection thing cat eyes did in low light, his short triangle ears twitching independently at every sound, and his well-groomed jet-black fur glistening over sleek muscles as he told me with slow, deliberate softness how he would shatter my legs with a twelve-pound double-faced sledgehammer if I didn't join his guild.

Since I decided I liked my legs whole and unbroken, Big Cat Smooth took me to Ignacio's chop shop downstate to do me up agha-bison after he brought me into the guild. Ignacio was the agha-geneticist whose team did up Big Cat Smooth, and was set up in Carbondale, on the Southern Illinois University campus. He had been this brilliant geneticist at Rush University Medical Center, but got caught in the middle of a black market organ ring run out of the hospital. Wasn't like he was the only one involved. But that was what happened when you were an arrogant asshole and pissed off your guildmaster.

Anyway, Ignacio and Big Cat Smooth had wanted to do me up agha-bison, but I figured I could have the same bulk and strength with bison muscle and bone grafts. I won't lie; I'm a pussy when it comes to agha-surgery. Grafting has been around for a few decades, but that symbiotic, cross-species cell-injection process bullshit is still new. Don't get me wrong, though. Ignacio is the best agha-geneticist there is, guild or no guild. I don't have to look any further than Big Cat Smooth and see that.

And it doesn't matter I would have been the first agha-bison. Usually, that's what you wanted; the less agha running around with the same skill set the better. Makes your merc services more in demand. No one would have been able to match my strength. Not even agha-gorilla. But had I went agha-bison, my days of getting ass would have been over. I mean, what woman would want to fuck a shaggy, bigheaded dumb ass with horns? And that was if I could still get a stiffy after the surgery.

Wasn't like I couldn't effectively use the added two hundred pounds of bison muscle and one hundred pounds of bison bone grafted to my frame, though. Ask those fucking wolves. They would have slunk back to Stanford Sutton if it wasn't for the alpha female. She made them regroup for another concerted attack. But they were tentative. Wary. They expected the roll.

Eventually the alpha male gathered his balls and leapt again, teeth going for the jugular. Broke his back with a bear hug. Vulnerable and exposed, the alpha female hamstrung me, but it was a superficial wound. Too much muscle back there. I lashed out with a size 18 EEE Bacco Bucci Crocket slip-on and got her in the hindquarters. Shattered her leg and hip.

Just in case you didn't realize, I'm fucking unstoppable. I'm PATH's worst nightmare. I'm the reason Stanford Sutton tours the neo-conservative television talk show circuit bitching and moaning about modified human beings. I'm the reason he and PATH have partnered with the Southern Baptist Ministers Coalition to protest me as a blasphemous abomination, saying I'm going to Hell for combining my flesh with the flesh of one of God's creatures.

Fuck 'em all, I say.

And fuck Fabien. He should have known some shit like this was going to happen. Each year Fabien does the Winter Convocation, I make sure I'm prepared to put my foot up Stanford Sutton's ass in case he shows up. I don't go over my protection schemes the night before Convocation with the Dean of the Chapel for the fuck of it. Skinny-ass bitch refuses to acknowledge my presence unless I use the correct terms for the chapel: narthex, chancel and ambulatory. Fuck her, too.

But like I said before, Fabien's death is all my fault. I had been expecting a close-range assassination attempt executed with a blade or some sort of short range, low-powered projectile. Made sense for me to stand in the ambulatory behind Fabien and off his left shoulder as he sat in the pew waiting to speak. Any assassin who knew his shit would have realized that was the best approach. But then Stanford Sutton got creative on me.

Now, I know what you're thinking and fuck you for thinking it. I'm a damn good bodyguard. I trailed Fabien three paces to the lectern, scanning the audience, right hand in my holster and on my nine millimeter beneath my black Dolce and Gabbana suit jacket. But who the fuck sends seven wolves into a church to kill someone?

Didn't matter, though. Fabien might have died, but none of those wolves got out of the chapel alive. After I shattered the alpha female's leg, she scrabbled across the chancel away from me, paws and good hind leg propelling her across the wooden floor. The other three wolves whimpered. Flattened their ears against their heads. Dropped their tails between their legs. Made to go after me a couple times. Thought better of it each time.

The alpha female stopped when she came up against Fabien's body, and, with a big fuck you to me, lapped up the blood pooling around his head. Unhurried. Slow. Like she was enjoying it.

So I did the only thing I could have done.

I rolled.

WC Roberts lives in a mobile home up on Bixby Hill, on land that was once the county dump. The only window looks out on a ragged scarecrow standing in a field of straw and dressed in his own discarded clothes. WC dreams of the desert, of finally getting his first television set, and of ravens. Above all, he writes.

NETHER-AIR AMBUSH

Flint strikes and sparks from steely eyes
light a tinder sky
the prairie underworld gone up to castles in the air
to lay seige, like the eggs of a salamander
in rings of Promethean verse
recurring incendaries
turned once more to stone (in death
our libations) *salut!*

Charon takes his pay from your abyss
and in the hollow of his hands a string of pearls
wiser than Solomon Kane
dances a cadenza

guns blazing
the James Gang on flying horses
dive-bomb the ferry shrieking like Ju-87 Stuka
harpies outside the Orpheum theater
in Memphis, TN

a sphinx uploaded in 3D
to snatch the rudder and patrol the Nile
hermaphrodite; death, the blending of a pair
bound in chaps and nylon fibers
for Pluto, god of wealth
confusion to tyrants
and the masses

Patrick Hurley lives in Chicago and works as Project Coordinator for the Great Books Foundation. His work can be found several anthologies, including the e-zines *Allegory* and *Niteblade*, the podcasts *Well Told Tales* and *Drabblecast*, *Ghostlight* magazine, and the humor/fantasy anthology *Strange Worlds of Lunacy* by CyberWizards Press. In between running marathons, he is at work on his first novel.

LUNA SPRINGS

"You can't wait to be rid of me, can you?"

"Dad, that's not true."

Arthur Prince looked away and mumbled, "Bullshit."

"Not in front of the girls, Art," Ilene chided. Arthur peered across the table at his giggling granddaughters and with grave precision, pronounced, "Bullshit."

His son, Ted Prince, sighed.

"Can't say I blame you," Arthur continued. "I'd want to be rid of me, too. I look half a corpse and smell like the other half."

"Dad—"

"Don't! I hate being patronized almost as much as I hate this wheelchair." Arthur tried to rotate his seat and failed. "You could have at least sprung for a hov-chair."

Ted tried to keep his voice pleasant. "I've been doing a lot of research on Luna Springs and it's top notch. The effect of lessened gravity and the increased solar exposure are supposed to—"

"Spare me the science lesson, son. It's one thing to cart Grandpa off to a home, it's another altogether to launch me to the fucking moon."

Both granddaughters gasped.

"Okay," said Ilene in her too-sweet voice, her eyes cold, "I think it's time for Grandpa's medicine."

Arthur grew pale.

"I don't want any," he whispered.

"Why ever not?" Ted asked.

"I don't like it."

"It makes you happy," they insisted.

"It makes me forget," Arthur mumbled between spoonfuls of Dolvertid. Soon, his eyes grew glassy and a dull smile creased his face. The girls giggled at the thin line of drool dripping from his chin.

"There, that's better," Ilene pronounced as Arthur drifted off into nothingness. "Really, dear, I can't wait until we get that man on the moon."

◊◊◊◊◊

Families crowded the launch platform, each with an elderly passenger in tow.

"See, they've got hov-chairs," Arthur grumbled, as Ted wheeled his father toward the registration center. The doors were opened for them by gentlemen wearing sky-blue uniforms, the sigil of a smiling silver moon gleaming on their chests. Inside, an old woman's voice could be heard screeching like a crow, "You're launching us into the sun! Admit it! You're shooting us straight into hell!"

Her family pretended not to hear her, smiling sheepishly at everyone else in line.

Some of the elderly stared silently at the shuttle with tears in their eyes. Some stared with anticipation. Most were on Dolvertid, and stared contentedly at nothing.

At Arthur's insistence, the family had *not* given him any of the wonder drug. Ted acceded to the request, in part because they'd run out and refills were expensive, but also because he thought his daughters' last memory of his father should be a lucid one.

When they reached the front of the line, Ted presented his ticket and signed the release forms. An instant later, two sky-blue orderlies appeared on either side of Arthur's chair, and began wheeling him away. Arthur looked back toward his family.

"Please, let me stay." Tears were running down his cheeks. They'd never heard him speak so humbly, so pleadingly before.

"I'll try and be more pleasant," Arthur continued, his voice trembling. "I'll even take the damned happy drugs." Ilene huffed.

The orderlies folded their arms. Ted paused. For so long he'd dreamt of a free schedule, an extra room, and a cease to unwanted querulous advice. Then he looked over to his wife.

"Bye, Dad," he said, kissing his father's forehead, "I know you'll like it up there."

Arthur's eyes widened in pain.

"Girls, hug your grandpa." They approached hesitantly, one and then the other. Arthur clutched them fiercely, until they started to shift uneasily and Ilene pulled them away. The family waved as Arthur was wheeled toward the rocket ship. With a face as still as stone, eyes red, Arthur stared blankly ahead.

The Princes went and stood with the other families on the observation deck as the shuttle began its countdown. As it reached ten seconds, everyone began chanting along.

"5...4...3...2...1!"

They all cheered, some louder than others.

As the Princes drove home, Ted's daughter Lisa asked, "Will Grandpa be okay?"

"Of course, he'll be okay," Ted snapped irritably. Ilene placed her hand on his arm.

"When can we visit him?"

Ted pretended not to hear the question and they did not repeat it.

◊ ◊ ◊ ◊ ◊

"Yes, I'm here to see Arthur Prince."

The receptionist looked up from her magazine.

"And you are...?"

"His son, Theodore Prince." *Who else would it be?* "I made an appointment a month ago."

"Let me see." The receptionist tapped her holoscreen. "Well, we received your request but it says here our resident declined."

"Yes, but there must have been a mistake." Ted tried to peek around at the screen.

"Not according to our files," the receptionist said in a serious voice, then tapped the screen dark.

"Listen, you don't know my father. He's stubborn, probably declined because he was upset or high on Dolvertid. He hasn't seen any family in a year. I'm sure he'd enjoy the visit. Look," Ted smiled, "I'm sure you can circumvent this, right?"

"I'm sorry sir, but we don't go against lucid residents' wishes here. It clearly states that he specifically does not want to see you."

"Lucid? My father's on a constant Dolvertid regimen! How does he know what he wants?!"

The receptionist's eyes narrowed. She'd seen the type before. The guy spends a month's salary to get up here only to be snubbed by a father he was probably desperate to get rid of. He was the fifth one she'd dealt with this month.

"According to my chart here," she said sweetly, "your father is progressing along nicely and hasn't received any Dolvertid in the last eight months."

Ted paused.

"Really?"

She nodded.

"There's no way, then, for me to see him?"

The receptionist consulted her holoscreen once more.

"Tell you what. I'll give you a two-hour visiting pass to the commons. If you don't mind visiting with the other residents, maybe you'll run into him."

Ted didn't relish the idea of being foisted upon a herd of insensate geriatrics, but this trip had cost too much to leave without trying.

Luna Spring's common room was not what he expected.

Rock music blared loudly over the speakers. There were no wheel- or hov-chairs. The residents walked around upright, laughing and flirting with each other like teenagers. They were...happy. Not the zonked out haze of Dolvertid, but the real thing.

And the smell! From visiting his grandparents as a child, Ted had memories of nursing homes smelling vaguely of piss and sour milk, but the aroma here was wonderful. Fresh flowers, perfume and cologne.

Ray Charles' "What'd I Say?" came on over the speakers as Ted watched an old man dance between three cooing grandmothers, alternately pinching and kissing each of them on the cheek. There was something familiar about him...

"Dad?!?"

The matrons unhitched themselves from Arthur. Ted's father whispered something to them, and they departed, laughing softly. For a moment, Arthur looked so angry that Ted felt like a kid about to scolded. But then Arthur broke into a smile.

"So, you came anyway, eh?" Arthur clapped Ted hard on the shoulder. They shook hands. Ted was amazed at his father's grip. For a moment, all he could do was stare.

"You're walking! You can walk!"

"Nothing gets by you, son."

"But how?"

"The orderlies gave me some mumbo jumbo about Daniel Stewart, this billionaire genius who wanted to live in the heavens before he died. I guess he did his research. They say the gravity's lessened here, air's purified, filtered with vitamins and proteins. Even the light's better. Luna Springs is on a mobile foundation timed to keep optimum reflected sunlight at all hours.

"But, you know what I think? Earth was holding on too tightly. Once it let go, we got something back. It's like being young again. The ladies here feel it, too." Arthur gave his son a wink.

"You can't mean—what about Mom?"

"What about her? I loved your mother. Always will. Everyone up here has lost at least one person they loved. Some were even forced up here by families that didn't want us anymore."

Ted looked away.

"I'm happy on the moon. Here, I get to have some fun before I die. Here, my mind is crystal clear. My memories come alive in the moonlight. Here, I have a new life…"

Arthur's face became cold.

"And I would rather not be reminded of the old one."

Ted flinched. Arthur smiled as if nothing had happened. "Don't feel bad, son. Think of me as I will think of you, as a memory."

"You won't visit?" Ted was surprised to hear himself ask.

"Return to that heavy, clinging bitch of a planet?" Arthur sighed. "No, I won't Ted. And I suggest you don't, either."

Arthur hugged his stunned son, then nodded. The two orderlies standing behind Ted came forward and escorted him back to the returning rocket.

Upon returning to Earth, Ted Prince refused to discuss his trip to Luna Springs. Ilene assumed the visit went poorly. It was too bad. All Ted had ever wanted, she believed, was for his father to be happy.

Jamie Mason is a Canadian science fiction writer and critic whose stories have appeared in *Abyss & Apex, On Spec, Not One of Us* and *Thaumatrope*. His young adult sci-fi novel *ECHO* is forthcoming from Drollerie Press. He maintains a website at: http://jamiescribbles.com/.

MY DUMB SUMMER JOB

I hate guarding the aliens. It's, like, so *boring!* I'm not allowed to take my eyes off the video monitor and my supervisor won't even let me talk on the phone. It's not fair and doesn't make any sense because there are Marines with rifles in guard towers all around the refugee camp who get *paid* to watch and the transport ships that keep landing to unload more aliens have guards watching, too. It's not like I can't *talk* and see the monitor at the same time! I tried explaining that to my supervisor but he just confiscated my cell phone and wouldn't even answer when I tried arguing about it, the rude bastard. Just wait 'til I tell my mom! She works for the doctor in charge, which means she's pretty important (which also sucks because if she didn't, I wouldn't be here). Adults are so frigging *stupid.*

My life was *perfect* two weeks ago. If I could go back in time, I'd choose that Friday. I was finally over at Jenny Cooper's house (yes, *the* Jenny Cooper!) after trying to get in with her crew for months and I was excited because now my summer was set and I'd get invited to all the cool parties. We were in the kitchen with the radio blasting, mixing margaritas and, like, dancing and goofing around and someone had just lit a joint when the announcer interrupted to say that a spaceship had begun orbiting Earth with aliens onboard and suddenly my cell phone was ringing. I wanted to cry because I knew it would be mom saying come home because the news meant she had to go be with her geeky scientist friends to work on their dumb secret project and it's just my luck that the government would ruin *everything* by picking that afternoon to make contact with aliens.

But mom ruined it even *more* by saying I had to go with her. I was, like, *mom, I can't believe this shit, are you serious?* And she said yes, the government was moving all the scientists and military people responsible for the aliens to this special camp in Nevada and that their families had to go with them because they'd be gone for months and the government couldn't, like, risk any leaks. So I had kind of a tantrum right there in Jenny Cooper's kitchen and started screaming and crying and I think I might have broken stuff I was so upset. I know Jenny was pissed but before I could apologize, this military guy came to the door and made me go with him in this black van to the airport. I had to board a plane with my mom and her geeky friends for this three hour trip and there wasn't even a movie or anything and I ended up here and it sucks because I have to stay in this stupid refugee camp in Nevada all summer and they won't even let me out to attend Burning Man, for Christ's sake!

Oh, *and!* I'm not supposed to call them aliens. They're *refugees.* Can you believe it? First they show up and ruin my summer and now I'm supposed to pretend they're from, like, *Viet Nam* or something. At first it was cool because all the networks sent reporters to cover the story and celebrities kept showing up to shake hands with the aliens (excuse me—*refugees*) and do commercials asking for donations. But that only lasted, like, *five minutes* before there was this earthquake or hurricane or something in Mexico (or somewhere) and suddenly everybody was more interested in that. The only thing left to look at since the celebrities left (besides the aliens) are the Marines and yeah, some of them are real hotties but they never say anything and won't look at me even when I wear my jean shorts with the flag patch on my ass. (Of course, I can't wear that to work. Mom got me this dumb summer job with the security company that has the contract to guard the alien dormitory and they've got this really gay cop-wannabe kind of uniform. It's so gross, I hate wearing it.)

So I work from, like, ten at night until six in the morning watching this monitor showing the dormitory hallways and exits because even though everybody knows the refugees are here, they still have to be protected. (*From what?* I asked my supervisor. *Angelina Jolie?* That was when he decided he didn't like me.) I leave work at six and sleep until one or two in the afternoon then make lunch for mom when she comes back to the trailer after helping the head doctor run tests on the aliens. Mom says they need to run these tests before the aliens are released into Earth's general population. *To do what?* I ask. *Find jobs at Walmart or something?* and my mom says yes that's more or less the plan. But not until she's sure they aren't carrying some disease that could kill us all. *Well, can't you, like, just call the planet they're from and ask?* and my mom says they tried that but couldn't get a response. (I guess they're not answering the phone up there on Mars or wherever. Which tells me that alien leaders are no different from ours. Once in charge, they stop answering questions.) I ask my mom why the aliens couldn't get jobs teaching us how to travel to other planets and stuff and she says the refugees are from the lower classes of their society and so don't have any smarts about spaceships or curing cancer or building awesome laser guns and I say if that's the case, then why are we bothering to help them? Then mom gets upset and calls me a selfish little bitch and I stay in my bedroom and play on the computer until it's time to go to work.

So, I'm still upset from my fight with mom and have some pot left over from the party at Jenny's so I decide to go get stoned. I wait until my dumb-ass supervisor takes his lunch then go outside to this area behind the dormitory building that's a kind of loading dock and, once the Marine patrol passes, I light up and take a great big toke of weed and look up at the stars. It's, like, really clear in the desert. As I start to get high, I feel a little better. I usually do. But that only lasts until I remember that I forgot to prop the door open behind me and now I'm locked out and the only way back inside is past the sentries at the front door and I know they'll smell pot on me and I start to get all paranoid. Will they shoot me if they know I'm wasted? Then I start to freak out and go all shivery like that time I did too many 'shrooms with my cousin Sara and we ended up in the Emergency Room getting our stomachs pumped together. (It made us closer, yeah, but it still kind of sucked.)

I'm thinking about all of this when the door opens.

I'm in that really freaked-out place people get into when they're too high, so the squeak of the hinges sounds like some monster screeching. And I feel like puking and screaming and peeing my pants all at once but I don't. Which is good because it's one of the aliens that steps out and I'm supposed to be guarding them and doing all those things at once would be, like, totally unprofessional. So, I try to man up and be all security guard-ish for this alien female. And I'm, like, *what are you doing out here?* And she tells me she comes out here all the time after curfew and that tonight's the first time she's ever, like, encountered anyone else, so she assumes I must be doing something *I'm* not supposed to be and she's all, *what are* you *doing here?* So we're at kind of a Mexican stand-off (which is such a weird expression because Mexicans are such totally mellow, non-confrontational people). I decide to kind of relax and see if that helps the situation any. *I'm on break*, I say and wait to see what she says.

And she stares at me almost like she can see inside me. And you know those big nostrils that they have? (Like, I'm assuming you've seen the aliens on TV, same as everyone else.) Well, she leans forward, her bald head touching mine and her blue skin jiggling with all that extra flab they carry around (being overweight is so gross) and she takes a good long sniff with nostrils the size of golf-balls and says I smell different from the others. (And so by now, I'm like totally paranoid. It would be just my luck to end up bumping into the biggest alien snitch in the dormitory but it turns out she isn't interested in being a fink.) She says I smell *relaxed*, which is a good thing because most of the humans she's met have been very tense and she says this causes her people to be frightened. So I tell her, yeah, I'm pretty mellow and she says that's good because it reminds her of this place back on her planet called a *do-em* where she says they gave everybody medicine to be relaxed and I ask what a *do-em* is and she looks at me kind of funny and says it's home. Then she says that she and her friends sneak out here all the time to enjoy themselves and that next time she'll bring some of them so we can hang and I say cool and slip back inside and return to the computer screen at my desk.

Next day I'm really excited because I start thinking about what the alien said about how back home they take "medicine" to be relaxed. And I think maybe she can turn me on to, like, some really wicked alien drugs and that maybe being out here all summer won't be so bad after all. So, I'm daydreaming about all of this while mom and I are having lunch and I'm not paying attention and she has to repeat herself when she says that the doctors have decided the aliens are more or less healthy and that we really have nothing to worry about regarding diseases and stuff. *Does that mean we get to go home soon?* I ask and mom says we'll be staying until they're sure the aliens are fitting into society okay, but that that might end up happening sooner than anyone originally thought. And I'm, like, so jazzed by the idea of getting home before summer ends and hanging out with Jenny and like that.

So the next night I'm out at the loading dock waiting for my new friend when the door opens and out she waddles with two other chubby blue alien chicks. And they're, like, *hi, how are you?* and I'm friendly even though they're overweight and have *no* fashion sense at all. Not the kind of girls I'd be seen dead with at school but out here in the middle of Nevada, it's, like, totally different. (Especially if you're, like, alone and don't know anybody and want to score some drugs.) So I turn them on to some pot and we all get high and they start giggling and jibbering amongst themselves about *do-em* this and *do-em* that in their funny language and I'm trying to follow along when suddenly I see headlights approaching and I know it's the Marine mobile patrol. So I get them to duck behind the dumpster with me and suddenly the car stops. I think we're about to get busted by the Marines until we hear footsteps crunching through the gravel and then the sound of a guy pissing. And by the way we all look at each other, I can tell that guys from their planet must do it the same way because suddenly we're all, like, stifling giggles and trying hard not to make a sound. Then one of the alien chicks makes a gesture like she wants to borrow my lighter so I give it to her and she sneaks away for a minute or so before coming back. Then we head inside. I make it all the way back to my desk before the patrol car explodes.

I watch it burn on the monitor at my desk for a while before my supervisor bursts into the room screaming at me to evacuate the building right away and I'm like, *duh—you don't have to yell* and I head home and change into my sweats and make a sandwich and download some new music onto my iPod before getting to bed (early for a change). And when I wake up and go for coffee, mom is at the kitchen table with this balding guy with little round glasses who she introduces as Dr. Ridley. (I don't like anyone who's older than about twenty-five so I kind of grunt at the guy and sip my coffee but when he starts talking and I discover that he has, like, a brain and a sense of humor, I have sort of a conversation with him.) Turns out he's a linguist from some place called MIT (why don't they just say "mitt"? Duh!) who's been brought in to help decipher the refugees' native language. He says the refugees are really brilliant the way they've been able to learn English so quickly but that acquiring their language might encourage the government on their home-world to respond to our radio messages.

So I tell him I've learned an alien word: *do-em*. Dr. Ridley says he thinks that's very interesting and asks my mom for a piece of paper and pencil to write it down (since his notebook and pen have gone missing from his office). While mom gets it for him, she jokes that lots of things have disappeared lately from her lab (which I don't believe because mom's, like, the obsessive-compulsive Queen of Clean—she's probably just saying it just to make the old guy feel better). So Dr. Ridley writes down my alien word of the day and waddles back to his office to do his lingual thing and I put on a Tae-Bo DVD. It's really important to stay in shape.

So when I get to work that night, they call a meeting of all the guards on night shift. And this really uptight Marine lieutenant comes in and starts barking at us about all the problems they're having with "containment" in the camp and that last night's explosion and all the recent thefts has everybody concerned about security and he talks in this alphabet soup of abbreviations and says things like "10-4" and "stand by" in response to peoples' questions. So I put my hand up and when he calls on me I'm, like, aren't the *Marines* really the ones responsible for guarding the camp, so why is he giving *us* such a hard time? And he goes all red in the face and upset and afterwards my supervisor says I'm a trouble-maker and I'm, like, *if I'm such a trouble-maker, then why not fire me?* And he says he can't because my mom works for the doctor in charge but that he'll add a formal Notice of Reprimand to my personnel file once he finds the proper forms (which have gone missing from his desk drawer), then he tells me to scram.

So by the time I arrive outside later that night, I've had enough grown-up bullshit for one day and I'm totally anxious to see my new alien gal-pals. But they don't show up, which really pisses me off. So I smoke the last of my weed and go back to my desk (I remembered to prop the door open; yay!). And it's, like, really quiet in the hallways, which is surprising since they have Marine guards *inside* the buildings now but there's no sign of them (which is fine with me 'cause I don't want to get into any trouble for being high at work). So I'm sitting at my computer screen, moping, when there's this knock on my office door and I open it and there's my alien girlfriend. And we're all, like, *hi, how ya' doing?* and I notice that she's carrying, like, a back-pack and a rifle. So I'm all, *what's up?* and she tells me to look at the camera by the main dormitory room, which I do, and I see a bunch of aliens sneaking down the hall and out the building past two Marine guards who they've got hog-tied on the floor. And the alien girl says thanks and it was really fun getting to know me and that it's been just like *do-em* and that perhaps we'll see each other again some time. Then she hugs me and leaves.

So I get home after my shift and mom's awake and drinking coffee at the kitchen table along with Dr. Ridley and that really uptight Marine lieutenant from the meeting I told you about and a guy in a suit from the Office of Science and Technology and they're all, like, really upset. And Dr. Ridley stops the meeting when I walk in and introduces me as the girl who found the key to the alien language. And I'm all, like, *huh? what?* And he explains that he ran something called a regression analysis on the word *do-em* and was able to figure out what it means and use that to decipher the rest of the language and communicate with the government of the aliens' home-world. And they're all sitting there staring at me and they still haven't told me what the word means and I'm confused so after a moment or two of silence, the guy in the suit clears his throat and speaks up.

"The alien government admitted the refugees were actually deported," he says quietly. "Turns out overcrowding is a problem in their prisons, too."

So now that all the aliens have escaped and are, like, robbing banks and convenience stores, I get to go home for the summer. (Yay!)

Despite the curfews and martial law, I guess Jenny's planning this big Fourth of July bash at her place and she's asked me to help organize it. (I'm, like, so jazzed!) I wish those alien chicks had cell phones so we could invite them, too, because they're really kind of cool (even if they are blue and fat). It's shaping up to be a great summer. The only bad thing is that all the soldiers driving around have really put a crimp in the street trade so I'm having a hard time scoring pot. You wouldn't know where to get any, would you? Here's my number. Call me if you find some and maybe you can come to the party. Oh, and don't worry: I'll, like, totally pay you for it. I've still got some money left over from my last paycheck.

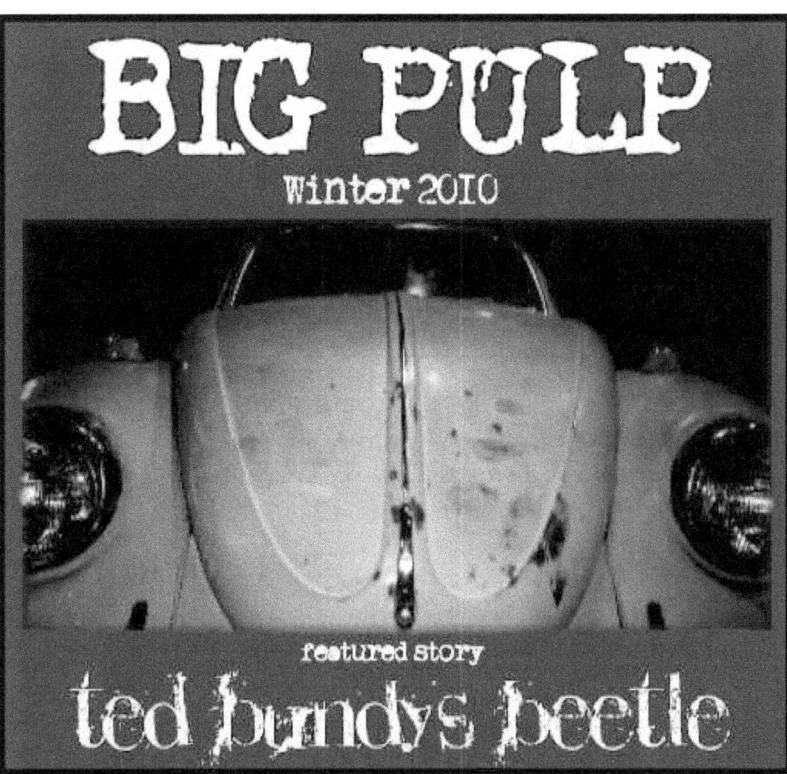
33

Vice for the Lovelorn

Romance, Heartache, Vengeance

As you may have guessed, VICE FOR THE LOVELORN isn't a typical romance magazine.. In fact, you might suspect a bit of cynicism influences our selections.

And you would be right.

However, even our cold hearts can be melted, and such was the case with Keyan Bowes' romantic fantasy "Sensitive Ice." We think you'll enjoy it.

Then, find out who's to blame for "A Kiss and Makeup" by Shannon Schuren; feel the charge when Michael Turner is "Struck by Lightning"; and unravel Walter Giersbach's "Misunderstood Identity."

Snuggle up and enjoy!

Keyan Bowes is frequently ambushed by stories, and took the 2007 Clarion Workshop for science fiction and fantasy writers in self defense. Keyan's work has been accepted by several magazines, including *Strange Horizons*, *Cabinet des Fees*, and *Expanded Horizons*, and is included in three anthologies, *Eight Against Reality* and *The Book of Tentacles* as well as *Art From Art* (forthcoming). Her story "The Rumpelstiltskin Retellings" was made into a short film by Justin Whitney (Sea Urchin Productions). She is currently working on two young adult fantasy novels.

SENSITIVE ICE

Tall, slender, dark smooth skin, and those eyes! Clear, glittering, the iris that looked like crystal. Those unearthly eyes were what made Anyango a super-model. They flashed above jewelry by Cartier, above perfumes by Xikain, above lipsticks by ReFactor, and today, above a small snow-leopard cub for a wildlife conservation group.

◊ ◊ ◊ ◊

Anyango hadn't been there when her family was killed, back in Nairobi, near the stadium where the marabou storks roost in the roadside trees. Instead, the death-scene played itself out before her mind's eye in a thousand variations, in clips from television news, from videogames, from action films. The tire marks where the red car careened out of control, crashed into a wall. The blood. The slumped bodies of her mother and father and little brother. The rush to the hospital, the frantic doctors who could do nothing. What she remembered was the gasp when her Aunt Mary took the phone, her scream, her words as she came over to Anyango who sat on the sofa, looking up startled from her Gameboy. "Oh, baby…"

Anyango was too frozen to respond. She stared at her Gameboy, pushing the same buttons over and over, her mind stopped. And the next day, Aunt Mary had screamed again. "Your eyes…Anyango, what happened to your eyes?"

It seemed strangely appropriate that the eyes she saw in the mirror were not the familiar dark brown, almost black irises. They glittered instead, like ice chips or diamonds shining where the light caught them. Anyango had not cried then or since.

An inexplicable pit had opened in her life where before there had been sunny savannah. Sometimes she dreamed about her family. She awoke a couple of times to Aunt Mary hovering worriedly above her. She looked at Anyango's blankly glittering eyes. "Oh, baby…" she said.

Eventually, Anyango and Aunt Mary left Kenya, moved to America. Aunt Mary got a job with the Refugee Reception Center, dealing with people as baffled as she had been by this new world. When she managed to scrape together some money, there had been doctors' visits for Anyango. The ophthalmologist sent her on to a series of specialists. Someone at UCLA got a paper out of it, a 19 year-old African female presenting with unusual crystalline structures contained in both orbits, no apparent effect on vision. No one could explain how the 32 degree Fahrenheit melting point of ice was compatible with the 98.6 degree temperature of the human body. No one tried. After a while, Anyango refused to see any other doctors. The diagnosis was idiopathic ocular aqueous crystallization.

It didn't usually affect her eye-sight, but when it was hot, Anyango sometimes felt her vision blur, and a ripple of panic. She took to wearing dark glasses all the time, even indoors. She told people she had sensitive eyes. Maybe they thought she was being cool. Boys in baggy pants with silver chains around their necks tried to befriend her, but their talk of gangstas and hos and bitches annoyed her. She finished community college, and went to work for a storage company, a climate-controlled environment where they stored furs and other delicate and valuable things for the rich and famous and couldn't-be-bothered.

In Cold Safe's office, out of the heat of the Californian summer, she felt protected by the gusts of cool air whenever she opened a storage locker. Sometimes she even took off her specs, put them down on the desk. They were very dark. She had bought progressively darker ones as her fears had grown. Now, she could barely see through them except in full daylight. She carried an extra pair for indoors.

◊◊◊◊◊

The doorbell rang unexpectedly. Clients usually called in advance to set up an appointment. Startled, she leaned forward to buzz the visitor in. Her glasses fell off.

"Fuck!" They were broken. She picked them up as the client entered. "Oh, sorry, Mr. Myrdal."

"Max," he said automatically. "Call me Max. I was on my way to the studio and thought I could drop this off..." He was carrying supermodel Sheliya's fur coat for storage. As Anyango looked up at him, he stopped short.

"Anyango! Your eyes! You have simply amazing eyes! Why do you always cover them?"

"Thanks, Max," she said with a courteous smile. "They're sensitive. I just broke my glasses. Shall I take that fur?"

But he wouldn't let the topic go. He invited her out for a drink. She politely refused. He suggested coffee instead. He called her home and spoke with Aunt Mary. Ten days later, he signed her with his agency, and Anyango said goodbye to Cold Safe.

◊◊◊◊◊

They were very careful. Anyango removed her glasses only for the actual shoot. The hot lights were focused on a substitute, and Anyango stepped into them at the last minute. Max ordered even darker glasses for these sessions, so dark that Anyango could not see anything at all except when under the lights. When she removed them for the shot, the dazzle glittered off her ice and gave her a brilliant dazed expression that became her trademark.

Other agencies and models tried to copy the effect with contact lenses, with digitally altered images, even with surgery. Nothing was exactly the same and Anyango remained unique. Max added no one else to his Agency list, and let his other clients go. Anyango seemed never to go out of style, never suffer from over-exposure. Her eyes were likened to diamonds. Her dark skin shrugged off the abuse of the hot lights and the passage of time. She was timeless, ageless.

◊◊◊◊◊

Timeless, ageless, and frozen. It seemed to Anyango that she saw no-one but Max and various camera crews, occasional marketing directors, a rival model or two, that she was alive only before the cameras. She had never been very good at making friends, not since Nairobi, not since the sparrow chatter of schoolgirls who did not know that Fate could swoop on them like a falcon. These days, the mystique of her super-model status seemed as much a barrier as her permanent dark glasses.

People had been good to her, and she was grateful. People like Aunt Mary, people like Max, people like some of her professors, even people like George Blair at Cold Safe. As a substitute for warmth, she practiced what she learned to call, in this America, random acts of kindness. A gift here, a note there, a new house of Aunt Mary's choosing. It kept her tenuously connected to the human race.

Max, Aunt Mary told her, might be interested in more than a professional relationship.

"He let all his other models go to rival agencies, girl," said her Aunt Mary. "That man is not hedging his bets. He goes out of his way to be nice to me, like I was family to him. A man does that for the future in-laws. I thought he would ask you out."

"He did, a few times, but I was too tired. My eyes are sensitive."

◊ ◊ ◊ ◊ ◊

Today's shoot was for Fauna Friend, a wildlife group. Anyango had waived her fees. Conservation was a cause important to her.

The session had gone on much longer than usual. She was tired. The snow-leopard cub had gone past curiosity, into playfulness, fallen into a nap, and awoken curious again. It had gotten away from its trainer a couple of times. She fondled the animal as it lay in her lap. It seemed about to curl up for another nap. It was really a delightful little creature. Her eyes closed to protect them from the glare of the lights, her mind drifted back to Kenya.

Instead of the endless variations on violent death, she recalled other cubs, lion cubs back in the savannah, where zebra grazed as casually as cattle in the Rift Valley. Clusters of shy giraffe stalking about the acacia-spotted plains. The protective mother elephant whose baby was always guided to the off-side, away from the vehicles and staring human eyes. Flying gazelles, and waterbuck and bunny-sized dik-diks that looked like plush toy deer. That had been their last trip together, just a few hours from Nairobi. The day they were leaving, they had come on the pride of lion lazing in the shade of a bush, two small cubs about the size of this one in her lap, playing with their mother's tail. The animals ignored their car with the air of bored celebrities.

It was a long time since she had thought of it, thought of her family in any way but the car crash. Tears welled up in Anyango's eyes. She quickly suppressed them, fearing what they might mean.

"One more shot and we're done!"

She shook her head to clear it, then picked up the purring cub, held him under her chin, and stepped into the lights. Max removed her glasses, she opened her eyes, there was a click. She closed her eyes and Max put her glasses back on for her. She cradled the sleepy animal. The lighting tech killed the lights. With her dark glasses, she could see nothing. Max rushed to her elbow.

"Here, give the little guy over here." He took hold of the animal to return it to its handler. "Ready?" he asked.

But before she could say anything, the cameraman exclaimed, "Oh, shit! Shit shit shit!"

Ten pairs of eyes turned to him.

"There's something wrong! Nothing's come out."

A technician hurried over and fiddled with the camera. "Nothing much," he said dismissively. "It needs a new chip. This one's worn. I told you to replace it this morning."

"But you never gave me one. It's your job to keep the spares."

"You should have asked..."

The Director took charge. "Stop squabbling, you two. Crew, stay where you are. Sorry, folks, we're going to do this over. Jen, bring Fluffles to the make-up counter, let's give him a quick brush. Max and Anyango, stand by. Shanika, we probably won't need to adjust the lighting again, but stand by anyway."

"Max, I can't," Anyango whispered. "It's taken too long. We'll have to come back tomorrow."

The Fauna Friend president, watching the whole process anxiously, overheard and shook her head. "Anyango, please? We don't have the budget to rent the studio and the leopard and the crew again. We're grateful, really grateful, that you're waiving your fees. But if we don't do it now, we can't do it at all."

"I wish I could, but I can't," said Anyango. "I have sensitive eyes."

The president sounded ready to cry. "We've spent a big chunk of our budget on hiring this outfit," she said. "We can't come back. We'd have to pay for it all again. And if we don't have the shots, it will all be wasted."

"I'm sorry," said Max brusquely. "Anyango supports your cause. But she can't do another shoot now."

"It's not just paying the studio," said the woman. "This was the only day they had available this month. You don't know what it took to pull this whole thing together on a small budget. The commercial is due to run early next month. We already paid for the space."

"I'm sorry," said Max.

"Wait," said Anyango. She turned to where she heard the photographer still arguing with the technician. "How long will you need to retake it now?"

"Hey, everything is already set up," he said. "We can do this in 20 minutes."

"Let's do it, then."

Max looked dubious. "Anyango, it's okay if we don't. The contract specifies..."

"I know," said Anyango. "But it's only 20 minutes. They can't afford to come back."

"You'll do it then?" said the president. She sounded jubilant. "Anyango, thank you!"

There was a whirl of activity as everyone took their positions. Fluffles allowed himself to be brushed and carried back to Anyango. She stepped into the light again. Suddenly, the cub raised a paw and batted her glasses off.

"Fuck!" she exclaimed, and bent over to pick them up. The cub scrambled out of her arms and escaped. Jen ran to intercept him as he scampered amidst the equipment. Too hot, too bright, thought

Anyango, and she stepped quickly out of the lights. Even with her eyes shut, the glare was considerable. She raised her lids for a second, and realized her vision was blurring. She covered her eyes with her hand. Someone retrieved the glasses for her, but the lenses had popped out of the frame.

"That damn fool optician !" swore Max. "I told him unbreakable."

"My outdoor specs are in my bag," Anyango said.

Jen captured Fluffles and brought him over. Everything was made ready for the camera again, and Anyango positioned the wriggling little animal under her chin. The photographer took a succession of shots. Anyango could feel her eyes beginning to burn.

As soon as the director said "Okay, that's it," she handed Fluffles to Jen and turned to Max for the spare glasses. Max was right there, holding her bag, a large leather bucket full of impedimenta. She reached in, feeling around for her shades. Her eyes felt as though they were on fire. She put on the specs, and stumbled out.

Max put his arm around her, guiding her. His face was very close to hers. She could feel his warmth, and leaned into it.

"Come on, Anyango, I'll take you home. Careful, there's a step."

It was cool and dark in his car. He had put in little curtains on the windows.

"My eyes, they really hurt. Did I overdo it?"

"Let's get you home." His tone was concerned, protective.

"I can't go home like this; Aunt Mary will worry terribly…"

"To my place, then. And a doctor if needed."

"Doctors," she said bitterly. "What do they know?" She kept her eyes closed under her sunglasses.

The car stopped. Max came around and helped her out of the vehicle and in through the door of his house. He had his arms around her.

"Let me look," he said. She put her face up for him to see her eyes, but kept them shut. He blew gently on her closed eyelids. "Let me look, Anyango."

His voice was tender with suppressed worry. Impulsively, despite the burning, she pulled his face to hers, and kissed him on the mouth, hard. Even as she did so, it seemed the pain lessened. Eyes still closed, she moved back until she felt the couch behind her. She sat, drawing him down with her.

"Anyango?"

"Shh." Her hands were fumbling around his collar now, down his shirt front. She put her hands behind his head, and pulled it toward her, and kissed him again. All the while, she kept her eyes tight shut. The pain was definitely ebbing. Her hands went to his waist.

"Anyango, are you sure?"

"Come on, Max," she said impatiently, and at last he put his hands over hers, helping her.

◊◊◊◊◊

Afterward, Anyango still dared not open her eyes, though she longed to look at Max. They no longer hurt, but were they well? She had to know but feared to find out.

"Max. Do you think I'm okay?"

He took her face in his hands. "Open your eyes, Anyango," he said. She could hear apprehension in his voice. What would he find underneath her lids?

She looked up at him, trying to read what he saw in his face.

He had a strange expression. "Your eyes, Anyango. They're different. Take a look."

They were. Instead of the cold clear crystal of ice, the eyes in the mirror were dark and bottomless and full of stars.

Shannon Schuren has been published in *Toasted Cheese Literary Journal, The Chick-Lit Review*, and **Big Pulp**, among other venues.

A KISS AND MAKEUP

"Don't." Annika waved the waiter away from the empty place setting on the other side of the table, her voice husky from too many cigarettes, too many drinks, too many lies swallowed year after year until she could no longer breathe. Explanations would be lost on the attending stranger, so she offered up her glass instead.

"Dirty martini."

He'd spit in it, retribution for the hours she'd taken up his table nursing her cocktails and despair, for the rings of dark lipstick she'd left on the rim of her glass.

Her roommate had done her makeup, the two of them clad only in lacy underwear, fishnet stockings, and padded bras. They'd done shots to calm her nerves and giggled at the names of the powders and paints. Brute Champagne for her eyelids, Arsenic Lace for the lashes, Maiden's Pallor on her cheeks. The perfect colors for an impending engagement.

Or a funeral.

Kevin perched backwards in his chair, his own peony lips pursed in an exaggerated pout as he lined hers with Blood Diamonds. When he finished, he blew her a kiss. "Gorgeous lipstick, darling. Almost as hot as my own."

His was called Lolly Pops, created specially for him by an adoring fan and named after his own one-man show.

"Are you sure you want to go through with this? You should leave him instead, before he breaks your heart. Hop a plane and charge it to the bastard's credit card. Fly to Fiji or Tahiti, drink spiced rum while nubile cabana boys lather your naked body with cocoa butter."

Kevin's fantasies were always sexier than her own.

There would be no naked cabana boys for Annika. Love, that was her aphrodisiac. A half-carat diamond nestled on her finger. A white satin gown with a train so heavy it pulled piles of rose petals behind her as she walked down the aisle. Tow-headed children who shrieked as their father chased them barefoot across a carpet of fern colored grass.

A rush of cold air and tinkling bells wrenched her from the fantasy and back to the candle-lit restaurant. And then he was beside her, her golden Adonis, her flawed Prince Charming.

Her Achilles.

"Sorry, I'm late," Graham apologized. "Work was hell. Traffic was awful."

The lies fell from his lips and lay discarded on the table next to her lipstick stained napkin. Neither virtue nor tidiness had ever been his strong suits.

"What's that on your collar?"

Her hands, naked aside from the Veiled Threat polish, remained folded in her lap as he struggled to view the pink kiss pressed against the cotton fabric.

"Smoochy." His voice was low, his eyes teasing.

The nickname always made her melt. Even now, she wanted nothing more than to sink into his arms.

If only it had been cheap makeup. Maybe then she could have ignored it. Forgiven him. Forgotten all of this.

But this lipstick had a name.

Lolly pops.

Michael D. Turner is a writer from Colorado Springs, Colorado. His writing has appeared multiple times in **Big Pulp**, and in *Aberrant Dreams, AlienSkin, Between Kisses, Flashing Swords, Every Day Fiction,* and *Tales of the Talisman.*

STRUCK BY LIGHTNING

Milo was struck by lightning.

He knew it was lightning because once, when he was a kid, he'd gone camping near the top of San Jacinto and a thunderstorm had come up right in the camp. He and the other kids had huddled in their sleeping bags under plastic ground-cloths folded over to keep out the rain while great bolts of lightning had flashed sideways through the camp, splintering a dozen trees, covering one of the adults with wood-chips blown out of a pine tree, filling the camp with the smell of ozone and making everyone's hair stand on end. It had been a joyful, terrifying experience and he remembered it vividly. So when he was struck by lightning thirty years later he knew exactly what it was.

What he didn't understand was how he'd been struck when, as far as he could remember, he'd been standing indoors. Was, in fact, still standing indoors, in the kitchen-like vestibule near his cubical where the coffee maker lived. Unharmed, as far as he could tell.

He'd definitely been lightning-stuck though. There wasn't a mark on him but his hair, or what was left of it around the ever-expanding bald spot, was standing on end and his shoes were smoking. When he took a step forward he saw that the rubber soles had melted right off the leather uppers and onto the tile floor with the gel insoles he'd started wearing two years ago stuck in the goo, leaving the uppers flapping loosely over his bare, unscorched feet.

Where were his socks? Details were a little confused but Milo was sure he usually wore socks. There were no socks in evidence now. He lifted the cuffs of his slacks to check. Just bare, hairy legs; one for each cuff. Maybe he'd been rushed this morning, or unable to find a clean pair?

Socks weren't the only things missing. There was no coffee-maker on the Formica counter near the sink. No fridge beside it either. There was a space for a fridge, an abrupt end to the counter despite a continuation of the overhead cabinets suitably raised to accommodate a full-sized refrigerator, but the flooring in that space was unmarked. No dust, no black footprint to mar the neutral pattern of the tile. No discoloration of the wall-paint to show an appliance had ever graced this space.

Nothing in the alcove showed any sign of habitation except the two blubs of rubber now cooling into the tile that marked where he'd been standing. Milo stepped out, off the tile of the break area and into the cheery blue of the office carpet. It felt soft and clean and new under his bare feet.

The office was silent. Not quiet like it was when Milo stayed late to finish some timely report due the next day and all his co-workers left before him, but silent. There was no hum of computer fans, no crinkle of Post-it notes and cut-out comics swaying in the breeze of the A.C. He looked into the first cubical, which belonged to Stan Williams, sales guru and office clown, but it was empty. Just slate-blue cloth cubical walls and an unused desk. No computer, no filing cabinets, no chair. Not even dust.

Milo wandered the cubical maze like a mouse in a lab and everywhere it was the same. No chairs, no computers, no office furnishings beyond simple desks, desks without drawers, mere faux-wood benches of desk-like potential, all the same. He looked for his cubical, his special place of belonging where he did his work but he wasn't certain he found it. They were all the same and they were all empty.

Empty also were the offices that lined the perimeter of the cubical farm. No brass plates slid into the holders beside each door, no signs of occupation. Just clean, unused desks, though the offices had chairs as well; cheap, impersonal swivel chairs with plastic backs and cloth seats. The office blinds were all closed.

He crossed an office, splayed two vanes of a venetian blind with his fingers to peek out the window. Sunlight glinted off another office building. He could not see the ground from here, could not see past the glare on the glass of the other office building. He crossed the cubical farm again, shoe uppers flapping on his bare feet, to the corner office on the other side. There he pulled the cord to raise the blinds and stared out the window.

And saw another office building, blue-glass windows between panels of pebble-textured concrete wall, with closed blinds. He looked down. From here Milo could make out the ground around the buildings, with concrete walkways between fake stone planters filled with neatly trimmed low evergreen plants. Small trees dotted the evergreen hedges like mile-markers along a highway, and neatly tended lawn hid behind the planters. Nothing moved; no breeze stirred the leafless branches of the trees, no stray papers tumbled along the walk edge. It was like the office, pristine and still. Unoccupied.

Yanking the cord on the other blinds revealed another faceless building. Something stirred in a window partway down, but Milo couldn't make it out. He dashed out of the corner office and partway down the floor to the middle office near the elevators. He raised the blinds and there, right across from him in the other building, was a girl.

Hair stood out in all directions from her head, frizzy not-quite-blonde hair. She was wearing a light-colored dress covered with little flowers. Milo waved his arms, frantically crossing them over his head, but she couldn't see him. The same sun that'd blinded him when he looked the other way blinded her.

Milo backed out of the empty office and looked out across the silent cubical farm. What was it that he did here? He wasn't sure. Whatever it was, he wasn't doing it now. He crossed over to the elevators and pushed the down button.

No light came on. The elevators were as quiet as the office. Across from them, behind a brass-handled door he'd never opened, the stairs. The stairwell was like the office, clean, new, unused, and empty. The stairs were grey-painted metal planks with raised cross-hatched markings and matching grey railings, never meant for workers filing in and out, just emergency evacuations. This seemed an emergency to Milo. His feet had grown accustomed to the clean soft newness of the carpet. The metal stairs were cold, the hatch-marks sharp-edged against their soft, uncalloused flesh. Four flights of stairs took him to the lobby. He wasn't even temped to test the other floors for occupancy.

Outside the air was crisp, a pleasant coolness. The smooth concrete pathways burned cold under his feet. He threaded the meaningless greenery to the next building, checking for signs of motion. The building lobby was as still as the one he'd left. Milo stepped off the path and worked his way around the building on the soft green lawn. He had to step over a planter to get back to the path as he came opposite the doors. The glass-paneled doors swung open silently when he pushed. That was good; Milo had been half afraid they'd be locked.

The lobby was the opposite layout of his building's, mirrored sameness. Elevators where stairs ran in his, just as dead as in his building. He pushed open the stairwell and started up the grey metal stairs. A sound came from above; door opening, soft foot falls.

Her feet came into view on the stairs above and Milo stopped. They were clean, pretty feet with nails painted light pink, the strap of a shoe still dangling from one ankle. Their owner worked her way slowly down the hatched stairs, and as she turned and looked down at Milo he stepped back, stunned. The snub nose, the light freckles marking her warm skin, the flowering dress over her slight frame, her poor, poor hair all askew. She was perfect.

"Uhh, hi!" Milo knew it was the dumbest thing he could possibly start off with, banal and content free. He never could talk to girls. She stared at him for a moment like a deer caught in the headlights of a semi-truck and he was sure he'd emerge from this with his record of success unaltered. Then she responded.

"Hi." For a long minute Milo thought that would be the whole of it, like a hundred thousand encounters with the opposite sex had gone for him. Then she continued. "I'm Laura."

Laura, that was promising. She stared at him uncertain, and Milo realized she was expecting some sort of reply. "Uhh, I'm Milo." Was he going to start every sentence off with that annoying *uhh*? "From the next building over."

"I didn't see anybody there," Laura said, talking breathlessly, "I couldn't see past the glare."

"I saw you." Milo assured her. Well, he hoped he was assuring her. He sounded stupid to his own ears. "You want to get lunch?"

Laura smoothed down her hair, sending a static charge crackling along her fingers. "Maybe something quick?"

"A dog?" Milo ventured. "There's usually a cart-guy around the corner."

"Okay."

He held the door, to the lobby, to the walk outside. Birds chirped in the distance. A pigeon cooed, ambling past their path. Their hands clasped as they waited for the elegant-feathered vermin to pass by.

Around the corner, the vendor stood at his cart.

"Two dogs," Milo said, glancing at Laura. "Everything?" She nodded and smiled. "Two dogs with everything."

"Here you guys are," the vendor held out two steaming dogs already covered with various vegetables. He handed her a dog and she took a bite. Juice, steaming hot, spurted out of the dog as she bit it, and she smiled. Together Milo and Laura walked back between their respective office buildings.

"Can I call you after work?" Milo asked.

"You can call me what you want, but I answer to Laura," she said, and then she gave him her number. He walked her back to her door, busy people walked around them. There was a crowd in the elevator he put her on. He had to hustle back to work.

His building was crowded now as well. He couldn't quite understand the looks he got while waiting for the elevator. He got off on his floor and headed back to his cubical. Steve from the next cube met him along the way. "Dude," Steve said in a whisper, "where are your shoes?"

Walter Giersbach's fiction has appeared in *Bewildering Stories, Every Day Fiction, Everyday Weirdness, Lunch Hour Stories, Mouth Full of Bullets, Mystery Authors, OG Short Fiction, Northwoods Journal, Paradigm Journal, Short Fiction World, Southern Fried Weirdness, Written Word* and **Big Pulp**. Two volumes of short stories, *Cruising the Green of Second Avenue*, have been published by Wild Child Publishing (www.wildchildpublishing.com).

MISUNDERSTOOD IDENTITY

The love letter in our mailbox Saturday was addressed to me. I had nothing to hide. Delores, who was looking over my shoulder, saw the "Darling Kevin" salutation, and freaked out.

"Is there something you want to tell me, Kevin?" My wife of 12 years put on her pit bull look, the one she wears when I forget to put out the garbage or miss the kid's school bus.

"Delores, I have never met this…this Sharlayne in my life. It's just another one of those mash notes that come every now and then. I mean, how could I even meet this babe? I go to editorial meetings, see my publisher. I come home. No business trips. And the letter's postmarked San Francisco."

"Then how do you know she's a babe? Maybe she's an editorial assistant. She certainly knows where the famous Kevin Alter lives."

Delores was right on one count. I'm Kevin Alter, mystery author and runner up for an Edgar Award two years ago. But now there's this bozo somewhere stealing my fame and identity, passing himself off as me.

This has been going on for half a year. Somebody had stolen my very being and was masquerading as me all over the country. From the letters and calls, I deducted he'd show some babe a copy of my latest book, *Prelude to a Killing*; point to the black-and-white photo on the back cover and, *Pow!*—next thing he was in bed with her. The babe would Google my name and *Pow!*—up would come Woodmere

Terrace in Oakville, New Jersey.

I guess the imposter and I looked somewhat alike. I told my editor I *had* to have a new photo—or no picture—when my next original Kevin Alter mystery novel came out.

Who *was* this guy highjacking my life? Did I deserve cooing voices at midnight telling me lust was acceptable until love came along? Could my marriage survive another love letter filled with purple prose? Even the florist's delivery guy was starting to wink as he dropped off new arrangements. Last week, someone even lipsticked my Toyota with an "I♥KA." I'm glad my ten-year-old spotted it before Delores did.

I'm a simple, hard-working writer. I don't think about sex all the time! I worry about how to pay for our kid's braces. Delores' clothes washer is broken. The neighborhood landscape Nazis are giving me dirty looks because the yard needs a little work. My life was becoming a disaster because of a body double who makes me look like a jerk. In short, my marriage was a ferry boat foundering on the shoals of suburban catastrophe. All I wanted to do was write mysteries.

With Delores on my back big time, I decided no more Mr. Nice Guy. I hunted up a phone number for Eddie Corelli, an old buddy with the Jersey State Police. "Eddie," I said softly so Delores wouldn't hear, "my reputation is being Shanghaied." I laid out all the embarrassing details.

Eddie asked if I'd had any credit card collectors calling. Maybe there were bills for big-ticket items I hadn't bought.

"Not yet. Just love notes, birthday cards, flowers, reminders of how ecstatic my love-making is. And today, someone named Sharlayne wrote that if she was pregnant she'd name the kid after me."

"Well," he said, summoning up all his police intelligence, "then it's not identity theft. It's identity *fraud.* This hotshot is using your rep to hit on women. Personally, I'd be proud to have someone polishing my reputation. I bet you get a lot of sly looks at the supermarket."

"Eddie, there's gotta be a law. Can I just start calling myself, say, Senator John McCain?"

"There's no law, but I don't think you'd pick up many women," Eddie said. "See, Kevin, Lover Boy doesn't really want to *be* you. He just doesn't want to be himself."

"Delores," I shouted, "I've had it!" She came out of the kitchen. "I'll hire a private detective and then sue the ass off this impersonator. It's been six months. He's making me look like a licentious bum. Like all I want to do is take women to bed."

Delores gave me her patient, self-satisfied smile, the one she wears when my socks don't match or I forget to zip my fly.

"No, darling, you're certainly not licentious. But, you can't sue your doppelgänger. Because he's me. I'm your alter ego. I sent you the flowers last week. My friend from the library made the calls. And she wrote today's letter from Sharlayne."

The world went into deep freeze, time stopped, and I'm sure my jaw dropped. "But, why would you want to think I'm some playboy on Viagra?"

"Kevin, darling, you're the mystery writer," she cooed, giving me a look I hadn't seen in a long time. A slinky look. "Figure it out. Why would a woman want to think her husband was the greatest lover in the world? Maybe one who lived up to a fictional reputation."

Now she had me. Was this a mating call or the plot of a new mystery?

...I'm a smart guy. I mean, I have this condition. It's not amnesia. I can't make new memories, is all. There was an accident, I got my skull smashed in, but I can remember everything up until then, and I was smart. I earned good money, lived well.

So when I find myself on my knees sucking off a total stranger in a room I've never seen before it's not because I'm stupid. I've got my reasons, I just can't remember what they are.

"Every Time's The First"
by Sarah Hilary

Basil Wolenski was allowed to have a minor superiority complex, being a gem of westernization, at least by Isobelino standards. He owned not one, not two, but three pairs of stonewashed Levis, while most of his friends rejoiced if they could procure a pair of Polish knock-offs on the black market. The pockets of those Levis were filled with condoms of all colors and flavors, while his friends were still relying on those Soviet-era torture devices that smelled like car tires and ripped after the first thrust.

"How Am I Gonna Play Guitar Now?"
by Marina Neary

FANTASY, MYTH, LEGEND

In this edition of LORE, BIG PULP's magazine of fantasy, myth and legend, we're pleased to present Conda Douglas' "Blood Tells", a fantasy/horror tale of Irish song and dance, and the price to be paid for each.

Afterwards, we invite you to spend "One Night in Manhattan", a twisty tale of alternate realities and the writer who may be creating them, by Edward Morris; and then stay tuned as Floris Kleijne fills us in on "What Happened While Don Was Watching the Game" in this modern urban fantasy.

Enjoy!

Conda Douglas blogs at Conda's Creative Center. Her story "Blood Tells" comes from a summer she spent in Dublin. It was an interesting time...

BLOOD TELLS

"I need a drink," Maud said.

I refrained from mentioning she had already drunk too much. "If we don't go now, we'll miss the bus to the airport," I said instead.

"Don't be so practical, Wren," Maud scolded. She signaled the pub man. He saw her gesture, shook his head, and turned away.

"It's because we're Americans," I said.

Despite Maud's classic Irish beauty, her red hair and green eyes, the Irish always recognized us as Americans. They always spotted the way we moved through the world, proud, arrogant and afraid.

We'd spent the early part of the afternoon pub crawling and music hunting. We'd followed the strains of Irish songs from one location to another, the music more intoxicating than the pints of Guinness stout ale.

This place was Irish Traditional, cheap linoleum flooring with scarred, rickety tables and benches scattered about, the smell of stale meat pies, ale and old-cigarettes-before-the-ban in the hazy air. Overheated, it was stuffed with the warmth and crush of human bodies. The windows were misted over, obscuring the rainy September day outside.

"They're starting another tune," Maud complained. "So why can't I get another drink?" She ran her hands through her short cropped hair, hacked away after the accident. Even in the fluorescent light of the pub, her dark red hair glowed, an aura of blood around her head.

I reached out to stroke a curl and she jerked her head away, our rhythm ruined.

"Your hair looks like a halo," I said.

"Saint Maud," she said, "the patron saint of losers."

The tables were pushed close together, so that the drinkers sat claustrophobic elbow to elbow. In the cleared space, a fiddler sat upon a bar stool. While he fiddled, patrons took turns dancing jigs. They earned applause and sometimes a drink, for their ability to go through the ancient dance steps. Steps I once knew well.

"Join in this time, Maud," I suggested.

When she played, she stopped thinking about drinking. She stopped thinking about the harp. I believed that she even stopped thinking about Aoife.

"No, I've not been asked."

"They don't know that's a harp you've got, and they never ask." I wanted to kick the wrapped canvas bundle at her feet, an addiction worse than the alcohol. If I could only get her home, back to America.

"Quiet, Wren, they're starting," Maud said.

During this last jig, an old man danced. He held his pint in one hand as he leapt around the room and never spilled a drop. He wore glasses with thick lenses that obscured his eyes. How could he see to dance?

My legs quivered with the need to join him, until a sharp jab of pain around my damaged knee stilled them, but not my desire.

The last of the notes died. The old man received a fresh pint for his dance. Everyone turned back to the business of finishing the last pint.

"You should have played, Maud," I said.

"Why didn't you dance then?"

I winced.

Maud touched my bad knee. "Never mind. I can't play well enough. In a year, then maybe. If we stay."

"We can't stay. We're due back tomorrow."

"It'd be easy enough for them to find somebody else to teach Music 101 and Modern Dance."

"And what would we live on?" I said. Our old argument, often repeated in this final week in Ireland, as both our time and money grew short.

"You never used to ask that before."

"Before is dead and gone."

Maud dropped her hand.

56

The old man appeared at our table. "It's Americans you are then?" he said. He grinned, with black stumps instead of teeth. A musty smell of old damp wool permeated his being. Old wool and worse, I caught the effluvium of rotted teeth and aged shoe leather, too long worn.

"So what is it you've have wrapped there, swaddled like it was your own wee babe?"

Maud unwrapped the harp from its blanket and carrying straps. She'd never been able to find a suitable carrying case. She cradled Aoife's legacy, a small Irish harp. Centuries of hands had worn the wood in several places, diminishing the deep cut grooves of Celtic swirls decorating the harp. Aoife died in the accident, but her harp survived, a memento of death, a reminder of despair.

Since she wouldn't play it, I wanted Maud to put away the dirty thing. I wished that she had never inherited it and Aoife's obsession.

She ran her hand over the strings. The string cut into her palm and left a trail of blood.

"Maud, your hand," I said. I reached out but dropped my own hand at her frown.

"It's the blood what tells," the old man said. He raised his pint in her hand's direction as if in a toast. "Feeding the harp, are you?"

Maud ignored the blood dripping from her palm. "Listen," she said. "Do you hear it?"

"What?" I heard only pub noise.

Maud tilted her head to one side. "Don't you hear it? The tune?"

The old man whistled a low heavy tune. Dark spit spewed from his lips.

Pain crawled along my knee. "Stop it," I said to him.

He ceased and wiped his mouth.

Maud stroked the harp as if it lived. "It sounded like the old original tune, the one from whence all the others came." Blood from her cut ran into the Celtic design and over the stain of Aoife's death mark.

I grasped Maud's arm. "What nonsense, let's go."

The old man placed his hand on my bad knee. I jumped. He held me fast. His fingernails, torn to the quick, showed blood around the rims.

"If it's the old traditional songs you're wanting," he said, "then I know a place, a grand place for the singing, dancing, and playing." The best music was played after pub hours, in tucked-away-out-of-the-way-hidden places, where the Irish congregate to dance and sing. "It's only the invited that go, because of the haunting."

"That's just tourist talk to spook us. You Irish love telling a tale to us gullible Americans," I said.

He tightened his grasp.

Heat crawled around my scars.

"For they're saying as how the place is the home of one of the old ones, the Sidhe. It's said this one's a priestess what sacrificed herself." He dropped his hand.

Maud sat frozen in her chair.

On the clouded window, the old man's twisted fingers danced as he drew a Celtic symbol that mirrored those on the harp.

"She cut the symbols deep into her skin, till she bled her life away," he said. He drank again, and smacked his lips. "And if you're willing to pay for it, she'll give you your heart's desire."

"Can she bring the dead—music to life?" Maud asked.

"Forget it, Maud," I said.

She gazed at me, her eyes clouded with drink and despair. "Can she make my friend here, Wren, fly through the dance again?"

"I want to go home," I said. I sounded like a petulant child. I wished we were on the plane already.

I caught sight of myself reflected in the old man's glasses. There was a smudge of ink on my nose and the humidity made my hair hang in stringy strands, like old brown rope. My long drab grey skirt covered the scars around my knee. What would I pay to dance again? I pushed the thought away.

"Closing!" the bartender shouted.

The old man got up and with a wink danced out the door.

Maud flung the harp back into its blanket and carrying straps.

"Maud—"

"We'll lose him," she said. She left, without waiting to see if I was behind her.

I limped after her, her follower as always, out into the Dublin street.

Overhead a solid wall of rain clouds blocked the sun. A light mist rising off the Liffey River muffled the sounds of the early evening traffic. I hoped the cold would dispel the froth of the ale from my mind.

We followed the old man into the winding back streets of the old part of the city. I struggled, moving as fast as I could to keep him in sight. He moved fast for an old man.

Maud stepped quick as if she'd forgotten my pain. Perhaps she had.

"Out of money, out of time, and with any luck, soon I'll be out of my mind," Maud sang. The harp thumped on Maud's back in counterpoint. Even in the failing light, her red hair glistened with the mist, a beacon. The Irish, as they hurried home, brushed past us, their grey-cast faces in the grey mist blurred.

We turned onto a street paved with old, broken cobblestones and patched with tarmac. My weak leg slithered over the wet slick stones and I fell. I felt a sharp edge tear into that leg, the pain a sudden heat, a reminder of great pain not long ago.

"Maud," I cried.

So intent she was on the figure ahead, she didn't answer. At last she turned around.

The old man looked back once, spun in a high twirl and vanished around a corner.

"Oh, Wren," Maud said as she helped me up, "now you've lost us again."

"Nonsense, we're not far from the Liffey," I said. I could still smell the dank river stench; hear the muted rumble of traffic.

"Wait," Maud said. She stood frozen, a blood-haired Virgin of Christ. "Listen."

I listened and heard the sweet notes of a tin whistle. What other people could coax such music out of a cheap toy, but the Irish?

We followed the high, thready sound. I spotted him first, a young man, a boy almost, as he walked along ahead and played. His clothes looked formal, stiff and uncomfortable, from the back.

"Hey," Maud called.

He turned a corner and the music ended. We raced after him and into the narrow dark street. The whistle player was nowhere to be seen.

I heard a whisper, like a prayer, that made me feel the cold of the mist. Georgian mansions crowded the sidewalk, aging spinsters gossiping together, their flaking facades old shawls around their crumbling dignity. I couldn't recall this part of Dublin, dirty and decaying.

"Maud, let's get out of here," I said.

"You go."

I sighed and followed her.

At the end of the alley, a woman swept the stoop of a large stone building, a church. She looked up.

At first I thought her a nun, then she smiled and I saw it was a wimple of black hair that framed her white face. She wore a long black dress that enhanced the effect. What looked like a rosary at first was a long knife, the hilt encrusted with jewels.

Her face shone white and all Irish, strong features over pronounced bones, so close to ugly as to be beautiful. And ageless. I could not guess if she was in her twenties or fifties. Thick, tangled black eyebrows marred her beauty, but leant humor to her face.

"Is this the place?" Maud said, walking toward her.

"If you need," the woman said. She dipped the broom into a pail of sudsy water and swirled the suds over the steps. In the weak light the water looked dark and thick.

"It's blood," I said.

"Aye, it's the blood what tells," the woman said.

"A pub fight?" I asked. Like the blood pulsing beneath the skin, Ireland seethes with violence, sometimes erupting like a cut artery.

"No."

"It's like someone painted the steps with blood," Maud said.

"Does it now?" the woman said. She picked up the bucket and slewed the water over the steps. "Look how dark the water runs, like the dark Liffey it is, stained with Irish blood."

The water wetted my shoes. Something black and oily, a blood clot perhaps, tumbled into the gutter. I limped back.

The woman laughed. "You frightened of a wee bit of blood, are you? You'll never last long here, then." She turned up the steps.

"You said if I need," Maud said to her, "I need a drink."

The woman turned back. "You can always find a drink in Ireland."

"It's not pub hours," I said. Would we ever get home?

"Aye and this is not a pub," she said. She smiled, white teeth bright even in the mist. "You can always get a drink in Ireland if you're willing to pay."

"I can pay," Maud said. She stepped toward the woman. She slipped on the steps and almost fell. Aoife's heavy harp slid over her back and gouged into her shoulder blade.

The woman grabbed her wrist. "Careful now, it wouldn't be doing to break that lovely harp of yours," she said.

Maud laughed and said, "It's not my harp."

I shivered with the cold in her laugh.

The woman's hand on Maud's wrist looked liked it was locked. I wanted to snatch Maud away.

"Maud, please," I said.

Maud looked at me then, looked at my leg, where the blood still trickled from the cut. "Your friend's marked," the woman said. "It's the blood what tells."

"Yes, marked with Aoife's death," Maud said and turned away from me.

The woman smiled and offered her other arm. I took it, if only to break her concentration on Maud. Beneath the cloth on her arm I felt ridged skin. Beneath my fingers the ridges moved.

"Battle scars," the woman said.

I hoped it would be warmer inside, though I doubted it. September in Dublin brought a damp, penetrating cold that blew in off the sea. I hadn't been warm since we'd arrived, perhaps before. Perhaps my heart had frozen.

A blue shield stood affixed next to the heavy oak door of the building.

"Blue plaque disease," I said. The name the Irish had coined for the myriad commemorative shields, always blue, that decorated so many buildings in historic Dublin. I squinted. "What's it say?" I peered closer.

Some vandal had scratched over the words. Odd, for the Irish are proud of their heritage and their freedom from British rule. Not even the children would be so bold as to mar a martyr's memorial.

The woman drew a dirty fingernail across the plaque and added another scratch. "During the uprising the British caught this fellow and shot him to death, making him a martyr to the cause."

"Why is it all scratched?"

"They found out later that he was a traitor and that it was his own people shot him to death on these very steps. He must have run here, for sanctuary. But this church has been deconsecrated. No sanctuary here. T'was a great pity, that young soldier dying, he could play the tin whistle like none other."

I heard the strains of a tin whistle, nearby, now. It struck deep within my wound. My feet shuffled in a never-forgotten step. I pulled after the sound, but the woman held me fast.

In the weak light, it seemed her face shone white and luminescent, as if the skull beneath the skin was about to reveal itself.

"The music," Maud said. She too tugged at the woman's hold.

The woman started to sing in a deep contralto, rough and rich. I didn't know the song, couldn't understand the thick dialect. The air around us vibrated with the wealth of her voice. The tin whistle stopped.

The woman sighed as she unlocked the door with a large, rusty key. "Didn't have to lock this place, not in the old times, there wasn't nobody coming in then."

"You mean because of thieves?" I asked. The increase in drug use had brought more crime and a different violence to Ireland.

"Oh no, had to start locking it when an old drunk crawled in here and died."

The place looked long abandoned. The pews remained from when it had been a church, only now they lay stacked against the walls. All the other church trappings were stripped away. Nails and light patches showed where crosses and religious paintings had once hung.

A table sat where the altar must have been and on the steps to the altar a few bottles and glasses stood. Even in the cold air, I smelled mildew and rot.

"Froze to death he did, the old fool," the woman said.

Cheap neon lights hung from the ceiling and I caught sight of

Maud's shadow. The harp slung on her back deformed her into a hunchback.

"Do they come and play here?" Maud asked.

"Oh, aye, every night there's a celebration."

The woman led us to the table. Maud eased the harp down onto a chair. She took off her coat and beneath it her white silk shirt, a gift from me, was spotted with blood.

"You've got blood on your back," I said.

"From carrying the harp," Maud said.

"You carry your own battle scars," the woman said.

Maud looked at me with the sorrow of forever in her eyes.

I heard a rustle under the table. A small mongrel stared up at me. The dog, black, brown and white and of no determinate breed, gave a tentative sniff at Maud's harp.

"Get away," I said. I pushed the dog away with my foot, not wanting to touch his dirty hide. He reminded me of the scrabble-haired mutts who followed the tinkers' carts. He growled and slunk away.

"Careful there, he bites," the woman said. She brought the drinks, generous ones of Irish whiskey, to our table.

"Will the musicians come soon?" I asked. We'd missed our plane by now. We'd be on the next one, I swore to myself.

"You impatient American, you have all the time you need."

A rustle in one of the high windows drew my attention. Ravens nested on the sill, sheltered beneath a cracked windowpane.

"Wasn't it a Celtic belief that ravens steal the souls of the dead?" Maud asked. She showed no inclination to leave and I resisted the impulse to pluck at her sleeve.

"And how did you come to be knowing the ways of the Celts?" the woman said. She refilled Maud's glass. She ignored my empty one.

"Part of learning about Irish music is the Celtic stories."

"Aye, Christians spent centuries trying to bury the old ways. It still lies beneath the skin." The woman stroked the ridges on her arm. "It still lives in the blood."

"Looks more like it's covered with dirt," I said. I rubbed my foot over the dirty floor. Beneath the dirt, a pattern was carved into the stone. "What's that? An old tombstone? Are there people buried under this place?"

"Sure, but that's no tombstone you're looking at."

I looked closer.

The marks whorled, lines curled back upon themselves. Somehow they reminded me of my dance notations. I followed the lines with one pointed foot and remembered when I danced barefoot, an elemental gliding along the music. "It looks like an old Celtic ceremonial stone."

"They built a church upon a Celtic altar? A place of sacrifice?" Maud asked.

"This site's been holy for a long time."

"Why was it deconsecrated then?" I asked. I never got an answer for a clatter pulled away my attention.

In one corner, the dog worked at a bundle of black rags tossed there. At least I believed it was rags, until I spotted the round whiteness of a skull and the tumble of bones among the cloth.

"The mad nun," the woman said. She refilled Maud's glass. "They say she broke her vows, went mad, and killed her lover right over this stone."

I swallowed hard. I prayed the bones were only fakes, placed to impress the tourists. I tried to make a joke out of those splashes of white against the black. "And I suppose they walled her up alive?"

"What would her bones be doing out in the open then? No, she danced herself to death and they left her unburied, out of consecrated ground."

"The Celtic priestesses danced till they died," Maud said. She stared down at the design on the floor as if all the answers were etched there.

"Maud, you know how the Irish love spooking the tourists," I said.

The woman laughed. "Don't worry," she said, "the lover's blood's long since soaked into the stone." Her sleeve pulled back revealing whorls of deep cut lines in her forearm, the ridged scars. Some of the wounds still oozed blood.

"How much are you charging for all this creepy-old-Irish atmosphere?" I asked.

"What price are you willing to pay?" the woman said. She took off her knife and placed it upon the table.

The old man from the pub came in, carrying a fiddle. He played the opening strains of an old song I at last recognized.

It strummed along in my blood. My good leg beat time, my heart along with it, desperate for the dance. "I guess I can get lost in Dublin," I whispered.

With the last of my desire for life, I grasped Maud by the arm. "Let's go home."

"I am home," Maud said.

I stared at Maud. Her eyes had glazed over and there was nothing in her face for me. She picked up the knife.

I reached for the blade. "No, don't."

"What price will you pay, dancer?" the woman said.

I dropped my hand. I wanted to dance. I needed to dance.

Maud plunged the knife into my heart. I staggered in a parody of dance steps before I fell.

My blood pooled over the floor, running into the grooves of the ceremonial stone. A raven landed upon my breast. He tore at the wound.

Rain beat against the stone walls, like a soft echo of gun fire. The tin whistle player came in and joined in the tune. I saw his face, the streaks of blood on his head from where the stones had struck.

A young woman, dressed in a nun's habit, danced over the carved stone in the middle of the floor. Her skirts fluttered over the carved pattern in the stone. Around her head ravens flew and the dog nipped at her heels.

Maud kissed me. The pain faded from my leg at last and from my soul.

The music thrums in my dying heart as Maud cuts the ancient lines deep into her arms. Maud picks up her harp and plays, while the nun dances, and the old man fiddles, and the boy plays. I feel my heart dance as my blood soaks into the thirsty stone. I've found it, the song of the blood.

For it is the blood what tells.

Edward Morris was a 2005 British Science Fiction Association Award nominee whose work has appeared in print on four continents, in three languages, and at such diverse publications as *Murky Depths, Nowa Fantastyka, Helix SF, Aeon SF* and twice in *Interzone.* In 2008, he was a guest author at the H.P. Lovecraft Film Festival.

ONE NIGHT IN MANHATTAN

My name is Harold Hart Crane. I am alone in my hotel room. It is Christmas Eve, in the Year of Our Lord 1941. I will not lose my mind.

The Herr Doktor told me to repeat things like this, when the "peak" of the drug happens, whenever that is. Time has turned to rubber, and the clocks have melted down.

My name is Harold Hart Crane. I will not lose my mind.

A thousand years ago, I got that package this afternoon from that quaint little bearded Kraut Dr. Rinkel at Boston Psychopathic Hospital. The stuff's an alkaloid that acts on several chemicals already in the brain. He orders it in microgrammes, do you believe that, at the most exorbitant rates from Sandoz Labs, in Chur, Switzerland.

Or did, a thousand years ago. Before the clock melted on the wall, and the trip to the store did not end. This room is tired. The velvet wallpaper spirals up into patterns of patterns toward the ceiling, beanstalks I have no heart to climb.

I am too fascinated by where I've gotten to down here on Earth, this warm radiator and the radio on just sub-audibly, a mad caterwauling counterpoint to the juke-joint Jezebels below.

A wall of silence rings my Moroccan portable typer in this restless one-night cheap room. Just beyond, I hear the blessed Andrews Sisters belting out "Bei Mir Bist Du Schöen" from the hotel bar while rhumba drums beat mad macumba, animal jungle rhythms of Science, Commerce and the Holy Ghost jitterbugging with my Lucky Strike Green that jitterbugs all by herself in the flying-saucer-shaped ash tray on my desk.

I, with them, want to dance my legs down to the knees at the sight of what I see my cigarette smoke doing, bending light around the strange typer that is harp and altar of my fury fused.

I started writing the thing I was working on before, an essay on the sub-genre phenomenon that Will Jenkins at *Amazing Stories* calls 'sidewise-history.' I was thinking of a few fanciful examples of this 'flash-in-the-pan': World War One never happening, the South being given modern fusion technology during the Civil War, a dozen other such...

As fast as I wrote and replaced scenarios on the page, the three framed photographs I've hung above the Burroughs cybernetical typer changed again, image shuttling past image like a Tarot hand drawn by a riverboat gambler.

The pictures are all wrong, now. I can't slot-machine them back to what's supposed to be there. And it's the typer...Me...That's doing it? I grab for my Lucky and smoke half of it off at one drag, never enough, never enough.

My typewriter. Mine. It did that. I have no tangible explanation for what I've just seen, and barely the capacity to describe it. The page went blank just as I started to come up on this LSD-25, and then...

I need to slow down. My God, how did I not see that I got into the wrong racket when I started publishing Scientifiction? I should have stayed a poet! But then there'd never be this moment now, the right sound of the right keystroke twanging the strings of the cosmic harp in such and such a way that it might ripple back, and change the shape of Not Quite All?

What the hell is History, anyway? And who writes it? How do we know we're not, at this very moment, living someone else's parallel world?

What does it matter what we do now? I could go rob a bank, assassinate anyone, sleep with anyone, abuse any drug, commit any crime, and then come back here, sit down at my desk, and write it out of existence, and it would have never...

There it is. I know I'll remember this in the morning. Damn it all, we should all just stop working and start doing what we want to do.

Then Society would have to change. We could do it. We didn't give away all our power after the Great War. Not all of it.

Did we? I don't know. I can't think about much, except the images hanging on the wall above my desk. I will write my way through this, too. Dear Bill Burroughs the computing-machine magnate tells me the gods smile on me when I'm in my element.

But this isn't my element, Bill. I'm somewhere else on the Periodic Table, tonight, in my sordid rooms at the Chelsea Hotel where I sit in front of my Aladdin Portable at the mirror and try not to fall apart...

I once told Bill my secret dream-job, when we were walking in Times Square and sucking on Italian sodas, stoned to the gills on Mexican brown ditch-weed through the water-pipe back at Huncke's squat.

Bill slapped me on the back, looking like a preacher in his loose, floppy gray suit, and said Kid, poetry isn't a career as much as it is a chronic condition. In your case, Campbell's boys have rooted it out to a ganglion, but usually it's terminal...

Poets extrapolate. So do I. The sounds in my head fade down now to zazen silence. Outside my window, the gray, dappled belly of pregnant sky threatens snow. There's nothing for me now but that blank page in the typer, healed to be broken again.

My hesitation melts away like the frost on my window as the radiator clanks into life once more. If my watch is even right. I have gone mad. I must have gone mad.

It happened like this:

I stopped cutting my latest serial, *Chaplinesque*, when I felt my pupils get big and my mouth get electric and came all the way up, staring stupidly at the wall behind my desk. What was hanging there formerly had been two photographs, one en collage. The one that caught my eye used to be a framed photo of Harry S. Truman grinning at the camera like a baboon.

I pasted Truman's portrait over a picture of the mushroom cloud he unleashed on Tokyo, and scrawled in the Missourian's own words below it, 'THE ONLY THING NEW UNDER THE SUN IS THE HISTORY WE DON'T KNOW.'

Right next to Truman was a picture of another young-old fascist,

Howard Hughes, behind the tiller of his Lockheed 14 after that first trans-global flight. I just final-drafted a very difficult novel called *Meet Me In St. Louis*, see, tying Truman and Hughes to the assassination of President-For-Life McArthur. My fictional Doug McArthur as Prexy is clearly modeled after our current, actual Caesar.

I gave the manuscript a slap and sent her onward just three weeks ago. It's a fine old vaudeville comedy of errors set in the Kremlin and the Oval Office as America and the NATO allies plunge hell-bent, headlong and breakneck into the Sino-Vietnamese Conflict, the bloodiest war in human history, a hypothetical Big Three.

My God, it was meant as a joke, like 'A Modest Proposal', just something to get people off their butts and thinking. I never meant...that is...

Wait.

Black Mountain College just published *Meet Me In St. Louis* as a mythopoetic curiosity. Their senior editor Bob Lowell compared me to the homespun Scientifiction Grand Master himself, Stephen Vincent Benét.

Bob also introduced me to Will Jenkins, who lives two floors up from me now and lets me bounce my stories off that fertile brain. Will's got a fine turn of phrase himself, especially in his newer epic works like 'Doomsday Deferred' or 'To the White Sea', where he talks about his experiences as a bomber pilot during the Berlin Siege in '47.

Will is riotously heterosexual, but somehow we hit it off anyway. The first advance for *Meet Me In St. Louis* came yesterday morning. After I got back from the bank, Will and I did some heroic drinking at Capote's little walkup in the East Village.

Truman was fit to be tied. We were up gossiping like a couple of high-school girls until dawn. Oh, heavens, Truman could set me straight on this now. I wish I could tell him, but...

Catch is, I'm not afraid that Capote won't see the difference in the photos.

I'm afraid he will.

Or Edward will, that columnist from *Vanity Fair*, infuriating Edward with the broken shift key on his typewriter, for whom Gay is just the captivating cognomen of some nerdy girl at Cambridge who didn't like going to the monkey house to make out.

Edward Estlin Cummings, if you please, understands me, though, which makes him all the more infuriating. He called my first Scientifiction novel, *The Bridge*, "a true portal to someplace I've never traveled, gladly beyond any experience."

But this morning, the wall above my desk and typer has quietly informed me that I have lost my natural mind and traveled someplace beyond. I like to have photographs of my subjects while I'm working, always did. Truman (Harry S., not my dear Holly G.) and Howard Hughes were the models for my villains.

Until a few minutes ago, the only art upon the wall above my desk was, ipso facto, the late Citizen Hughes, with his smarmy prep-school good looks, gone down in his Hercules somewhere off the California coast; and Give 'Em Hell Harry looking old and broken after he dropped The Bomb, the year before they found him hanging in the Oval Office.

I framed the Truman photo. Hughes just got masking-tape. That three feet of wall Harry and Howard occupied was reserved for photos pertinent to whatever story I was working on, currently a kind of altar to the unquiet dead. But behind the glass of the cheap frame just now is…was…

General Dwight David Eisenhower, out of uniform, wearing a black suit with a thin black tie, in a Lincoln limo with the top down, surrounded by Secret Servicemen (and…women?) The picture of Ike's motorcade in Tiananmen Square is on grainy new color stock.

Saluting him from a ceremonial throne at the other end of the shot is a skinny man with a mustache and an overbite, with shining diamond-coal eyes. Chiang Kai-Shek, garbed in the robes of a Han Emperor, leading a Komodo dragon on a gold chain…

Where Howard Hughes just was, there's now an 8 ½ x 11 glossy of a blonde tomboy with rakish good looks and a bomber jacket that's to die for, standing on a weed-choked runway beside a Fokker F-7. The woman looks all-in, and is supported on either side by what are clearly G-men in identical suits, leading her to the 1932 Packard touring car just out of frame.

"Amelia Earhart," I mutter, able to think of nothing but my first internationally published short story, 'Atlantis Regained'. In the story, Amelia was the first pilot to fly around the globe instead of Hughes, because of...

"Because of that weird fuel tank Amelia designed, the one she never got to use, the one she called the three-hump camel..." Then I stop muttering to myself. The picture is no collage.

Where the masking-tape has peeled back on the upper right corner, I pull the picture further away from the wall and behold only the Op-Ed page of the Times for March fourth, 19...

"...Thirty-two." I feel very cold. "Six years before Howard Hughes flew around the globe."

I'm not leaving my room now. Now it's dark, and I'm lying down, with a cold cloth on my forehead. I don't want to look at those pictures again.

I have to get out of this room. I'll leave, come back in and everything'll be hunky-dory just as it was, nice vanilla bread-and-butter missionary 1941...Slowly I turn, inch by inch, step by step, to the cracked Motorola radio on the end-table by the window, and turn on its warm, comforting little console-light and the tinny squawk of WRNY News.

"...Hughes ToolCo formally disbanded today, on the anniversary of the former President's impeachment hearings. President Albin Barkley, who himself gained plenty from the impeachment, was strangely temperate in his criticism of former President Hughes' mad, short-lived term in office.

'Howard Hughes desegregated the military,' Barkley eulogized at a press conference on the West Lawn of the White House this Saturday past. 'He put our Liberty satellite into space at the private level way ahead of the Rooshians, and helped us put Al Boyd and Bud Anderson on the Moon seven years later. I knew Howard for many years, and I can tell you...his heart was in the right place. America has lost one of her true visionaries...'

Protest marchers in Washington, D.C. said differently, however. At four o'clock this afternoon, Your Reporter caught up with Carolyn Cassady, ringleader of the—"

I reach up and shut off the radio. Barkley was a fool with no vision who did what he was told and very little else. Never President! Never! I never voted for him, I voted for Adlai Stevenson, who won, and—But they just said—

Someone's putting me on. We have yet to reach the Moon. Howard Hughes, too, has never been President of any United States where I lived, worked, grew up…Neither, for that matter, has Eisenhower.

I mean, come on! Eisenhower was blown to bits at Normandy just like every other Kraut or Yank who was at Ground Zero when the Niebelung detonated! I've tried to write my way out of all my nervous breakdowns, with some success, but…

The pictures didn't come from my condition. I am not nuts! Nobody tell me I'm nuts! All I did was come home last night drunk and pass out in my clothes!

And who the hell is Carolyn Cassady? I—

I look out the window, then, the dark, cold hotel window with its slight gray tint, its old pine sill marked with the ashes and energies of every lonely beat mendicant who ever sat in it and watched the Manhattan neon and the cars on a cold night or morning. I wipe off the condensation, peering out like a child. Then I forget how to blink.

Snow tumbles down out there through the grey-blue light, like stars seen traveling close to the speed of c, scribbling frosty sagas on my eyes, the gleaming cantos of unvanquished Space. It's been a long time since I heard such stillness dumping down in sheets as it is now, a million stars, a million dreams, a storm of ticker-tape just for me, an endless sky you could sled in, one that tastes as fresh and immediate as a nosebleed.

The sound makes me look down. The car bumbles around the turn, its tyres higher and thinner than I'd consider trustworthy. It's metallic blue from stem to stern, and looks like a teardrop or a diving-bell with elaborate finned fenders, low-slung and gleaming with purpose, humming like bees in a lion's skull. MILBURN-STUDEBAKER Bateau, it reads across its hood in raked-back silver letters.

There is no exhaust pipe. Only that hum, hum, hummmmmmm… The old lady steering the contraption is having the time of her life doing spins in the snow. (That 'Milburn's' electric motor is apparently strong enough to climb a damn tree.)

She sees me, and raises a silver hip-flask. I wave back, hoping for her sake that the cops don't come. Her round of "dough-nuts" (as we called such manoeuvres when I was an under-grad) is done now. She turns away, driving out of sight.

Merry dough-nuts to all, and to all a good drunk. Her license plate reads NYC. I wonder if that is a new boro of Nieuw Amsterdam, perhaps somewhere close to this one. Either way, the plate is too large, and done up in the wrong colors.

Where did I put that Scotch? By the phone across the room, right where I left it. Nothing's changed, not even the...

Numbers on the dial. The words dry up in my mind. The phone-shaped thing has more buttons than the squeezebox end of an accordion.

All this was my fault. Somehow. I wrote this into being. Me, me, Hart Crane, the most frustrated writer in New York since Joe Gould! Hard to imagine me as...

God?

I go back to the window, watch the snow listen down inside, to the secret self who finds the words in a simple declarative, Yes. Then I go sit in front of the typer again, awash in the melted Italian soda of neon from the street outside, cold and sweet and rare. Flakes of snowy silver sentence scroll down past my still-open window with the crocus luster of stars.

Rage, blow, thou sermons' flashing roar, scattered chapters of living glyph! TAP. TAP. RATTATATATTATATATTATA—

But I write 'sidewise-history'! If I do this right, I WILL PUT MYSELF OUT OF WORK!!!

Yet all my fine collapses weren't ever lies. My frosted eyes raise altars, and silent answers stutter back across the stars. This game enforces breakdowns, but I have seen the moon in lonely alleys. I can still love the world, and sidestep the worst of it with a fatal smirk.

Who can end up blaming me if my heart lives on, completes the dark confessions spelled out in my every cell, and closes round the jewel of this instant with its floating lotus flower? This fabulous shadow could not be quenched by any sea.

Edward, I—

RATTA-TA—

My name is Harold Hart Crane. I am alone in my hotel room. It is Christmas Eve, in the Year of Our Lord 1941. I will not lose my m—

(then white)

Floris M. Kleijne was born in Amsterdam in 1970, and then nothing of consequence happened to him until 2001, when he traded his mother tongue for the English language. (His mother still resents the trade; she's not spoken to him since.) Since 2001, he's published stories—some of them award-winning—about space travel, time travel, an axe murderess, people with gills, and—even though he's happily married—a naked man in a cage. His first novel, a road movie with werewolves cast as the good guys, is only two rewrites, an agent, and a publisher away from becoming a best-seller. Floris likes to claim he prefers writing to Real Life™, but the truth is he loves both with equal passion.

WHAT HAPPENED WHILE DON
WAS WATCHING THE GAME

The baby boy, exhausted with the exertions and impressions of the day, slept through it all. Through the rough shunting of the parking platform in the automated car park, and the metallic clang of the platform being locked down, he snored peacefully, his little head leaning obliviously against the car seat headrest. When the car door clicked open, he only made a tiny dissatisfied sound. The guttural muttering of the two that slid into the car and temporarily shared the back seat with him didn't penetrate his dreams. He never felt their small hands opening the clasps of his security harness, nor did he wake as they lifted him out of his seat, with a gentleness that belied their fierce appearance.

They maneuvered their tiny, sleeping burden out onto the platform and towards their exit, leaving the car empty and silent, as if no child had ever been in it at all.

"Hey, where's the kid?"

Marjorie froze with her back against the front door, balancing four grocery bags on her arms. She was torn between blind panic, and annoyance bordering on anger. Her rapid understanding of what had happened enabled her to quell the panic. It did nothing, however, to stop her other reaction from blossoming into fury at her useless sack-of-shit excuse for a husband.

The worst of it wasn't that Don had shown no inclination to help carry the groceries, concentrating instead on sorting the mail as Marjorie struggled with the bags. Nor was it his trance-like preoccupation with the upcoming game.

At the moment, even leaving their child in the car came in second to calling him 'the kid'. This was taking his lackluster approach to fatherhood to new depths.

"His name," she hissed, "is *Donny!*"

To her satisfaction, the inane expression on his face was replaced by guilt; for an entire second, there was more than just the prospect of home runs and no-hitters on his mind. Unfortunately, it was still not enough for him to draw the obvious conclusion.

"Yeah, Donny. Where is he?"

"You left him in the car, you idiot!"

He smiled sheepishly.

"Oops," he said.

Marjorie kept her cool. Donny had been tired enough to sleep for at least another hour, so there was plenty of time to get him before he noticed anything wrong.

Still, she had every reason to be concerned about him. He was still lying buckled into his car seat, which was on the back seat of their MPV. Which had been shuffled into the dark robotic bowels of the autopark.

Marjorie hated the autopark. She hated waiting her turn at the entrance. She hated operating the control panel. But most of all, she hated waiting minutes for the car to appear. She knew too well how long it took the system to retrieve their Buick; she'd left enough house keys, handbags, or sunglasses in it.

But never Donny. Never her own flesh and blood.

Don made no move to go back down for his son, instead looking pointedly at his watch. She considered standing her ground and making him choose between the first inning and the safety of their child. But that was a choice their marriage might not survive, and a confrontation she wasn't ready for. Yet.

"For God's sake!" she said. Shoving the groceries into his chest, she made her way around him and pressed the call button.

Behind her, she heard paper tearing and heavy objects thumping and crashing to the floor. A cloud of flour billowed around her as she stepped into the elevator.

◊◊◊◊◊

Of course, it was only her imagination that the autopark took twice as long to produce the Buick. Or so she told herself.

Down in what she refused to call the control room, she'd operated the control panel with an efficiency born of concern for her baby. Instead of her usual fumble around the different buttons and switches, she went rapid-fire through the entire sequence, pausing only, in irritation, when she had to enter their four-digit PIN number.

Of course, Don had selected the PIN digits, and every time she had to operate the autopark, she squirmed at the memory of his almost religious rant about the mind-numbing statistics of long-dead athletes. Who *cared* about the difference between batting average and slugging percentage, or whatever they were called? If he would spend half the brain power he wasted on Lou Gehrig's statistics on remembering her birthday, their marriage would be in half the trouble it was.

3-4-0-4, she punched in, and through the large window into the autopark she could see and hear the device come alive with metallic grumbling noises. An interminable period of squeaking, clanging and grinding later, the garage door rumbled up that separated the parking bay from the autopark. Any moment now, the robotic parking platform carrying their car would grumble gracelessly into the bay. Marjorie made her way around the control panel to the door leading down into the bay. She didn't want to waste a single *minute* rescuing Donny from the car seat.

When the platform slid into the bay and the garage door closed, it took a moment for Marjorie to understand what was wrong.

The car wasn't there.

Marjorie fired off a string of curses that would have impressed her husband. This was the third time this had happened since they'd moved into the building. She toyed with the idea of calling Don down and have him deal with the problem. But she still didn't feel up to wrestling with his precious baseball fetish. Calling Maintenance wasn't a real option, either. Their dim-witted handyman Jake needed three weeks to replace a busted light bulb, and two months to deal with boiler problems. And the last time the autopark had malfunctioned, all Jake had done was hand-crank the inner garage door and retrieve the purse she'd left on the passenger seat.

Marjorie could do that much herself.

As she edged past the empty parking platform, a little voice whispered that she wouldn't be acting this rashly if Don hadn't been so useless. She knew a part of her was doing this to prove she didn't need him. Let him cheer his slugging heroes, slump in his favorite chair and drink his Bud, while she saved Donny, presented him to his father in triumph, and then…Yes, that was the question, wasn't it? What then?

The inner garage slid up as she worked the manual crank. With apprehension, she looked into the widening hole. When it was high enough to pass through, she took the small stainless steel flashlight from her purse and stepped onto the platform. She hesitated for a moment, wondering if she was really doing this. A fleeting thought made her take out her cell phone and quick-dial 1. Don answered after six rings.

"What!"

"Don, the car won't come out. I'm going into…"

"HE WAS SAFE, GODDAMMIT!"

It was a measure of her faith in her husband that she didn't think for a moment he was referring to his son.

"Yeah, what was that, hon?" Don added.

"I'm going…"

"HOLY COW, STOLEN BASE!"

"He's taking a pretty big lead down there," Marjorie added automatically, and that seemingly innocuous quote gave her a disturbing sense of urgency, making her shiver.

"Enjoy the game," she said, and snapped her phone shut. Then, flicking on the flashlight, she stepped into the autopark.

◊◊◊◊◊

Finding their car in the autopark was easier than she'd expected. There were rows of parking platforms packed closely together, the tracks that carried them to the entrance crisscrossing between them. Metal walkways paralleled the tracks, with a set of rungs against a pillar near the elevator mechanism in the center. There were naked light bulbs everywhere, but Marjorie hadn't found a switch, so her flashlight was her only illumination. It flickered occasionally, but that was the least of her worries.

She climbed to the top and walked a complete circuit of every level, turning around only when the beam of her flashlight hit the concrete walls of the cavern.

She frowned. A cavern? What kind of word was that for a man-made, concrete structure? But it felt appropriate. Maybe it was the darkness and silence. Maybe it was the way her footsteps echoed. But there was something else, a faint, earthy smell, and the air felt moist.

She found their car on level 5. Only in the relief flooding her did she realize how much she'd tensed up. It was difficult to see into the car, and with the beam bouncing off the rear window, it might be just a trick of the light. But something seemed wrong.

When she stepped onto the platform and edged to the back door, she saw the door was open. Shining her weakening light into the car, she saw the car seat was empty. And when she leaned into the car, she found dirt on the back seat.

At first, the narrow beam made it impossible to see any pattern. But after adjusting the beam's spread, she saw a trail from the car door to Donny's seat. Climbing out of the car, it was unmistakable: there was a trail of dirt leading along the edge of the platform, back to the walkway. And where it reached the walkway it resolved into clearly separate tracks.

"An animal," she thought with a tightening stomach. But that was almost impossible to believe. It didn't even matter what it was. A fierce sense of protectiveness occluded all other considerations. Driven by huge, bright fear, fear for herself and for Donny, she stepped onto the walkway and followed the tracks.

Which dead-ended twenty feet further on against the concrete wall.

There were two columns of rough indentations in the wall to her left, forming another kind of trail leading down into the darkness. For someone with her indoor climbing experience, the handholds were a freeway down.

She gave no thought to who or what would kidnap a child, leave a trail of dirt, and carve out a ladder in concrete. She didn't dare.

◊ ◊ ◊ ◊ ◊

Twelve feet down, she found out what caused the moist and earthy smell.

Moist earth.

Suddenly, she also understood that the term 'cavern' wasn't as misplaced as she'd thought. She stood at the edge of a forest of metal supports. As she'd climbed down, the smoothness of concrete had given way to rough bedrock. And when she stepped down onto the floor, it gave slightly, and a musty smell rose. Her flashlight confirmed what her feet felt: the bottom of the cavern was bare earth.

Marjorie set off to her right, following the cave wall, dodging around metal supports flecked with rust, until the rock suddenly opened up into a passageway to her right. She shone her light into it, but the diminishing beam failed to illuminate anything beyond the first fifteen feet. The tunnel looked wide and high enough for two people to walk abreast.

Marjorie didn't hesitate. Part of her knew that she was riding the momentum of her first impulse, driven by her anger with Don, and wondered at the wisdom of what she was doing. But stopping to think now would confront her with everything that was weird and terrifying about it all. Being rational and sensible, as Don always admonished her, would freeze her in place, or worse, scare her into going back home. And her son was down there.

◊ ◊ ◊ ◊ ◊

The air in the tunnel was cold and damp. The only light was the beam of her flashlight. Here and there, mushrooms grew, and several times she thought she saw something scuttle from her peripheral vision. The corridor seemed to be sloping slightly down. Marjorie realized she was more scared than she had ever been in her life.

There were cables and pipes and ducts running along the ceiling, and she spotted an unlit neon light high on the corridor wall. A bit further, an extinguished torch leaned from the wall. Still further down the tunnel sat another neon tube, and when she felt the little box she thought of as its motor, it was still warm. The strangest assortment of lighting fixtures sat at regular intervals along the tunnel wall. A huge light bulb here; more neon there; a candlestick, a caged security light, and even, connected to a bit of copper tubing, what could only be an old-fashioned gas lantern. And each light was still warm to the touch.

Only people used artificial lights. There was a person ahead of her, and he had Donny, and he was leaving the tunnel in darkness. But she would still catch up with him. She had her own light.

Which flickered and went out.

A yelp escaped her lips. She pressed the switch a few times, but got only a weak glare that died as soon as it appeared. She switched the batteries around like she'd seen Don do. The flashlight didn't even flicker any more.

"BASTARD!" she screamed, not sure if she meant her quarry, or Don. He'd promised to buy fresh batteries at a gas station last week.

When she lifted her hands to her face in despair, Marjorie realized she could see her fingers.

She reached for the wall to orient herself, and peered down the corridor. It was faint, but there definitely was an orange glow in the distance. It wasn't enough to make out details, but it gave her an idea of where the walls were, and to see the direction she was heading. With her determination renewed, she set off towards the flickering light.

◊ ◊ ◊ ◊ ◊

After about half an hour, she was close enough to see that the tunnel turned sharply further ahead, and the light was sufficient to make out details. When she was close enough to clearly make out the corner in the tunnel, she started to run.

Seeing what lay around the corner, the sheer force of

incomprehension brought her to her knees.

She'd sprinted headlong into a huge space. The wall behind her curved round to form a dome at least sixty feet high. The cavern was roughly elliptical, and she thought the mall parking lot would have fitted comfortably. The cavern was lit by countless campfires sprinkled around the floor. By their light, Marjorie saw other tunnels open into the cavern at regular intervals.

But it wasn't the cavern itself, or even its occupants, that blanked her mind with incomprehension.

There were piles against the wall, between the tunnels. To her right, a pile of sunglasses rose. The next pile seemed to be of thousands of pens. There was a pile of grease-stained McDonald's takeout bags. Cell phones, notebooks, soda bottles, paperback novels, coats, purses, CDs. One section of wall was covered with at least two dozen back seat LCD screens, most of them, she noticed with renewed fury, tuned to sports channels. To her left was a pile of keys; next to that, what must have been a fortune in small change.

Scuttling from pile to pile, emerging from tunnels or disappearing into them, sitting around the campfires, running around, were countless…creatures. They were the general size and shape of children, though brown, and furry. They had small, bright eyes in pointed faces; knobby limbs, clawed hands; a stoop to their walk and a jitter to their movement.

It took Marjorie mere seconds to take it all in. Then she spotted Donny and spurred herself into action.

Donny was on the floor near the fast food pile, wrapped in some kind of blanket, between two of the…Goblins, she admitted to herself. They had to be Goblins. They were facing away from her, and seemed to be in a heated discussion with another Goblin, larger than the rest, wearing more and better clothing, as well as a weird kind of crown.

A faint childhood memory surfaced, of a teenage girl in some movie mumbling, "You're him, aren't you? The Goblin King." Fury rose in her. Ignoring everything else, she strode towards the three Goblins surrounding her baby.

She'd crossed half the distance when the creature she'd dubbed the Goblin King noticed her. He silenced the two others with a gesture.

They turned around and watched her approach.

A few feet away, she stopped. Ignoring the other two, she faced the King. Half-remembered ritual words bubbled from her lips.

"Give me the child! Through dangers untold, and hardships unnumbered..."

Startling her, the King spoke. His voice rattled and squeaked.

"Oh, rubbish! Don't come to me with your movie nonsense!"

"Don't tell me what I can't do!" she burst out. "You stole my baby, and I'm taking him back now!"

Squatting, she gathered Donny and his rough blanket into her arms.

"Of course you are," the King said. "It's all a terrible mistake."

"What?"

"These two," he bit, gesturing at the embarrassed youths, "have a lot to learn."

They hung their heads and shuffled their feet with eerie semblance to abashed children. Marjorie felt the wind dropping from her sails.

"What do you mean? What were you doing with my baby?"

"These...*idiots* stole him."

Explaining took a while. Apparently, what the Goblins did was steal stuff. Where humans advanced by discovering, inventing, developing, the Goblins stole. The King made it sound like two equivalent and equally honorable paths, and Marjorie held her thoughts about that to herself.

Originally, they stole whatever they could get their hands on, including treasure, livestock and even children.

"Changelings!" Marjorie exclaimed.

The crowd gathering around them snickered as one.

"So easy to blame us, isn't it? No, changelings were just an easy excuse whenever a really ugly child was born. I don't know how *you* define stealing, but *we* never replace what we take."

Centuries back, somewhere in the Middle Ages, humans had had enough. They had tried to hunt down and kill every last one of the thieving creatures. They would have succeeded too, but a particularly diplomatic Goblin had intervened.

"We made a truce," the king said. "We agreed to take 'only that which is lifeless, and has been lost or abandoned through carelessness or purposeful action'. In exchange, humans promised to leave us in peace."

"*Lifeless?* You think my Donny is *lifeless?*"

The two young ones squirmed, and the King said:

"Clearly not. These two will be on fast food sorting detail for two months. They thought they could cross the line, but they were *wrong!*" The last word was shouted at the two offenders, who looked like they wanted to disappear into the ground. "I apologize. Please take your child back."

"There is one small problem," a voice sounded from the gathered crowd. One of the Goblins was making its way through the audience. It was grey and bowed and moved with slow care.

"What's that, counselor?" the king asked.

"The terms of the truce are clear," the counselor said. "What we steal is *ours*, no matter what the circumstances. Nothing can be *given* back; it can only be *exchanged.*"

From the crowd came a murmur of agreement. The King frowned.

"I'm afraid my counselor is right," he said. "Even under these circumstances, we are bound to the terms of the truce. Giving back your child would be as grave an offence against those terms as the theft itself. It must be exchanged."

Marjorie was only half-listening. She had an idea that made her chuckle as it blossomed.

"Tell me, king: I saw the cables and ducts and tubes in the tunnel. Do you steal utilities as well as forgotten items in cars?"

"Yes, we have gas, water, electricity…everything. Why do you ask?"

"Do you have cable, too?"

◊ ◊ ◊ ◊

Hours later, Marjorie was having a luxurious soak, lavender bath oil spreading its calming scent. Donny was splashing and spluttering in his own little bath, gurgling happily as he pounded the water with a rubber duck.

"Dada?" he muttered.

Marjorie pictured the wall of LCD screens. The king had assured her they regularly stole crates of beer and bags of chips, and the fast food pile yielded plenty of leftovers.

"Daddy's downstairs, sweetie, watching the game."

The Chill of Night

Crime, Mystery, Suspense

Strange things can happen in THE CHILL OF NIGHT, everything from a hard-boiled crime tale to a locked-room mystery, from a ghost story to a serial killer thriller.

This issue, we have two longer tales, led by Jason Ridler's "Flight Risk," the story of a traumatized girl who discovers an unusual link to the former tenants of her new home.

We're also pleased to present Paul Von Hippel's "Virus", a tale of suburban paranoia set in the early years of the war on terror. It begins when two young Muslim men move into a quiet Ohio neighborhood and ends with a devastating twist.

Jason Ridler has published over 30 short stories in venues such as *Brain Harvest, Not One of Us,* **Big Pulp**, *Crossed Genres, Chilling Tales, Tesseracts Thirteen,* and more. His non-fiction has appeared in *Clarkesworld, Dark Scribe,* and the *Internet Review of Science Fiction*. A former punk rock musician and cemetery groundskeeper, Mr. Ridler is a graduate of the Odyssey Writing Workshop and holds a Ph.D. in War Studies from the Royal Military College of Canada. Visit him at his writing blog, Ridlerville, http://jsridler.livejournal.com/, Facebook, and on Twitter at http://twitter.com/JayRidler.

FLIGHT RISK

The spicy oregano stink of Dad's version of Mom's spaghetti filled the house. Tamara shut the door, slipped past the half empty boxes she'd filled at Mom's, and checked her email. Zero. Daniel was waiting for her to send one, to say she made it all right. But Mom said that hard to get always gets what she wants.

A big green and empty backyard looked back at her through her temporary bedroom window. She imagined the grey and yellow parking lot view from the apartment, the changing patterns of the little cars, the packages that changed hands as dusk hit. She missed the stairwell, playing cards with Daniel, sharing one of his mother's menthol smokes; each drag like a winter breeze indoors.

Grass? Fresh air? "Boring," she said to her reflection.

The scar on her forehead was barely visible, but it still hurt. Lucky. That's what the doctor called a mild concussion from the car accident. Said she had to be careful and take it easy and maybe she'd remember, but who the hell wanted to remember an accident?

"Dinner's on, Tam!" Dad yelled.

God, she thought, what is this? The Marines?

Her computer chimed. An email had landed. Mom was right again. She smiled, then flipped through a *Sandman* comic on her new bed until Dad called again.

Yellow light from weak bulbs covered the big, orderly kitchen. She liked his spaghetti better cold and played with it until the steam eased.

Dad's shirt gripped him tight. He's too cheap to buy a new one, she thought, admit he's gained weight. His rough face looked older in this cheap light. "Do any more exploring?"

"Found some whisky bottles and condoms behind the dumpster of the Seven-Eleven."

Dad's granite face chewed slowly. "Huh. Made any friends in the neighbourhood?"

"Not yet. Maybe if I hang out at the Seven-Eleven long enough, though." The granite reddened. She smiled inside. This beat reality TV any day. She ate a warm mushroom. "I'm stuffed. Can I be excused?"

"You should really try to make some friends here, Tamara. This is a nice neighbourhood."

"If nice means *boring*."

"Nice means safe." She prepared to hold her breath until Dad finished his "I was an orphan in Bonnie Rig" speech. Instead, he said, "This is a good place to come home to."

Home. Another four-letter word she didn't say in front of her father. He wanted her to stay put. For good. She remembered overhearing the first counselor, the bottle blond with bad teeth, say that Tamara might run away. Disappear. Unless she had a stable home. Tamara smiled: Mom had told that bitch to go to hell, that she didn't know her daughter at all. Not Dad, though. Didn't make a peep.

She forked a pepper. "I liked it better with…at the apartment." She chewed on the cuff of her long sleeve shirt. "Sorry."

Dad nodded, took a moment, then spoke. "It's ok. It's normal. She's your mother." God, he almost sounded like the judge awarding custody three years ago, word for word. "But she's sick. Until she's well again," he smiled, "I guess you're stuck with me."

She sighed. "For how long?"

His lip trembled once, but he ate the rest of his dinner in cold silence. The spaghetti she'd been playing with now looked like blood and stringy hair and her stomach tightened. She asked to be excused again. He nodded.

Daniel's sappy email made her groan. He hoped she was ok. Things sucked now. There was no one to stay out with all night, smoking and talking comics and boo freaking hoo. He asked if she'd borrowed his

Sandman volume II, he was scared he'd lost it.

"Borrowed?" It sat on her bed. She touched the scar. Stupid. Of course. She'd borrowed it. She finished the email.

"why don't you come back to Toronto, just for a weekend, could you stay with your mom's new boyfriend?"

Todd? Old news after the accident. She hit delete and wondered how many heart attacks Dad would have if she vanished and then reappeared? Would he send her back?

◊◊◊◊◊

Tamara lay the parcel containing Dan's comics down on the post office desk. She figured he'd like the surprise. "How long will it take for this to get to Scarborough from here?"

The overweight woman with glasses and a bucktooth mouth gawked. "Where?"

"Scarborough. You know, Scarberia? In Toronto."

"Oh," she took the parcel and read the address. "A few days. Week on the safe side."

"Damn, that's a long time," Tamara said.

"Not like you're mailing it to yourself." She weighed the package. "Five fifty. What's inside?"

A smart-ass remark almost left her tongue when a question popped out instead. "How long does a letter take to arrive at your own house?"

"One to two days if it is picked up before 3 p.m."

She paid for the parcel's postage, a book of stamps, and some envelopes. At home, door shut, she began to write.

Dear Dad,
If you're reading this, I'm already gone.
Tamara

She smiled at the ambiguity. She could be dead. She could have run away. She could have gone for a donut! She'd spend the day in town, smoking and reading more of Daniel's comics, then reappear. He'd crack worse than a trembling lip! She'd be on the next bus back home before his last tear dropped!

But Tamara didn't trust the ugly lady. This had to be perfect. She'd do a test run. She put the letter in the envelope, signed the new address, and slapped on a stamp. She said she was going for a walk, but he was crouched over his desk, typing up reports or whatever, and didn't hear her. Let's see if he misses me when I'm really gone, she thought, lighting a cigarette against the wind.

She finished her smoke, found the nearest mailbox, and fired it into the chute. A block away in the shade of a birch tree, some girls in summer dresses, each a different colour, stopped walking and stared. Tamara lit another smoke and gave them the finger. They muttered swears at her as she walked back home.

Days later, Dad knocked on her door. "Tam? Can I come in?"

She had almost finished the *Preacher* comic she'd found in a box of other comics she must have borrowed from Dan. "Sure."

He looked awful, almost like the post office troll, and the bags under his eyes were almost blue. "I've got some time off this afternoon. Thought you might want to see a movie. We could go to a matinee. Like we did for your birthday."

She turned a page. "Kinda busy." She'd noticed yesterday that the mail came around one p.m.

He nodded his head seriously. "Right, right." Then turned around and left. Face twitching. She closed her eyes against the guilt swelling in her gut, then blurted out, "Maybe we could do it, uh, Friday?"

Dad's head popped back. "Friday." He nodded his head, doing some kind of mental math. His face hardened. "Absolutely. Why don't you pick the film? My treat." A smile broke through his hard Scottish face before he left. It looked weird. The guilt faded.

Later, she heard the sound of the mailbox's squeaky hinges. Dad, back at his desk, told her to slow down. She popped outside to see the mailman's blue and white form jut around the hedges and head for the next house. She grabbed the letters and rifled through them. Bills. A *National Geographic* magazine. And a plain letter with no name, just an address. She shoved it in her pocket, put the other junk on the kitchen table, and marched to her room to read the letter.

A different envelope. Tougher. A date was branded to the stamp. 12

April 2004. "Postal Troll lost my letter," she muttered, opening the envelope. She dropped on her bed, reading the first line.

"Mother. If you're reading this, I'm already gone."

She read it a dozen times but the stunned sensation never left her face.

"I want you to know that this isn't about you. I just can't pretend anymore. It's too hard. I don't feel real, but it still hurts. No one thinks I can be sad. No one sees me. Not the way I am. The way I feel. I'm lost in this skin. But it's just a pretty shell. That's all everyone wants to see. To touch. But I don't feel anything good. And that scares me.

"I love you, Mother. But I'm not a toy, or an appliance, or a showpiece. They can't leave their trophy shelf. I can. Please don't be too sad.

Love, Emily."

Chimes rang out of her computer. She ignored the message from Daniel and tucked the letter beneath her pillow and walked through the day in a haze.

She woke the next morning, shivering. She'd dreamed of broken glass and ghosts in mist. She dressed quickly, reading Daniel's email, and ran into the afternoon sunlight, packages in hand.

The same postal troll stood behind the office desk. She fired off the latest batch of Daniel's comics Tamara had discovered in her boxes, but wouldn't give the forwarding address to the old owners of Dad's house.

Stumped, she walked back home, past the Seven Eleven, her mishmashed dream following her, a dark memory swirling.

"Hey!"

She'd walked toward the field, behind the Seven-Eleven parking lot, when three girls appeared from behind a car. The summer dress rich kids, Tamara figured. Red, Blue and White. Like a box of crayons. Each of them held unlit cigarettes. "Hey what?"

"You're the new girl," said the one in the blue dress and ponytail.

"On Twine street? You moved in this week."

Tamara lit a cigarette and blew a thin stream of smoke into the mid morning breeze. "Yup, Sherlock. That's me."

"Oh my god!" said the red one. "Emily's house."

Tamara wiped the sweat from her face with her sleeve. "Who?"

"Emily Painter," said the third, in white. "She was our friend."

The tone made it clear: Tamara was no Emily Painter. "Oh," Tamara said, playing dumb. "She move away or something?"

The crayon girls looked at each other. The white one spoke. "She died."

"You don't know that!" said the red.

"Where could she be, Samantha? The moon?" said the blue.

"No one found her!" said the red.

Tamara repeated the name in her head, worried she'd forget: Painter, Emily Painter, Emily Painter, Painter, Painter.

"Hey," said the white, approaching her. "You have any matches? We forgot to get them."

"Rookie mistake," Tamara said, then flung them her matchbook.

They lit them eagerly, but only puffed. "Wanna hang out?" said the blue. "We're going to the mall later." She handed back the matches.

Tamara took a step back (Painter, Painter, Painter). "Nah. Gotta get home."

"I told you she was stuck up!" said the red. Tamara flicked her cigarette at her and she squealed. Leaving the crayon girls behind, she realized something. She'd called the house "home."

Three Painters were in the phonebook. Each time, she asked to speak to the mother of Emily Painter. The last one held her breath for half a minute. "This is Doris Painter."

"Uh, hi. Name's Tamara McTavish. I live in your old house and——" Her mouth dried as the words hung back in her throat. "See, I have something."

"Yes?"

"Something of your daughter's. I found it in the house and I'd like to return it to you."

Heartbeats passed, then. "Fine. Come tomorrow. I'm very busy right now." She gave her the address and hung up. Mrs. Painter's voice almost echoed after the call. Tamara found the address on MapQuest. It was not close.

"Tam? Lunch is on."

She ate the egg salad sandwich and cold lemonade without saying a word, trying to calculate how long she'd be, while Dad read the paper. If her bike hadn't been stolen from the apartment last year, she'd make it home quick, no sweat. Now, she'd have to start in the morning. But why? Tomorrow. Something about tomorrow...

"Plans for the rest of the afternoon?" Dad said, folding the financial section over and scrutinizing the tiny print.

"No," she said, nibbling the crust, heart thumping. What was it hiding in her head? She rubbed the scar. Got up, went to the post office—

"I met some girls from the neighbourhood."

"I hope not by the Seven Eleven." He raised an eyebrow comically.

She smiled. "They seem ok."

He smiled back. "Good."

She told him they had plans tomorrow morning.

"Great." He swallowed dryly. "But we won't miss the movie, right?" Dad said.

The movie, she thought, that's it! She sighed. "No chance."

"Grand. You didn't forget, did you?"

She flinched. "No."

"The doctor said you might have some trouble—"

"I didn't forget, damn it! I'm not some basket case."

"I just meant—"

"Can I be excused?" She didn't wait for a response.

Friday morning began warm and bright. Dad? Long gone. A note on the clear kitchen table said he was at the office, but he'd be back at eleven, and that she should take an umbrella when she went out. Then, PS "I'm sorry." Tamara crushed the note and tossed it near the garbage. Apologizing? How weak was he? Mom never apologized.

She jogged as the dew began to vanish from the lawn-strips on the sidewalks. When she'd reached Roberts Road, the clouds had thickened and moisture infected every breath. Hugging herself, she hurried, double-checking her back pocket crammed with the address, 243 RR.

And the letter for Mrs. Painter. She smiled. She hadn't forgotten a damn thing.

At 100, the rain sprinkled, at 120 it dribbled and by 200 it smacked her in buckets. Dark thunder kept her running, lungs tense and charred from too many morning smokes. The rain soon eased, blocked by the canopy of large elm and spruce trees on this stretch of the neighbourhood. But her long sleeve shirt was still a hundred soaking pounds.

There was 244 Roberts Road.

"Shit," she said, listening to herself drip.

A wide front porch and a second story balcony sat before her. The bedrooms had large bay windows. The wet limestone made everything dark and warm and blue. A big crabapple tree stood rooted in the lawn and the rain, now a mist, tapped off of the leaves on to the rich, green lawn. An SUV, covered in rain bubbles, sat in the driveway like a crimson tank.

Rolling up her soggy sleeves, she walked to the grey front door and hit the doorbell. The wood creaked under her feet as she leaned back and forth. A distant sound. Footsteps. Closer.

Opening the door was a woman in a light pink blouse and white pants. Thin. But not jagged like Mom. Elegant. Strawberry blond with a very white face. Queen of the WASPs. "Mrs. Painter?"

"Yes." Her face barely moved. If she had wrinkles, they were drowning in botox.

"I'm Tamara McTavish. I called yesterday."

"I remember. You have something of mine?"

Tamara's lip twitched as this rich bitch gave her an "I don't have all day" look. Tamara smiled, dug out the letter, and pushed it at the elegant waif. "Enjoy."

She did an about-face and saw the tree bend against the downpour. The porch had kept her dry and it was a long walk home. A whisper made her turn.

"My Emily."

Mrs. Painter's face tensed, stretching near a breaking point. "Oh god." Her eyes shut and she pressed the paper to her mouth.

"Uh, I'm sorry," Tamara said. "About your—" a gust of wind chilled her and tickled her throat. A cough crept out. Then another. And another. Her chest raged with tremors and her eyes watered.

"Good god, you're soaked," said Mrs. Painter. "Get inside." Tamara did not resist, chest heaving. Mrs. Painter pulled Tamara through a huge kitchen and down a dark hallway, Mrs. Painter's low cut heels thudding down the dark, enameled floors. A bright light came on in a rose coloured bathroom that looked brand new. "The towels are there. I'll find you something dry to change into."

She closed the door and Tamara shivered. She dug her drenched cigarettes out of her pocket and tossed them and the matches into the garbage, then dried her heavy hair with the fluffy, white towels.

Two knocks. "Dear?" Mrs. Painter didn't wait for a reply. Her make-up redone, her face firm. "Here. You can't go home in that." She offered Tamara a thick, pink sweater.

So Emily was the pink crayon, Tamara thought. Or what her old Crayola packs called "skin" colour. "Thanks, but I—"

"Please?"

She nodded and took the sweater to keep the old lady from crying.

"She was beautiful. Great rider. Top of her class."

"Grand," Tamara said, holding the pink sweater. It smelled like expensive perfume.

"Just perfect." Mrs. Painter gazed somewhere past the immaculate bathroom and relaxed until that old doll face held itself still. "Gerald said we sold the house too quickly, but I didn't care about the loss." So that's how Dad could afford it! "It was too full of…We needed new memories. You know, she was so beautiful…"

Tamara tried holding her breath while this woman spoke of the daughter she didn't even know. She gasped and sucked in more air three times before she stopped blabbing about riding lessons and awards and other shit that apparently Emily had bolted from into nowhere. Mrs. Painter sniffed. "Sorry, what was your name again, dear?"

"Tamara McTavish."

Her eyes narrowed. "What an odd name."

"Not if you're Ukrainian-Scottish."

"Well, dear, I believe I owe you a thank you." Tamara waited, then realized that *that* was the thank you.

"Oh. Sure."

"Well, I'll let you get changed." She blinked. "Then we'll do something about your hair." She closed the door and Tamara dried herself and dropped the soaking, frigid sweater on the ground. But she kept her undershirt on, drying as best she could, before putting on the sweater. When her head went through the hole, Mrs. Painter walked in.

"Well. Don't you look nice." She frowned. "Except for that hair. Come on. Can't have you leaving my house looking like this." She dragged Tamara into the kitchen, sat her down at a glass table and began to brush out her tangled mane. "You really need a haircut. These split ends won't heal themselves."

She gritted her teeth. "Fine. You have the time?"

"Twelve thirty."

Dad. The movie. She pulled away from the brush and it pulled back. "Ow! Damn!"

"Language, dear. I'm almost done."

"But I gotta go."

Her scalp burned as she tried to pull away.

"I said easy, dear." Tamara covered her scar with her hand while Mrs. Painter finished. Dull pain echoed in her head.

"See," she said, holding her by the shoulders in front of a giant hall mirror. "Isn't this better."

Tamara's hair was smooth and long and felt like a wig. Mrs. Painter brushed a lock over her scar. "Look, thanks, but I gotta run."

"Not in this weather. Let me give you a lift."

"No, that's ok—"

Mrs. Painter held her hand tight and walked her to the SUV as the rain started to pound. "Don't worry. I know the way."

Rain blurred the windows and Tamara, hugging herself in the pinkness of her sweater, swallowed pasty spit. The huge car engulfed her small body. Mrs. Painter babbled but Tamara didn't hear it. Something tugged on her mind.

Hail hit the window like gunfire and Tamara gasped.

"Rotten day," Mrs. Painter said.

Breathless, Tamara nodded. Hail kept tapping the glass in sharp rhythms. Harder. Softer. The neighbourhoods melted down and up along the windows. She was boiling. The pink darkened.

"Do you like my house?" Mrs. Painter's voice warbled.

"Sure." She kept blinking. But the world was melting in rain outside.

Hail tapped the window so hard she expected cracks. She closed her eyes to avoid it, but mom's voice ran through.

"Might take my license, but no man tells me I can't drive my daughter around to look at new houses, because baby when I get that next win we are moving. You gotta be the boss, baby, or else they'll take it all, like your daddy, and you saw the way the judge looked at me, right, baby? Hey, anything left in Momma's drink? Pass it here. Careful, don't spill it! Jesus Christ!"

"Mom, don't!"

Tamara opened her eyes. Rivers of water dissected the window like spiderwebs of broken glass. She smelt pungent rum. He stomach twisted and blood ran out of her face. Cars rushed passed her head, sending gooseflesh down her spine. She gasped.

"Hard to see the house, all this mist." Mrs. Painter's said, driving steady. "Maybe we should go back, wait until it clears."

Tamara's head swam in the hazy shapes of the rain until it eased into a fine mist. Where was the house?

"Do you want to go back, Emily?"

Her lip trembled. The car kept moving, inching along the curb. "Tamara."

"Pardon?"

"My name is Tamara. Stop the car."

"Are you alright?"

"Stop the car, bitch!" Tamara opened the door before the car stopped and hit the wet ground running.

The mist thickened. She ran across the lawns until she saw the porch. Dad held an umbrella in one hand, a letter in the other.

The letter! She ran, chest heaving. The soaked envelope sat at his feet. "Dad!" Her voice coughed out, weak and tinny. He unfurled the letter. "Dad." She swallowed the phlegm and pain. "Don't read!"

It fell out of his strong hands.

She tore off the sweater, undershirt drenched in sweat. "I'm here, Dad! I'm home!"

Paul Von Hippel is a writer from Columbus, Ohio.

VIRUS

Sunday, October 17, 2004

The mansion across the street had stood empty since the All-Star break, and now it was nearly time for the World Series. So we were relieved when a moving truck finally pulled into our dead-end street, a mile north of downtown Columbus, Ohio. Our dog, Pudge, noticed it first—not the truck, but the dog sitting erect and regal between the two dark men in the front seat. Broad-shouldered and shaggy as a wolf, the dog was taller when seated than the passenger on his right, and just a little shorter than the driver, who was so lanky that he had to duck his head to peer under the sun flap.

Pudge thrust his boxy head through the porch balusters and barked at the wolf-dog as he would at any intruder. After the mansion was taken from the previous neighbors—either repossessed by the bank, or seized as part of a meth bust, depending on who you asked—Pudge's territory had grown to include not just the brick mansion and pillared front porch, but also the yard with its bare patches under pine trees, its sagging white fence, its cracked sidewalk next to the weed-choked grass along the curb, and even a length of the street where the moving truck had now pulled up and stopped.

The cab door opened, and the driver dropped soundlessly to the street. Standing upright, he was as long-limbed as a catalog model, and he was dressed in the fall collection: khaki slacks and a beige corduroy jacket over a matching turtleneck sweater. The fall colors continued into his face and hands, whose skin was tawny as an oak leaf.

The passenger—shorter and darker, wearing jeans and a black leather car coat—jumped down from the far side of the truck and landed heavily on the curb. He fastened the wolf-dog's leash and led it through the white picket gate into the back yard. Tail high, the wolf-dog trotted imperiously around the inside of the fence, sniffed the crabgrass as though sampling the house merlot, and raised its leg approvingly against a white pine near the house's foundation.

Pudge's barking rose to an hysterical pitch.

"Pudge!" My husband Brad stood up, wiping his hands on his jeans. He'd been stuffing wet maple leaves into a paper yard sack. "Pudge, that's enough!"

I leaned forward on the porch swing to grab Pudge collar. Or I tried to: like an air bag, my pregnant belly kept me from reaching very far. "Do you want to play?" I asked Pudge. "Do you want to meet the big doggy dog?"

"Wants to kill him, looks like," Brad said.

I stood, then crouched open-kneed to pull Pudge back from the railing. His nails scrabbled on the concrete. "Don't listen to Brad. Brad's just grouchy because the Red Sox are losing."

"You call this grouchy?" Brad crimped the mouth of the yard sack. "If the Sox lose again tonight, there are men in Boston who won't say a pleasant word until spring."

"Let's greet our new neighbors, then." I led Pudge down the stairs and took Brad's damp hand. "While there's still time."

Pudge tugged us across the street, and we reached the moving truck just as the tall driver finished raising the door on the cargo bay. The passenger stood in the back yard, making the wolf-dog sit before he opened the gate.

"Hi," I said. "Need a hand?"

When the driver saw my belly his eyes widened. He raised his palm. "We are all right." No one ever accepts help from a pregnant woman.

"We live across the street," I said. "I'm Vickie. This is Brad."

"I am Faisal." The tall man shook Brad's hand and nodded at me. The shorter man closed the yard gate and joined us. "And this is my brother Samir."

"Pleased to meet you," Brad said. "So. Where you from?"

"Boston," Faisal said.

"I mean originally."

I shot Brad a glance, but he wasn't looking at me.

"Of course." Faisal smiled. "We are from Cairo. But it is seven years since we left."

"Really?" Brad said. "What brought you over?"

"We were students," Faisal said. "I trained at M.I.T. as a civil engineer. Samir works in computer security."

Brad nodded. I could see he was about to ask another question, so I broke in. "I'm a lawyer," I said. "I work downtown at a family law firm. Brad writes a column for a sports website." The column was a minor part of Brad's job; he spent most of his time managing relationships with advertisers. But Brad had just started the column, after months of wheedling his boss, and it was the only aspect of the job that he wanted to talk about.

Samir scowled. "Web advertising," he said, as though he knew what Brad really did for a living. "Many security issues there. Click fraud. Denial of service attacks."

"That's right." Brad nodded, impressed. "You looking for a job, Samir?"

Samir shook his head irritably. I dug my nails into Brad's palm.

"Where do you work, then?" Brad asked.

I interrupted. "Did you say you were from Boston? Brad's from Boston, too. Grew up in the western suburbs. Newton."

"Ah, Newton." Faisal nodded and smiled broadly, as though the name brought back fond memories. "We lived more centrally, near Fenway Park."

"Fenway Park?" Brad brightened. "Are you watching the Sox tonight?" He looked at his watch. "Game four starts in half an hour."

"Unfortunately, no." Faisal said. "Even were we to unpack our television, our cable service is not yet active."

"You can watch with us," I said. "Come for dinner. We're having pork chops." The Muslims exchanged glances, and I felt my face redden. "Or something else. Pizza?"

"You are very kind," Faisal smiled again. "But no. We have much unpacking."

"Can't say I blame you for skipping it," Brad said. "No team's ever come back from three games down. And with Hernandez pitching, there's not much hope, is there?"

Faisal glanced confusedly at me and I shrugged, giving him

permission to smile. "If you say so," he said. "You are the expert, Brad."

Pudge sidled toward the fence, sniffed one of the pickets, and raised his back leg. The wolf-dog snorted and trotted out from under the pine trees, hackles raised, yellow eyes slitted. Pudge dropped his leg and started forward.

"Sit," I said, and snapped his leash. Pudge lowered his haunches slowly, as though unsure that I could handle the situation. "This is Pudge," I told Faisal.

"Budge," he said.

"No, *Pudge*." Brad broke in. "Like Ivan Rodriguez. But really he's named after Carlton Fisk."

Faisal squinted, confused.

"The catcher," Brad said. "For the Red Sox. You know. Hit that home run in the '75 Series." When Faisal didn't answer, Brad went on. "Now *Budge*—Don Budge—was a tennis player."

I broke in. "*I* always think of his breed. He *is* a pug. His *name* is Pudge." I looked down the leash and clucked my tongue. "Isn't it? Isn't your name Pudge?" Pudge stared up at me and panted anxiously. His back legs trembled. The wolf-dog stood behind the fence and looked entreatingly at Samir, as though awaiting permission to start on dinner.

Brad nodded toward the wolf-dog. "Impressive specimen," he said. "What's his name?"

Samir turned his head slowly toward Brad. "Beedoos," he said.

"Sorry?" Brad asked.

"Virus," Faisal said. "With a *V*." His teeth buzzed his bottom lip emphatically, as though the letter took special effort to pronounce.

Brad said, "Oh. Okay," which unfortunately is the signal that releases Pudge from his most-recent command. Pudge sprang up, barking, and Virus lunged toward him, snapping, trying to shove his jaws through the slats of the fence.

"*Beedoos!*" Samir shouted a short command in Arabic, and Virus dropped to the ground. Suddenly calm, he looked up at Samir for further instructions.

"Pudge!" Brad said. "We told you to sit!" When Pudge continued barking, Brad knelt next to him and pressed his hips to the ground. But as soon as Brad let go, Pudge stood up and started to bark again.

"I'm sorry," I told Faisal and Samir over the barking. "We'd better go."

"A pleasure to meet you." Faisal waited for Brad to straighten, then shook his hand. I reached for a handshake, too, but Faisal simply dropped his hand and nodded.

As I led Pudge back across the street, I snapped his leash, less for his benefit than to show Faisal and Samir I was in charge. "What's *wrong* with you?" I said. I climbed the front stairs and let Pudge into the house ahead of me. He ran to the front window and set his paws on the sill. He stared across the street into Virus' yard, and let out little wuffing under-barks.

After we'd closed the front door, I turned to Brad. "And *you*," I said. "What was *that* all about?"

"What?" Brad hung his jacket in the front closet. "What did I say?"

"You were interrogating them. I half expected you to ask their mother's maiden name."

"Their mother." Brad started for the back of the house. "That's funny."

I followed him through the dining room and into the kitchen. "What's funny? You think they don't have a mother?"

"Not the same one." Brad opened the refrigerator and pulled out a beer. "They look like brothers to you?"

"They *said* they were brothers."

"Samir's dark and short, with a thick beard, and stubble halfway down his neck. Faisal's light-skinned, taller than me, looks like he's never had to shave in his life."

"And my sister has bright red hair. They *said* they were brothers, Brad."

"They said they were from Boston, too." Brad popped the top of the beer can. "But they'd never heard of Carlton Fisk?"

"Why would they?" I asked. "He hasn't played baseball for a million years."

"Eleven."

"Whatever. They haven't been in the country that long."

"He's part of team lore."

"Maybe they don't care about baseball, Brad. Not everyone works for sportfreak.com."

"So why say they lived near Fenway Park?" Brad picked up his laptop computer and headed for the TV in the living room.

"Because they *did*?"

"They could say they lived near B.U. Kenmore Square. Back Bay."

"Or they could tell the truth, right?" I blocked Brad's exit at the kitchen doorway. "That they hate America. That they've come to strike at the heart of American power and depravity. Right here. In Columbus, Ohio."

Brad shook his head and smiled. But the smile faded quickly, and he said, "Don't tell me you didn't think about it."

"No," I lied.

"Come on. If something happened and the TV news came around, you'd tell them you never suspected a thing?"

I pantomimed a reporter's microphone in front of my mouth. "They seemed so quiet," I said. "They kept to themselves."

Brad glanced down, then looked into my eyes. "Somebody trained that dog to attack."

"Or not to," I said. "At least he's trained. *We* can't even get Pudge to sit."

"And that name: Virus. Creepy."

"Not really," I said. "Not if his master works in computer security."

Brad help up a surrendering palm. "Okay," he said. "You win Most Tolerant Spouse."

"It's not about that."

"Can you let me through? The game'll start any minute."

I stepped out of the doorway and let him pass.

He's not himself, I thought as I got the pork chops out of the refrigerator. He wasn't himself, and it didn't have much to do with terrorism—it had to do with baseball. Brad was ebullient, of course, when Boston made the playoffs, but if they'd been knocked out early, say back in August, he probably would have recovered quickly. It was this tension—with the Red Sox almost out, but still clinging to a sliver of hope—it was the tension that set Brad on edge. Maybe that's why Boston has so many hospitals.

Maybe they'll win tonight, I thought. That ought to help. But no, then they'd still be down three games to one. Winning tonight would only prolong the agony.

I glanced up to assure myself that Brad was out of earshot, then told the pork chops what I'd only then realized.

"I hope they lose."

Monday-Wednesday, October 18-20

But the Red Sox didn't lose. Not only did they win game four, on a twelfth-inning home run, but they won game five in extra innings as well. I was asleep before the end of each game, but Brad's bellowing from the living room let me know the outcome. On Tuesday, the Sox led game six from the fourth inning on, and won four runs to two to force a seventh game.

Wednesday evening, when I came home from work, Brad stood with his back to the television, staring out our tall front windows at the house across the street. Pudge stood next to him, his paws on the windowsill, his ears making soft corners on his head, like a stocking cap.

"Evening, boys." I hung my coat in the front closet. "Interesting goings-on chez Virus?"

"That dog is out all the time," Brad said. "They've tied a rope between those two pine trees, and rigged up a kind of harness and pulley for him. All he does, all day, is run along the rope from one tree to the other. He stares through the side fence, then the back fence. Side, back, side. Patrolling."

I came over to the window and scratched Pudge's head. "Thinks he owns the place, huh?"

"There have been comings and goings all day," Brad said. "Cable truck, plumber, electrician."

"They're fixing up. Great. That place has a lot of potential."

Brad pointed to a white van parked near the alley. "That van's been here at least four hours. No markings."

"A one-man shop making a long service call. We should get his card."

He pointed at three sedans along the curb by the front porch.

"Those arrived about thirty minutes ago, and six Arab men got out."

"Good," I said. "Good for them. I'm glad they've got friends in the area." I remembered Faisal nodding at my outstretched hand, as though contact with a Western woman was taboo. I fully expected that every visitor he'd have, as long as we lived here, would be Arab and male.

Game seven started at 8:30, and it was effectively over by 9:15. Boston opened up a six-run lead in the second inning, and stretched their lead to seven runs in the fourth. Brad sat back on the sofa, open-mouthed, and the break in the tension made me feel very tired. I went to bed at the start of the fifth inning, around ten-thirty, and I was fast asleep when Brad woke me at 12:45.

"Can you help me?" he said. "Please. I can't get on to the Internet."

"Really?" I said without opening my eyes. "Something's wrong with the cable?"

"The cable's fine. I just watched a four-hour baseball game on cable TV."

"Good," I said. "I'm glad you figured that out." I sank back toward sleep.

After a moment, Brad repeated, "I can't get on the web, Vick. Something happens after the cable comes into the house. Maybe the splitter, in the basement?"

"You want to go to your office?"

"The office is half an hour away." When I didn't answer, Brad continued, "This is a huge story, Vick. The Sox are going to the World Series. They haven't been there in eighteen years, haven't won in eighty-six. The Red Sox just beat the Yankees, on Mickey Mantle's birthday, to cap the most surprising comeback in baseball history." He paused. "If my column goes up late, our advertisers are going to notice."

No, they won't, I kept myself from saying. The effort to be polite made me open my eyes.

"Who am I kidding?" Brad said. "Nobody comes to sportfreak.com for my column. But this is a chance to *change* that, Vick. There'll be thousands of sleepless Red Sox fans clicking deep into the Web tonight, looking for a fresh angle, a reason to stay up a little later, a way to make the glow last."

And thousands of wives who wish they'd just go to bed. During Brad's speech, I'd come fully awake and realized that the fastest way to get back to sleep was to help him. I turned on the bedside lamp. "What do you want me to do?"

"Help me fix it?" The lamp shadowed the furrows in Brad's forehead. "Go down to the basement and check the connections."

"Can't *you*?"

"I'd have to keep running upstairs to try the laptop."

Right, I thought, because you need to plug into the router. Eighty dollars. For eighty dollars, we could have bought a wireless connection.

"It'll go much faster if you help," Brad said. "Can you take your cell phone down to the basement and check the connections? Call the upstairs stairs and keep me posted. I'll keep trying the router."

I stared at the ceiling. The lamp made a little circle of light there, in the darkness. I had just got to sleep half an hour ago, after willing the baby to take his knee out of my bladder. Sleep deprivation. Better get used to it.

It took me a couple of starts to roll out of bed, but once I did, momentum carried me to my cell phone on the bedside table and my robe in the closet. I stepped heavily down the stairs, and when I reached the ground floor Brad called down to me. "Hon?"

I turned and saw him at the top of the stairs. My "Yeah?" was all exasperated sigh.

"Thank you. Thank you, sweetheart."

I nodded. It didn't seem like much, but as I walked toward the basement stairs I felt a little lighter. The Red Sox were in the World Series, and if that meant a happy husband I was all for it. I dialed upstairs on my cellphone. Brad picked up. "Hello?" he said.

"You're welcome."

"Who is this?" Brad demanded. "Do you have any idea what time it is?"

I was too groggy to play along. "I'm just going down into the basement now. Descending, descending. Turning on the light. Ah."

Our house is a hundred years old, and in the basement every year shows. Cold War bomb shelter in one corner, open toilet and showerhead in the other. Holes bashed in the interior walls to cram through ductwork and pipes. It's a wonder the house is still upright.

"Looks good," I said. "We should entertain down here."

"I'll send out invitations. Can you find the cable?"

A cluster of wires ran through the cottony insulation on the ceiling. I didn't know what most of them did, but the thick black coaxial cable wasn't hard to pick out. It ran from the cinder-block foundation to the foot of the stairs, then split into two branches. One branch continued along the ceiling toward the bomb shelter, and the other branch disappeared into the filthy little crawlspace under the porch. I peered into the crawlspace and a filmy cobweb stuck to my nose.

"I don't know which cable goes to your router," I said. "But if it's the one in the crawlspace you better look for a new line of work."

"I've thought of opening a check-cashing franchise."

"Sounds good." I backed away from the crawlspace. "Nice clean work."

"How's the splitter?" Brad asked.

"Let me check." I ran my hand along the cable and grasped a little brass fastener at the split. Over the phone, I heard a short *bzzt* like the touching of two high-voltage wires. "Hey!" Brad said.

"You've got a connection now? I barely touched—"

"Just a second. Okay, okay." I heard Brad tapping on his keyboard, then the buzzing sound, again. *Bzzt. Bzzt.*

After the fourth buzz, Brad said, "Oh," in a tone of slow wonderment. "Oh. Shit."

"What?" I asked.

"No!" More tapping on the keyboard, louder this time. "*Stop!*"

"Brad!" I said. "What's going on?"

"I don't know," Brad said. "Can you come up here? Fast?"

"You want me to let go of the splitter?"

"Yes. No. It doesn't matter. Just hurry."

Hurry is a relative term when you're seven months pregnant. I kneed my belly up the basement stairs, going just slow enough to keep my sore breasts from bouncing. On the first floor I resisted the urge to stop for breath, and shoved round the corner to climb to the second floor.

When I arrived, panting, in Brad's home office, he was standing at his desk and stuffing his laptop into his carrying case.

"You're done?" I asked.

He shook his head.

"What happened?"

Brad zipped the case. "I was in a hurry. When you were messing with the splitter, I saw a message on the screen: 'A wireless network is in range. Do you wish to connect?' Lucky break, I thought, and clicked OK. Then it said, 'Do you wish to upload files,' and I said OK again."

I nodded. "The buzzing sound."

"Right. Then after the upload started, I though, wait a minute. Upload *which* files? Upload them *where*? I hadn't highlighted my column, and selected a connection to the office network. So God knows what files I was giving, and to who. I tried to stop. And you know what? I couldn't move the cursor."

"Like something took over."

"Oh, yeah," Brad said. "That computer's a zombie now."

"What are you going to do?"

Brad stood and slung the computer case over his shoulder. "Get out of range. Go in to the office, I guess. This story is going up way late, though, because I'm not going to connect an infected computer to the office network. Or copy the file over on a thumb drive. I can type the first screenful just by reading it off the screen, but if I still can't move the cursor I'll have to write the rest from scratch."

I nodded sympathetically.

He started for the stairs. "Then tomorrow I'll have to show it to our network guy. But he's such an idiot, I doubt he's even updated the anti-virus software. This wouldn't have happened if he did."

"Maybe you could show your computer to Samir," I said. "He's in network security."

Brad turned around, his hand on the banister. "You don't get it, Vick. Samir *did* this."

"Don't," I said. "How could he?"

"He's got a wireless router, that's how. Probably hooked it up today, after the cable truck left."

"It's not possible, Brad. Their house is clear across the street."

"You think someone closer hooked up a wireless modem? Maybe Roxie, next door, with her hearing aid and her walker?"

"But why would Samir care about your column?"

Brad patted the computer case. "All our banking information is on this machine. Balances, passwords, check routing numbers." He started down the stairs, then stopped halfway down and turned around. "You should probably get on the phone right now and report our credit cards stolen."

I followed him down the stairs and into the living room. "This is crazy, Brad," I said. "Sunday they were terrorists. Today they're identity thieves?"

"They *need* identity theft. They need it for financing, for disguise. You think Faisal and Samir are their real names?"

"You really believe this?"

"I don't know." He opened the front door. "God damn Red Sox. Even when they win, they give me a heart attack."

"Honey," I said firmly. "The Red Sox didn't infect your computer. They didn't, okay? And neither did Samir."

Brad backed onto the porch and looked protectively at my belly. He shook his head. "I hope you're right." He climbed down the porch stairs, sat down in his car, and drove away.

In the yard across the street, harnessed to the rope between two pine trees, Virus stared blankly at Brad's empty parking spot.

Thursday, October 21

One nice thing about Brad: when he's anxious, he does a ton of housework. Brad didn't get back from his office until three-thirty, and he was still asleep when I left for work on Thursday morning, but when I turned onto our street at the end of the day, he'd evidently been hard at work. Three yard bags stood on the curb, puffed out with maple leaves. Red Sox pennants flanked our front door and our cast-iron yard gate. In the myrtle by the curb, Brad had erected yard signs for two other not-yet-lost causes: one sign supporting the Kerry/Edwards presidential campaign ("A Stronger America") and one opposing the proposed same-sex marriage ban ("No On Issue 1").

The yard signs were for me—a thank-you for my waking up to help him last night, and for my putting up with him, generally, over the past week. Politics is my thing, not Brad's—my law firm had worked hundreds of pro-bono hours trying to get the gay-marriage ban struck from the ballot. Brad votes the way I do, but he's about as invested in politics as I am in the Red Sox. If he weren't from Boston, if he'd married someone else, he could easily live out in the suburbs with a Bush/Cheney yard sign.

The signs of Brad's handiwork continued into the back yard, where a fresh layer of wood chips had been poured into the dog run. Pudge galloped through the wood chips to greet me, a clean Red Sox kerchief tied around his neck.

I let Pudge out of the run, and he trotted ahead of me into the kitchen. His steps were quiet on the tile floor, which meant that his nails had been trimmed. As I hung my coat on the back hook, I heard a vacuum humming upstairs, and I noticed a marvelous homey smell, like cinnamon sticks in hot apple cider.

Pudge noticed the smell, too, and quickly tracked it to its source. He stood on his hind legs next to the oven, nose twitching, front paws balanced on the lowest drawer pull. Above him, next to the stovetop, atop a wire cooling rack, sat a warm apple pie. Strips of golden crust made a lattice over the top, and the mounded apples were dusted with rich brown cinnamon and nutmeg.

Pudge followed me to the foot of the stairs. "Hon?" I called up to the second floor. "This pie looks amazing. It *smells* amazing."

The vacuum shut off, and Brad appeared at the top of the stairs with the cord bunched in one hand. "Thanks." He climbed down the stairs, the vacuum bouncing ahead of him. When he reached the bottom, he said, "It's not for us, though."

"It's *not*?" I stuck out my lower lip, pouting.

"It's for Faisal and Samir."

I thought about this for a moment, then squinted. "*Why*?"

"I don't know." Brad crouched to wrap the cord around the back of the vacuum cleaner, and didn't look up at me when he continued. "I want to get a look inside their house."

"Brad," I said, "there's nothing to see."

"Then we're just nice neighbors welcoming them properly to Columbus."

"With pie?" I asked. "Nobody does that anymore. Not in the city. Not even here in the wholesome Midwest."

"I know that. So do you." He finished rolling up the vacuum cord, and stood to face me. "But *they* don't."

Pudge trotted away and curled, dejected, in front of the old gas fireplace.

I started to unbutton my peacoat, but Brad stopped me. "Better keep that on," he said. "We've got a pie to deliver."

"We?"

"I was thinking you could carry it. They'll be less suspicious if it comes from a woman."

I sighed and rebuttoned my coat. "I take it your computer's definitely infected."

"Unusable," he said. "Andrew found a keystroke logger and a routine that transfers new files out at startup. If you don't start up often enough, there's another program that freezes you up and makes you reboot every couple of days."

"Andrew found this? Andrew from work? You said he was an idiot."

"It's a well-known attack pattern, he said. I said, if it's well-known why aren't we protected from it? And he said, why was I connecting to a strange router?"

"Sounds like a productive conversation."

Brad shook his head. The corners of his mouth pinched in frustration. "Anyhow, neither one of us was sure he'd found everything, or cleaned it up thoroughly. So he sent it out to a specialist."

"Can you still work at home?"

Brad shrugged. "He gave me a loaner. A guy from Time Warner is coming out tomorrow to look at our connection. If he can fix it, I guess I'm in okay shape for the Series." He handed me the pie and ushered me out the door.

Virus' barking started as soon as we crossed the street. After four days harnessed to the pine trees, his possessiveness had turned frantic.

He chased us along the fence, barking and lunging, the harness snapping him back. I found myself shying off of the sidewalk and walking along the grassy easement.

We rang the front doorbell. No one answered.

"Maybe they're not home," I said.

"Someone's here." Brad pointed to the cars parked along the curb: the Oldsmobile and the two Toyotas. "Listen."

He rang again, and inside someone shouted in Arabic. Feet thumped up a flight of stairs. Finally Faisal opened the door.

"Hi, Faisal!" I said brightly, doing my best to sound wholesome and Midwestern. "How are you?"

"I am well, thank you." Faisal glanced down at the pie, then looked at Brad, questioning.

"It's for you guys," Brad said. "We wanted to welcome you to the neighborhood."

"Ah," Faisal said. "Thank you." He reached toward me hesitantly, as though touching me might burn his fingers. My first impulse was to make things easy for Faisal—just hand the pie over and leave. But Brad wouldn't let me hear the end of that. So I restrained myself and kept the pie pressed close to my belly.

"I am being impolite," Faisal said. "Please. Come inside."

"Thanks," Brad said, and stepped over the threshold.

The house was filled with unopened boxes. Furniture sprouted here and there amid the cardboard. Brad found a coat rack behind the front door, and hung up his Red Sox windbreaker to show we'd be staying a while. I started to unbutton my peacoat, then stopped myself. If Brad wanted to make himself at home, fine. But I didn't have to play along.

I couldn't have hung my coat anyway, because all of the hooks were full. Next to Brad's Red Sox windbreaker hung the corduroy jacket that Faisal had worn the day we met. And on the other hooks were two denim jackets and a trench coat. In the living room, we met the coats' owners. Three young men—two with mahogany skin and thick beards, one lighter-skinned and balding—sat hunched around a large set of paper plans unfolded on the coffee table.

They looked surprised to see us.

"Oh," I said. "We didn't know you had guests. We would have baked *two* pies instead of one."

"Brad, Vickie," said Faisal (again, he worked conspicuously at buzzing the *V* in my name). "These are Zia, Ulhar, Habib." Each man stood in turn to shake Brad's hand. They all ignored me, and I started to feel annoyed. I made a mental note to google how a Western woman should greet a Muslim man.

Faisal said, "They are helping us with some work in the basement."

"Really?" Brad said. "What kind of work?"

I broke in. "These old houses can be so much trouble."

"Indeed," Faisal said. "Yet Victorian homes have great character."

"We're lucky," I told him. "The owners before us fully renovated our place. All we had to do was move in and unpack."

Faisal didn't answer, and I wondered if I had overstepped by suggesting that he would be renovating. Maybe his guests were just helping with a superficial repair.

"So," Brad said to the men around the table, "you guys neighbors? Friends?"

"Relatives," said one of the darker men, the one with the longer beard—Zia, I think.

"Habib is an old friend," Faisal explained. "Zia and Ulhar are Samir's cousins."

"You mean *your* cousins?" Brad asked.

"Faisal?" I said. "Where shall I set this pie?"

Brad said, "I'll take it." He reached for the pie without taking his eyes off Faisal.

"It is confusing, I know," Faisal said. "Samir and I are half-brothers: we share only our father. Zia and Ulhar are from the side of Samir's mother."

Brad nodded and raised the pie. "Should we serve this? I didn't expect all of you, but there should be enough to go around."

Zia and Ulhar looked confused. Faisal exchanged a look with the bald man, Habib.

"It's still warm...," Brad cajoled.

"You are very kind," Faisal said. "And the pie looks tasty indeed. But it is now Ramadan. We cannot eat until sundown."

A flush of embarrassment climbed the back of my neck. "I'm sorry," I said. "I wish we had known."

"I'll just set this down into the kitchen," Brad said. "For later."

When Brad left the room, the men looked at Faisal, then at me. I shifted my weight uncomfortably; my swollen ankles were starting to ache.

"Sit down, Vickie," Faisal said. "Please."

I lowered myself to the sofa, then looked up, giving them permission to join me. Instead all the men remained standing. They smiled and nodded at each other as though the situation were satisfactorily resolved. I made a note to google "Muslim pregnant."

"So," I said after a moment's silence. "Quite a game last night, huh?"

Ulhar and Habib looked at each other helplessly; Zia shook his head.

"I did not watch," Faisal said. "But I am aware of the outcome."

"Hey." Brad returned from the kitchen, with a question that he pretended had just occurred to him. "Hey, where's Samir?"

Faisal turned to face him. "Samir is in Boston. Finishing a project for his former employer."

"Cool," Brad said. "Who'd he work for?"

"Why do you ask?"

"No reason," Brad said. "Pie's in the kitchen. We won't keep you gentlemen any longer. Pleasure to meet you, Zia, Ulhar, uh…"

"Habib," said the bald man.

"Of course."

As we crossed the street back toward our house, Brad started talking under his breath. "Little alcove off the kitchen," he said. "Little alcove with a writing desk, a laptop computer. And a wireless router."

"Doesn't mean a thing," I said, echoing his conspiratorial tone. "I'd be surprised if a couple of engineers didn't have wireless."

A muffled ring escaped from the pocket of Brad's leather jacket. He quickened his pace.

I sped up to keep alongside. "Aren't you going to answer that?" I asked.

He stepped onto the sidewalk. The phone rang again, and again.

Brad walked briskly past our front gate and into the alley, where he reached into his pocket and pulled out a chunky green cellphone.

"What's that?" I asked him. The phone he usually carries is smaller, and black.

"Shhh," he said. He didn't answer the phone, but stared at the display screen. "Write this number down: 617 235-5612."

"I don't have a pen," I said.

"617 235-5612," he said. "I think that's in Boston." He tucked the phone back in his pocket.

"That's not your phone," I said. "Is it?"

He opened the back gate. "I found it in Faisal's kitchen."

"Brad." I stopped in the alley, then hurried to catch him as he climbed the back stairs. "This has to stop. You have no right to take that man's cell phone."

"It's just a cheap prepaid thing," Brad said. "The kind they sell at that sleazy convenience store on Fifth."

"That doesn't matter," I said. "It's not yours."

"What I mean—" Brad hung his coat on the hooks next to our back door—"is what's Faisal doing with a phone like this? He's an engineer. He should have a sleek gray cellphone that can navigate the web."

"Oh, that's *very* suspicious." I rolled my eyes. "*Not* conforming to stereotype."

"Nice thing about these prepaid jobs, though: You can buy them for cash and they'll never be linked to your name. He can call anyone, say anything. No one will know it's him."

"Maybe it's not Faisal's," I said. "Maybe it's Zia's. Or Ulhar's. Or what's-his-name's."

"Habib's. What's the difference, Vick? They're all working together."

"Yes, they are," I said. "They're working in Faisal's basement."

"On what?" Brad asked.

"It's none of our business."

Brad opened the refrigerator and pulled out a beer. "You see those plans they were looking at?"

"Sure," I said. "I mean, not really. I didn't *scrutinize* them."

"What'd they look like to you?"

"I have no idea, Brad. Like plans. Probably for whatever they're working on in the basement. If it's anything like our basement, I'd say they're closing off the crawlspace, removing the toilet, installing wall-to-wall carpeting."

Brad nodded his head skeptically.

"Why?" I asked. "What'd they look like to you?"

He popped the top of his beer can. "Fenway Park," he said.

It was a restless night. Since my fifth month, I'd been getting up every two hours to use the bathroom, and I'd felt chronically overheated in our stuffy bedroom. Ordinarily, I could get back to sleep if I woke up, but tonight I kept thinking about Brad and his stolen cell phone, which since dinner had rung three times from two different numbers in the Boston area. I should steal it back, I told myself. Just slip it out of Brad's coat pocket, sneak across the street, and place it quietly in Faisal's mailbox. It all sounded like a great plan, until I realized that I couldn't be inconspicuous about it. Virus would be barking the whole time.

Around midnight I threw off the covers, and at one-thirty I opened both bedroom windows and set up a fan.

It didn't help. Cooler air poured in, but within ten minutes Virus started barking and whimpering. His harness whirred along the rope between the two pine trees in his back yard. He'd whirr to the tree near the foundation and whimper, then whirr to the tree near the back fence and let out three sharp alarm barks. Whirr. Whimper. Whirr. Bark bark bark.

At the foot of our bed, Pudge snorted. He trotted to the window and began to whine.

"Can we close the window?" Brad asked with his eyes closed.

"No," I said. "It's too stuffy." I'd been thinking of closing the window myself, but Brad's asking made me stubborn. If his stolen cell phone was keeping me awake, it seemed only fair to keep him awake, too.

"You can sleep this way?" he asked.

"No."

Brad covered his head with a pillow.

I shut my eyes. Virus' noises had a sort of regularity, and I tried to convince myself that they could be soothing if I tapped into their rhythm and counted. One. (Whimper. Whirr.) Two. (Bark bark bark.)

When I'd counted to twenty or so, Virus' rhythm accelerated, and then changed. Less whimpering, more barking. Faster whirrs. Brad pulled the pillow off of his head. "For Christ's sake, Vickie," he said. "Can we just close—"

A loud blast swallowed his words. First a crack like wood splintering, then a few seconds of debris pattering the ground, like the afterburst of a firecracker. Our open window shook in its frame.

I didn't recall getting out of bed, but I found myself standing at our bedroom window. Brad, whom I didn't recall getting up either, stood behind me with his hand clutching my hip protectively.

"Do you see anything?" he asked. "I couldn't find my glasses."

"Sort of," I said.

There was a four-foot hole in Faisal and Samir's basement wall. Large chunks of broken brick and cinder block lay in concentric circles around the foundation, and rubble had leaked through the fence and strewn the sidewalk. A section of the fence around Virus' yard had collapsed, the slats broken and splintered as though someone had kicked them with an impossibly heavy boot.

"I don't hear any barking," Brad said.

"The fence is down. Maybe Virus escaped."

"How could he? He's chained to those trees."

"It's not a chain," I said. "It's a rope harness."

Pudge started to whimper again. He set his front paws on the windowsill and started to shake.

"I don't like this," Brad said. "I'm going down to check it out."

"*Don't.*" I grabbed his hand and clutched it to my belly. "It isn't safe."

I had just found Virus. He lay at the foot of the tree near the broken foundation, still harnessed to his rope between the trees. He lay on his side as though he were asleep, but his ribs weren't moving. A sharp chunk of cinder block lay on the grass above his muzzle, and the white fur in front of his ear was stained dark. Behind the stain was a dent where his skull had caved in. The dent glistened with blood. Blood, or maybe exposed brain. Not that it made any difference to Virus.

By now some neighbors had straggled into the street. Nobody pays attention to sirens in our neighborhood, and even gunshots get ignored if they're far enough to the east. But a close-range explosion will get people out of bed. Our next door neighbor, Roxie, wearing a nightgown and a hairnet, had pushed her walker out onto her front porch. Some of the other black families—the ones that lived here before the neighborhood started to turn—walked cautiously toward the mansion, gawking.

A guy I'd never seen before—white, sixtyish, bald—flipped open a cell phone, and within five minutes a cruiser pulled up in front of Faisal and Samir's porch. Two young cops climbed out, and Faisal let them in the front door. After a few minutes the street cleared. I lay down on the bed, listening, while Brad sat against the bedroom wall, stroking Pudge's back protectively. When we heard Faisal's front door open across the street we sprang up again to watch through the window. I don't know what we expected to see; only a cliché comes to mind, the cops shoving Faisal, head lowered, into the back of their cruiser. Instead, the cops came out alone, and let themselves out the front gate. One shook his head and smiled faintly.

I got back into bed, suddenly exhausted. "That's a relief," I said. "I'm glad it was nothing."

At the window, Brad turned to stare at me. "Nothing?"

"I guess," I said. "At least, we don't know any different."

Brad closed the window and got into bed next to me. He lay on his back. Just as I was drifting off, he demanded, "How *old* were those cops?"

I thought about not answering, but if I fell asleep, he might ask again and wake me. "Twenty-five?"

"At the most." Brad threw himself onto his side. "Incompetents. Fresh out of the academy. Who else would work this shift?"

Saturday, October 23

Saturday morning, we were walking Pudge out our front door

when we saw a strange man across the street, standing outside Faisal and Samir's back yard. The man was short, bald, pushing sixty, with a heavy-but-not-soft build that said ex-football player, ex-cop. He scribbled notes on a wireless device I hadn't seen before: not a Palm, not a Blackberry, not a Treo. When he stopped writing, he held it up like a camera, and snapped a picture of the hole in Faisal and Samir's foundation. Evidently he wanted a closer shot, because he opened the gate and walked into the yard.

"Hey," I called out.

The man ignored me. He knelt by the hole in the foundation, and took a flash picture of the basement interior.

"Great toy," Brad said. "I've got to get one of those."

We crossed to Faisal and Samir's side of the street, and I rapped on the fence picket. "That's my neighbor's house," I said. "Can I help you?"

The stocky man took two more pictures with the flash, then rose from his crouch and walked slowly to the fence. He reached over and shook my hand. "Frank Arthur. You said you're a neighbor?"

"Across the street," I said before realizing that I had no obligation to respond. Something about him made me needlessly forthcoming. "I'm a lawyer. What are you doing on this property?"

"They know I'm here." Frank wrote something on his handheld. A pair of half-frame reading glasses rested on the bridge of his nose. "I'm an adjuster for Grange Insurance."

Brad said, "They filed a *claim* on this?"

"Sure." Frank turned toward Brad. "Why? You see what happened?"

"Not really. We heard a bang, and then, well, you can see as well as we can."

"This was the night before last?"

"Maybe two a.m. We were sleeping, so we didn't see what happened before the blast. What do they say in the claim?"

"Brad," I said. "He's not going to answer that."

"Act of God," Frank said, "They called it an Act of God."

A shiver ran up my spine. "What?"

"Or maybe bad workmanship. Some cousin, I guess, was over earlier in the day, fixing the hot water tank. And maybe he didn't fix it right, because the valve stuck, steam built up, and boom."

Brad said, "That can happen?"

Frank shrugged.

I thought about our own hot water tank, in our haunted-house basement. When was the last time anyone checked the valve? "Wouldn't there be some kind of warning?"

"Maybe," Frank said. "If the valve wasn't absolutely tight, there might be a few minutes of whining, really high pitched, almost too high to hear. I wouldn't hear it, not at my age. I doubt you would, either. Maybe a kid, though."

"Or a dog?" I asked.

"A dog? Sure."

"Their dog was barking a lot, right before the explosion. But you probably know that."

"I did not." Frank wrote something on his handheld. "Haven't seen a dog at all. Haven't heard any barking, either."

"Well, he died, I'm afraid. One of these cinder blocks hit him in the head."

"That's sad," Frank said flatly.

"He was a big dog." Franks' coplike manner made me want to provide a physical description. "Over a hundred pounds. Lots of energy, too. I'd guess he was less than five years old."

"I just," Brad broke in. "I can't help thinking. I mean, a water tank? It seems like an awful lot of damage for that."

Frank stopped writing and looked at Brad over the rims of his reading glasses. "That's what I think," he said.

"The cops came," Brad said. "But they didn't do anything."

"You think they should have?"

"I don't know," Brad said. "But we did notice some young Arab men—Muslim men—coming in and out of the house during the week. Thursday we dropped in with a pie, and found them looking over some plans. They said they were working on something." Brad paused.

"They say what it was?" Frank asked.

"No," Brad said. "But it was in the basement."

"So it could have been the water heater."

"Of course it was the water heater," I said. "Of course it was an accident. What else could it be?"

Frank shrugged. "You see a lot of strange things in the insurance business. Couple guys move into an old house. Needs more work than they realized, more than they can afford. So they take out a big policy, and…" He tilted his head at the foundation.

"What has me concerned," Brad said, "is this might have been just a practice run." He turned to me. "You know, like the radical group in that movie you dragged me to?"

I shook my head, annoyed, then realized what he was talking about. "Oh, the Weathermen. Accidentally blew up their own townhouse in 1970. Killed three of their own people."

"I remember that," Frank said. "Those were different times."

"But they weren't trying to blow up their own house," Brad prompted. "Weren't they screwing up a practice run for something else?"

"Right," I said. "They were going to blow up, what, the State Department?"

"An army barracks," Frank said. "But what's the connection? You think these guys are practicing?"

I glanced at Brad. "No," I said.

"But one of them's in Boston," Brad said. "Samir. Just got there on Wednesday, I think. I might have his number."

"The State Department's not in Boston," Frank said.

"No," said Brad. "But the World Series is."

Frank nodded.

Brad continued, "Game one is tonight,"

"I get you." Frank jotted in his handheld. "You said you might have a phone number?"

"Not with me," Brad said. "I could get it."

Frank dug a billfold out of his back pocket, and handed Brad a business card. "You find it, give me a call. Either number will do. I've got them both forwarded to this thing." He patted his handheld.

"Oh, man," Brad said. "It's got a phone, too?"

Frank turned the handheld toward us and clicked around with a stylus. "Phone, fax, voicemail, voice recognition. You leave that number, I'll just click the recording and it goes right into the Rolodex."

"Fantastic." Brad shook his head. "What'd it cost you?"

"Me? Nothing." Frank turned the handheld back toward him. "I don't think you can buy it retail, actually. The company's got some kind of a deal."

Brad nodded sadly. "I'm glad you're taking this on, Frank. The cops seem pretty clueless."

"I'm not taking anything on." Frank tucked the handheld in his pocket. "My role is limited to protecting the Grange Insurance Company and its policyholders. For me, the key question is this: was the explosion in this house deliberate? If it was, we don't pay. Some other building, in some other city—if we don't insure it, it's not my concern."

Saturday, October 23 – Wednesday, October 27

Within a hour, Brad called Frank's handheld with the Boston telephone numbers that he had read from Faisal's cell phone. But instead of Frank, a computer-generated voice answered with a prerecorded message that the (unnamed) subscriber was unavailable; please leave a message after the tone. Around five o'clock Brad called again and asked Frank to confirm receiving his message. Frank didn't call back.

By the time the Series started at eight, Brad was so agitated that he could hardly sit down for the opening pitch. The Red Sox won the highest-scoring game one in Series history—eleven runs to nine—but Brad was too distracted to enjoy it.

On Sunday, a few hours before the start of game two, Brad gave up on Frank and called Fenway Park instead. I felt sorry for the security officer who took Brad's call. I mean, look at it from his point of view: a stranger phones from Ohio with a theory about an explosion planned by young Arab men. The only detail he can give is the name Samir. If no one else calls with corroborating information, you go right back to worrying that some fan might sneak in with a beer bottle and throw it at the St. Louis dugout.

Game two started at 8:30. Boston took a 2-0 lead in the first inning, then stretched its lead to 4-1 after four. During the commercials, Brad kept running upstairs to troll the Internet for rumors of a bomb threat. When I caught him checking the Drudge Report, I made him stop.

Boston won again, 6 to 2, but Brad had hardly paid attention. The column he wrote was perfunctory, little more than a rehash of the box score.

On Tuesday, the Series moved to St. Louis, where the Sox won game three by a score of 4 to 1. On Wednesday, in game four, the Sox scored three runs in the third inning and still led 3-0 when Derek Lowe left the pitcher's mound after the top of the seventh. It was ten p.m. in St. Louis, eleven in Columbus. We sat on the sofa, watching a light-truck commercial with the television on mute.

I patted Brad's leg. "Looks like they're home free."

"Don't *say* that." Brad tapped the coffee table with his knuckles. The commercial ended, and Fox ran a montage of the Sox blowing a tenth-inning lead in game six of the 1986 World Series—the long montage that begins with Dave Henderson smiling as he catches an easy fly for the second out, and ends with the winning run scoring after a slow grounder rolls through Bill Buckner's legs.

I held my tongue.

In the top of the eighth, Boston led off with a single and followed with a double to put runners on second and third. The Cardinals brought in a new reliever, but he immediately gave up a walk to load the bases with no men out. Boston put a pinch runner on first, and brought in a pinch hitter for Lowe.

"This is it, don't you think?" I asked.

"I don't know," Brad said.

"I can see them losing a three-run lead, but it looks like it's going to be more like five."

Brad didn't respond.

The reliever struck out the pinch hitter, and got the next batter to ground into a fielder's choice. When the final batter struck out to end the inning, Brad smacked the coffee table with both palms.

"Honey," I said. "It's okay. They're still up by three runs."

"With a new pitcher." Brad sat back and folded his arms. "I just hope they can hold on."

We sat in silence through a beer commercial, and then the local affiliate ran an ad for Senator Kerry—the one where he promises to hunt down and kill Osama bin Laden.

I pressed the mute. "Hey, at least there's no bomb. You can rest easy on that."

"What makes you say that?"

"Even if the Sox lose *this* game—"

"Stop."

"—the Series won't go back to Boston unless they lose game five as well."

"You trying to give me a heart attack? The Sox are *notorious* for blowing big leads."

"Maybe they are," I said. "But do you think al Qaeda knows that?"

Brad looked at me. "What?"

"If you were planning to bomb Fenway Park, wouldn't you have done it game one or two? Wouldn't you have allowed for the possibility that, once the Series left Boston, it wasn't coming back?"

"What do I know, Vick? Maybe they have another cell in St. Louis."

Pudge sprang to his feet and snorted. The front gate squeaked open, and a few seconds later the doorbell rang. I stood up, leaving Brad on the couch with his scorecard and his laptop computer.

When I opened the door, Faisal looked down at me from our front porch, his head lowered, his shoulders hunched.

He looked straight into my eyes. "Hello, Vickie," he said. "I am very sorry to disturb you so late. You said, I think, you are a lawyer?"

"Come in." I stood aside.

Faisal walked quickly into the living room. Brad stood up and nodded with bare politeness. "Faisal."

"Hello, Brad," Faisal said. "Let me repeat my apology. I did not realize your game was still being played."

"That's all right." I fixed Brad with a look before he could say anything. "It's recording on TiVo. He can pause it and skip through the commercials later."

Brad hesitated, then pressed the pause button. "I guess that's right," he said. "At least for a couple of minutes."

Faisal didn't remove his coat but sat immediately in the low armchair next to the couch. He opened his hands. "Samir is gone," he said.

"What?" I asked.

"Sure he's gone," Brad said. "He's in Boston, right?"

Faisal shook his head. "He was supposed to return this evening. But when I went to the airport, he was not among the passengers."

I sat down on the sofa next to Faisal's chair. My first impulse was to put my arm around him, but I stopped myself, afraid that would make him more uncomfortable. "That can happen," I said. "Samir probably just missed the flight. Traffic in Boston must be crazy right now."

"Not yet." Brad pointed at the television. "The game's still on."

I fixed Brad with a stare. "Some fans celebrate early," I said.

"Not in Boston." Brad shook his head. "Anyhow, Samir wouldn't be driving now." He turned to Faisal. "You said he was scheduled to arrive in Columbus, what, an hour ago?"

"Two hours," Faisal said.

"Even so—" I started.

"Brad is correct," Faisal said. "I strongly doubt Samir is stuck in traffic. Actually, I have not known his whereabouts for three days."

I sat down. "Oh."

Faisal continued. "Before Samir left, our telephone service was still inactive, so I bought a temporary mobile phone at a convenience store. But the phone went missing. Yesterday, when our home phone started working, I called Samir's hotel in Boston. He was not checked in. I phoned a friend at his old employer, where he was supposed to be finishing a project. The friend had not seen him since Friday. Monday morning he did not come in."

I was out of my depth. In my work, I hear a lot about husbands running off with their mistresses, or abused wives disappearing with their children. Neither situation seemed to apply here. "This isn't my specialty," I said. "But I have to ask. Did Samir seem upset when he left? Was there someone in Boston he was exceptionally attached to?"

Faisal's eyes narrowed. "Samir didn't run away," he said. "He was *taken*."

We were silent. After a moment, Brad said, "What?"

"For some time we have been under surveillance. I had thought it might stop when we left Boston. But it continued. A few days after we arrived, an unmarked van parked on the curb. Not long after, it tried to wi-phish us."

"I'm sorry," I said. "Wi-phish?"

"They set up a wireless router, and tried to induce us to connect. Of course, only a fool would do so."

I glanced at Brad, who had lowered his eyes.

"And of course," Faisal said, "Samir is far from inexperienced."

"Of course," I said.

"I am quite sure they have tapped our phone as well. It took several days to connect, and the man who did it spent an exceptional length of time in the circuit box."

"But who would do this?" I asked.

Faisal shrugged. "FBI?" he said. "Homeland Security? Defense Intelligence? I may finally have seen one of them. A short, thick man, bald, perhaps fifty-five years old."

"Oh, that guy?" Brad said. "He's not a fed. He's an adjuster for Grange."

"For whom?" Faisal asked.

"Grange Insurance. He was checking out your homeowner's claim."

"We have not yet filed a claim," Faisal said. "And our insurer is Amica."

"Amica?" Brad said. "Well, maybe that's what he said."

"No," I told Brad. "He said Grange. Faisal, where do you think Samir is now?"

"I wish I knew."

"Have you called the police?"

"Yes, in Boston. They will not tell me anything."

"They have to," I said. "You have rights, Faisal. You're his brother."

Faisal looked away for a moment, then lowered his eyes bashfully. "We are not brothers."

I glanced at Brad. His eyebrows were raised politely, but his eyes darted toward me, and for a second I thought that he might be right about Faisal and Samir. But when I looked again at Faisal and saw that his cheeks were flushed, I realized what he must be saying. Of course. Two young men from an intolerant country, fixing up an old house in a gentrifying neighborhood. Why hadn't I seen it before?

I thought of the sign in our front yard, opposing the same-sex marriage ban. Faisal must have felt safe with us.

"Oh, Faisal," I said. "We're so sorry."

His shoulders started to shake. "My greatest fear," he said, "is that they have rendered Samir back to Egypt. I cannot bear to think what would happen to him there."

I couldn't, either. And I couldn't imagine it would help him to be homosexual.

I couldn't stop myself now. I laid my hand on Faisal's arm. "We will find him. Don't worry."

"You are very kind," Faisal said, and when he looked from me to Brad his eyes were wet.

"I do family law," I told him. "So I wouldn't know where to begin. But there are people in my firm who work with private eyes. And first thing in the morning, I'll call a friend who does immigration. I don't know if she's the right person, but she's a start."

"Thank you." Faisal rubbed the side of his face with one shoulder, and we stood up. He looked intently into my eyes, and if his background had allowed him to hug a woman I'm sure he would have. On his way to the door, he stopped and shook Brad's hand, clasping his shoulder as he did so. "You are good people. I knew this even before, when you brought the pie. You are the only people in this neighborhood who have showed us any kindness."

After Faisal left, I closed the front door, and stood for a moment, watching him cross the street. He was standing a little straighter than before, though I doubted he would sleep well tonight.

When I came back to the sofa, Brad was skipping through the end of the Kerry ad. I took the remote and set it back to pause.

"We are going to bust our *asses* for that man." I said. "We have a lot to make up for."

"Vickie." Brad reached for the remote. I tucked it behind my back. "Come on. You think the government's watching them for no reason at all?"

Michael tested the water with his toe, then lowered himself gingerly into the bath. Try to relax, she had said. Easier said than done - strangely, the lack of sexual advances from Susan had made him more uncomfortable, not less. He leaned back and closed his eyes. How long had it been since he'd had a hot bath? He thought of Susan pressing her bony little naked body against his, the two of them lapped by the warm fragrant water, and his penis stiffened against his belly. He lifted a languid hand, then dropped it, suddenly too tired to masturbate. His erection subsided, and he did as he had been asked, drifting off into a state of semi-sleep.

"Life in Miniature"
by Tracie McBride"

Then they punch her. They are laughing about it. And they hit her again. Every time she gets more weepy until she just shuts off. Yes, like a robot. I don't know. Ok, she looks at the camera and she's a blank like all the shit in her life and all the bad times just lead up to this. She doesn't care about Kathy or her parents or her bitch older brother Todd who keeps fucking her boyfriend like she doesn't know. She is not giving the director the finger. Blank. Totally blank. Like you gave up. Come on, Tanya. Work with me here.

"Snuff"
by Tim Lieder

THE FELLOW TRAVELER

WAR, VOYAGES, ADVENTURE

In THE FELLOW TRAVELER, we follow adventure wherever it takes us, from the old west to the wrestling rings of the *lucha libre*, down to the ocean's depths or to the deepest forests of bear country.

First up, we have "Promises", a super-hero tale by Fred Warren, in which childhood vows are fulfilled with serious adult consequences. Then, we're pleased to present "Thirst," Jens Rushing's tale of piracy and revenge on the high seas.

Grab your rucksack and follow along!

Fred Warren works as a government contractor in eastern Kansas, which is a lot like being a superhero minus the special abilities and cool costume. His short fiction has appeared in a variety of print and online publications, including *A Fly in Amber, Mindflights, Bards and Sages Quarterly, Brain Harvest, Kaleidotrope,* and *Allegory,* and his first novel, *The Muse,* debuted in November 2009. You can find him online at http://frederation.wordpress.com.

PROMISES

It begins in Kansas, as I suppose these stories always do. Donna and I played in the back yard, while our parents sat in the living room drinking lemonade and talking about wheat prices, and farm equipment, and how best to keep the varmints out of the fields.

We didn't care about any of that. We were half a world away, rescuing our planet from the latest incursion of evil villainy. The giant robot had just clocked me a good one, on the chin, and I lay prone, watching little stars and birdies circle my head as the mechanical monster clanked relentlessly onward, an impressive cluster of weapons spinning into firing position as it prepared to finish me off.

"Don't be afraid, Titanic Man!" Donna shouted, swooping in from above. "I'll save you!"

I shook off the glittering lightshow and struggled to my feet. "I don't need saving. Girls can't save boys, anyhow."

She launched herself from the rope swing to a perfect two-point landing a few feet away. "Why not? If I was a superhero, I'd save anybody who needed it—especially you."

I held the robot monster at bay as he slobbered all over my face. "Especially me? How come?"

"Because you're my friend, and that's what friends do. They save each other."

"Whatever. Robo Dog of Doom is killing me here, if you haven't noticed."

Donna was always there—at the farm, in school, at church, around town. She was a part of my landscape, like the wind and sun and the wheat fields that surrounded us like a golden ocean. But when we turned thirteen, everything changed. The fever and convulsions took her one day at school, and I watched, numb, my stomach knotted, as they strapped her onto a gurney and loaded her into a brown-mottled military ambulance.

She cried out once, a thin, strangled sound. I thought she'd called my name, and I struggled against the principal's grasp on my shoulders as the medics slammed the ambulance door shut and drove away.

◊ ◊ ◊ ◊ ◊

Donna was one of the Empowered. One in five million. Their immune systems ran wild, shuffling their DNA. Sometimes it killed them. Sometimes it transformed them into a superhuman. It happened to animals, too, but they usually mutated into huge, grotesque varmints beyond the capabilities of conventional pest control, one reason the Empowered were handy to have around.

They were heroes, most of them. They rescued people and warded off disaster. Sometimes, though, the thrill of power would corrupt one of them, and we'd get a villain. The government scientists weeded out most of those before they caused trouble. The others they hunted down and sent to a special facility somewhere in the Mojave Desert. What happened after that was anyone's guess. One of my friends said there were experiments, digging around inside the villains' bodies to figure out what had made them Empowered, so heroes could be created at will.

For five years, I waited and worried about Donna, wondering if she'd survived, praying she hadn't ended up a lab rat, dissected on some mad scientist's slab. Life plodded on, bland and lifeless without her. Finally, at my high school graduation, Donna's parents took the stage, eyes brimming, voices choked with relief and joy.

She was alive, and she was coming home.

◊ ◊ ◊ ◊ ◊

Donna returned on a sun-drenched Fourth of July, fresh from post-transformation training. She was the stuff of every teenage boy's dreams. She could fly, and she had enhanced senses and strength. Her perfect curves were accentuated by shimmering carbon nano-mesh armor that clung in all the right places and revealed much more than necessary. Marketing was a big part of the superhero gig, and the community wasn't above providing a little fan service for their audience.

I felt dizzy. This was my buddy, the rowdy girl who helped me fight imaginary monsters in my backyard, who rode bikes with me, who called me after dinner to ask for help with her homework. I stared at her with a mixture of joy, fascination, confusion, and a couple of other emotions I didn't want to think about as she stood on a rickety platform in the town square, thanking us for welcoming her home and explaining her new mission in life.

Her colors were red and white, and they called her Rockette. A little silver missile was emblazoned below her décolletage, and pinstriped flames adorned her thigh-high boots. A short cape, more decorative than practical, covered her shoulders. She carried a tranquilizer gun in a holster slung low on her right hip to, she said, "Rockette my enemies to sleep." It was more corn pone for the masses, but she said the cartridges had enough punch to drop any varmint, big or small.

As she looked across the crowd, our eyes met. She paused her speech, her brow furrowed and head tilted slightly, then a glowing smile spread across her face, and she said, "I see someone I've wanted to talk with for a very long time. Please excuse us."

Faster than I could react, she leapt from the platform, grabbed me around the waist, and vaulted into the air. We landed atop the school gymnasium as gently as a soap bubble floating to earth, my stomach lurching but my dignity intact. We talked for nearly an hour.

Her face was mature now, the familiar childish features perfected. Her skin was radiant, clear and smooth, framed by glossy auburn hair bobbed to her jawline. Her brilliant blue eyes were the ones I'd always known, but they never met mine precisely—she seemed preoccupied with some point on the horizon, just over my shoulder, as if she was seeing her future in the distance or scanning for a threat I couldn't see or hear.

I wasn't sure what to say at first—how do you talk to a girl who's been gone for five years, then comes back a goddess? I tossed a few half-baked jokes about old chorus line dancers, and battle bikinis, and not forgetting about the little people. It was lame and awkward. She took it all in stride, her laughter a gentle, musical sound that set me at ease and brought all the old memories rushing back.

Far too soon, it was time for her to go. We strolled back to the square, hand-in-hand, like two ordinary teenagers, and as we parted, she gave me a platinum disc embossed with her rocket insignia, a tiny button at the center. "If you ever need saving," she said, "just press the button, and I'll be there, faster than you can imagine."

"Girls can't save boys, remember?"

She smiled, but her eyes were moist. "I remember, but it's even less true now. Call me, and I *will* save you. I promise. That's what friends do for each other."

Donna—Rockette—walked away then, back to the plywood dais hung with patriotic bunting, a gaggle of adolescent boys, plus a few dirty old men who should have known better, drooling in her wake. As the crowd cheered and the high school band struck up a fanfare, I whispered, "And if you ever need me, I promise I'll be there to save *you*."

She might have faltered in her stride, just for an instant. Maybe her Empowered hearing was sharp enough to make out the words, but it was probably my own wishful thinking. She climbed the stairs to the platform, closed her eyes for a moment, then shot heavenward, out of my life forever, a dwindling mote of brilliant red against the blue Kansas sky.

◊ ◊ ◊ ◊ ◊

As I toiled through college, her fame grew. She joined the Devastators. They were a prominent and successful super-team, but I didn't like them very much. There were three members besides Rockette. Bulldozer was 350 pounds of idiot in construction-zone-yellow tights and a bullet-shaped helmet. He broke things, and he was an arrogant jerk, but people never looked deeper than his chiseled physique. Blue Streak was a speedster, and a narcissist. Rumors about his sexual preference kept the tabloids buzzing, as if he could possibly love anyone, male *or* female, more than himself. He was as slick as his glittering turquoise unitard and never admitted anything, one way or the other. Finally, there was Calculus. He was an anomaly among superheroes, artificial intelligence housed in an android body, shining green armor giving him the look of a huge, iridescent beetle. Though the government was silent on the issue, most people figured he was created as a sop to the A.I. lobby in the World Congress—one more step toward their vision of equality between human and machine. He was an expert tactician with a supercomputer brain, and his calculating prowess bordered on clairvoyance.

Nothing happened that Calculus didn't anticipate. It was the key to the Devastators' success, since Bulldozer was stupid, Blue Streak was self-absorbed, and neither of them listened to anything Rockette had to say. She sent me a few e-mails about their adventures, until the government tightened the security protocols and blocked her messages. She never complained—she was loyal, a real team player. I wished for her sake she'd get fed up with her teammates one day and stand up for herself.

I wound up in the construction business, or, more precisely, the re-construction business. When superheroes fought either varmint monsters or supervillains, it made a super *mess*. Somebody had to clean things up and reassemble the broken pieces of civilization, and I became pretty good at it. I didn't just repair broken buildings, I sculpted them with nanotechnology and resurrected them as works of art. I streamlined the whole process and hired the best work crews and civil engineers. There was good money in city restoration, and the job kept me as close to Rockette as any Normal could get. I set up my home office in New York City, a few blocks from the Devastators' headquarters.

I even made it into a news feature once. They called me "Doctor Disaster," like I was some kind of superhero myself. I laughed it off, but in my heart, I wished it was true. I wished I could live in her world, that I could match her blinding speed and dance with her among the clouds. Sometimes I'd glimpse her darting across the sky like a jet-powered ballerina in scarlet—curving, spinning, and pirouetting in maneuvers that would make a falcon dizzy.

I loved her.

Everybody loved her—even the press, who began to suggest the wrong hero might be leading the Devastators. She brought in the lion's share of her team's income from product endorsements, action figures, and public speaking engagements. They were lucky to have her. Bulldozer could barely put two words together, Blue Streak only wanted to talk about himself, and nobody could understand *anything* Calculus said. There was gossip of a secret romance between Bulldozer and Rockette, but I never believed it. She had far too much common sense to hook up with a knucklehead like that.

At least, I hoped she did.

I was supervising the final touches on World Trade Center Four when it happened. The Devastators were fighting Baron Tempest, a pesky weather-controller who should have been well within their capabilities. He was giving them a run for their money that day—he'd added directed lightning to his repertoire, and brilliant arcs of electricity crisscrossed the stormy sky over New York Harbor. Rain pelted my office window as I watched the live news broadcast, sipped my coffee, and tallied up the damage.

Blue Streak dashed hither and yon, dodging thunderbolts as Bulldozer tossed automobile parts and building materials in the general direction of the Baron's cloud platform. After ten years or so of practice, I mused, he should have been a better shot. Calculus stood safely in the lee of a mothballed Navy cruiser, chattering orders into his communicator. Maybe it was all part of the plan, though it didn't look like a very good plan at that moment.

He stopped talking and looked up. Rockette blasted out of a cloudbank and arrowed in on Tempest from behind, tranq gun at the ready. I smiled as she flashed across the vid screen. I thought it was all over.

At the last second, the Baron whipped around and flung a

thunderbolt at Rockette, transfixing her in a crackling auriole of ionized air. She plummeted from the sky, like Phaeton struck down from the chariot of the gods, a smoldering ember quenched in the roiling black waters of the harbor below. A moment later, Bulldozer connected with a concrete block, plucking Baron Tempest from his cloud and flattening him against the Chrysler Building. Emergency crews converged on the urban battlefield, and the broadcast went black. My stomach clenched. Voice shaking, I ordered my salvage team to begin the cleanup.

Rockette survived, but invulnerability wasn't one of the prizes she'd won from her spin of the mutagenic wheel. She healed incompletely. Scar tissue marred the left side of her flawless face, and she walked with a limp. Only in the sky was she as graceful as before, but she flew with none of the joyful abandon that was her trademark.

Her trademark. In the end, it was all about her trademark. Perfection was the essence of a superhero's allure, and demand for Rockette's image in any form dropped to zero. She tried adopting a rakish mask that concealed most of the scarring, but everyone knew what lay beneath. To the marketing wizards, she was damaged goods, and they dropped her from the team. Calculus issued a convoluted press release. Trimmed to its essentials, it thanked her for her service and declared it time for the Devastators to move on.

They signed a fresh new teenager named Sirene. She was a sonic screamer, and pretty. She couldn't fly, but Calculus bought himself a jetpack and began directing battles from the air. Sirene also wasn't much of a public speaker. Calculus assumed that role, adjusting his speech subroutines to make his orations more audience-friendly. He was almost charming, in a shiny, green, insectoid sort of way. His numbers rose in the polls, and the ad agencies plastered his picture on billboards and cereal boxes.

Soon afterward, Rockette disappeared, leaving the world to wonder about her fate. There were whispers of a lady in red who flashed from the dark crevices between buildings to catch suicide jumpers and steelworkers who missed their footing. I believed the rumors. Perhaps it was wishful thinking, but it is exactly what she *would* do, because for Rockette, it was never about the cheers, or the honors, or the money. She saved people because they needed saving.

I found a note on my desk one morning. Old school—a plain white paper envelope with a little card inside. Handwriting full of loops and curlicues in bright red ink.

I have to go away. None of the other teams want me, and the Empowerment Monitoring Agency plans to bring me in for re-evaluation. It's what they do with villains, and nobody ever comes back from that. I thought you should know. Guess my luck's run out—the first time Calculus ever makes a mistake, and it's with me. Tell the folks back home goodbye, and I'm sorry.

Your friend,

Donna

P.S. If you still have the coin, I still remember my promise.

Finally, it hit me. *Nothing* escaped Calculus' computations. He anticipated every scenario and planned every countermove. I went to my computer and pulled up the video file of the battle with Baron Tempest. I watched it over and over again, from every camera angle, not sure what I was looking for, certain only that something was there that would reveal the truth.

On the twentieth replay, I found it. As the Baron spun around to attack Rockette, I saw a tiny flash at his wrist. I zoomed in and cranked up the magnification. The edge of his gauntlet had flipped over in the wind, revealing a silver bracelet with a cluster of LEDs.

A Devastators wristcomm. Custom electronics from the government labs. Every team member had one, and only the team leader had the authority to make another.

The Baron hadn't sensed Rockette's approach in the air currents, he'd been listening to Calculus' orders from the beginning. He knew she was coming.

The video played on. As Rockette tumbled earthward, I forced my attention to Calculus, who looked on in icy cybernetic detachment as she dropped from the sky like a shotgunned swan, his eyes tracing her trajectory all the way into the greasy black water, showing no sign of alarm, making no effort to help.

Every action he'd taken since that moment served to boost his public image. It seemed so obvious now. Calculus wasn't content to lead the Devastators. He wanted the acclaim, the glory, and perhaps even the love that flowed past him to his charismatic teammate. So he set her up.

Somehow, I should have seen it coming. Somehow, I should have saved her, like I promised. I switched off the computer and stared out the window for a long time, watching clouds gather over the city, and remembering.

That evening, I planted a vial of construction nanobots, with a very particular taste in building materials, inside the ventilation conduits of Devastators HQ, timed to release during Calculus' recharge cycle. *Let him try to compute that.*

His teammates discovered an attractive abstract sculpture in his command chair the next morning, iridescent green chromalloy contorted into an intricate knot. I left his brain untouched. Calculus understood jealousy and treachery. Perhaps, fused inside that twisted metal prison, he'd learn about pain, and regret, and loneliness, like Rockette. Like me.

The world collectively shrugged, writing off the incident as some supervillain's revenge, and the Devastators began shopping for a new leader. They're still looking. Maybe this time, they'll find someone with both a brain *and* a heart.

◊ ◊ ◊ ◊ ◊

It ends in New York, as I suppose these stories always do. Atop the rebuilt Trade Center, polished onyx surfaces shine with mirrored moonlight, testament to my small, mundane power to mend what has been broken. It is glistening and perfect, as *she* once was, as she still is within.

I have wealth enough to hide her, and people of influence owe me favors—people with the skill and leverage to exonerate her. This time, I have the power to act, and I won't miss my chance again.

The wind howls, and the platinum disk is ice between my fingers as I reach skyward and press the button again and again, calling to Rockette, to Donna, *my* Donna, praying that she'll hear and answer, because without her, I'm lost, and my world is no world at all. We'll save each other, like we promised.

That's what friends do.

Jens Rushing is a widely published writer, originally from Texas and currently living in South Korea, where he teaches English.

THIRST

Twenty-two cannons boomed. The merchantman's mainmast shattered and splinters hailed the deck. Another shot from the barque burst the forecastle and sent sailors flying. Everywhere men lay dead and dying from the pirates' assault. The foremast buckled and crashed to the deck. The torn and burning sails fell loose and swathed the bow. From the aft cabin Miranda watched the shape of the wounded captain moving feebly beneath the sheet; soon he did not move at all. The bombardment ceased and in the sudden calm Miranda heard the rush of water into the hull, the groans and wails of the dying sailors, and the creak of oars in locks.

This last sound set her heart racing. She peered through the porthole, and too, too close, three large boats freighted with dark and desperate men crossed from the barque to her own sinking ship, oars dipping into the placid Caribbean sea. The pirates drew near; she could make them out now. A rogue with a long musket stood in the prow of the forward boat, scanning the deck for survivors. Miranda shuddered at the sight of him. He was tall and broad, with one milky eye and a bald scalp leathery and brown from the sun. A cutlass hung at his waist, tucked into a green silk sash.

"What are we to do?" Nona bawled. "Mistress, what are we to do?" She sobbed and wrung her hands. Her face was red from two weeks of crying. From Bristol to the Caribbean she had wept silently over Miranda's imminent marriage: "Oh, my wee baby girl," she said time and time again, shaking her head and annoying Miranda beyond telling. "Oh, my darling lass." Then her crying became intense and urgent when the captain sighted the red flag and commanded full speed and battle stations. Nona's sobs leapt to deranged shrieks when the first broadside crashed into the ship, and now she sputtered like a dying flame. "Do we conceal ourselves below and hope they pass? Or—do we destroy ourselves, mistress, before they, before those rough men…" She trailed off.

Miranda seized a bulkhead as the ship listed suddenly. "We're taking on water," she said. "We can't conceal ourselves, Nona! The ship will plunge under the sea and take us with it."

"A better end than whatever those brigands plot!" Nona dabbed her eyes. "I would rather see that, mistress, than you in their foul, wicked hands. Let the sea take us!"

"I have no wish to die. And I won't." Miranda said it simply, and knew it for a truth. "In two weeks, Nona, I'll be Mr. Fraser's wife and mistress of Averslay, and you'll be couched in luxury. Don't talk of death. I won't allow it." She closed and barred the door while she spoke.

Nona smiled for the first time since Bristol. "Oh, mistress. And my divan."

"Of course, good Nona." Miranda heard footsteps on the deck and raised her voice to cover them. "I'll have it stuffed with hibiscus blooms if you like! And a servant of your own! Never work again, good Nona!"

From outside a shouted command: "Stove it in!" And a thundering crash of metal against wood. Nona shrieked. The door shook, but the bar held. Nona held out her arms and Miranda flew to them.

"Pray with me, mistress, pray!"

"No need, no need. We'll live, Nona."

"You'll die this day, lass, and never prayed a word in your life."

Miranda pursed her lips but said nothing. She didn't flinch, not once, as the door shattered under the blows and the bald man strode into the little cabin, brandishing his cutlass. Nona clung to Miranda as a drowning man to a piece of lumber. She twisted out of Nona's grasp and lifted her chin in defiance. "I am Miranda Davenport," she said, and her voice had never rung so clear or so proud, "daughter of Sir Richard Davenport of Gloucester. Affianced to Samuel Fraser, captain in His Majesty's Royal Navy."

The pirate bowed low. "Captain Joshua Barclay," he said, "of no nation and no king, at your service." A redheaded man appeared in the doorway behind him. He wore a tattered blue Navy jacket, and his beard was full and bushy. He eyed Miranda. "And this here's Frederick Wickliff, bosun, Royal Navy—retired." Wickliff nodded. Nona moaned, and irritation flickered across Barclay's face.

"Captain," Miranda said, "I have made you familiar with my position. I hope I can trust you to deliver me safely to the nearest port. You will be amply rewarded, of course, for—"

Barclay cut her off with a wave. "Say no more, lass," he said, and Miranda smiled. "You'll bore me to tears. Aye, you'll come with me. A sweeting like you, to have and to hold." He gripped Miranda's wrist. Her nails raked his face, gouging long red slashes across from brow to cheek. Barclay howled and pressed his hands to the wound, then took them away and saw blood. Fury flared in him and he struck Miranda with the back of his hand. She reeled with the powerful blow—no one had dared strike her before—but didn't fall. Barclay drew a small dagger and moved on Miranda. For a moment she stared death in the eye. Wickliff shouted, "Captain! Havana!" and Barclay returned the dagger to its sheath.

A smile snaked across Barclay's face. "Right," he said. "Havana for you. Such a lovely face. Such fine skin, that none ever took a knife to." He stuck his thumbs in his sash and roared with laughter as blood dripped down his face. "To Havana, then!" He crooked a finger at Nona. "We'll not be needing her. Wickliff!"

"No!" Miranda cried. She seized a bottle from the table and sprang at Barclay, poised to crush his tanned skull. With a laugh he disarmed her and flung her over his shoulder. She kicked and pounded on his broad back with her fists. He grunted.

"Keep it up, lass, and you may not see Havana after all. You'll just make it to my bunk, and then it's the knife for you. Understand?"

Miranda lay still. She wanted to fight this man with every fiber of her being, but her desire to live was greater. "Wickliff," she said.

The bosun glanced at her and looked away. Drawing his cutlass, he moved past Barclay and into the room. His shadow fell across Nona, who whimpered and crouched in the corner. "Wickliff, you can't do this!" Miranda shouted. "Bring her, too! You can't—you can't!" And then Barclay was carrying her away, over the ocean, away from Nona, from Samuel, from life, from everything.

Insensate rage followed. Miranda lurked in a sullen fury for three days, the image of Nona's fear-frozen face her only company. Barclay imprisoned her in an aft cabin, quite small, and twice a day he or Wickliff brought her food and drink, which she left untouched. Miranda lay on her cot, turned to the wall. The only sounds were the babble of the sea and the no-quieter babble of laughter and clanking dishes from the chamber adjoining hers.

But love of life was bright within her, and her grief quickly gave way to anger and hatred for the men who had slain her old friend and abducted her, and soon an ambition, hateful and necessary, germinated like a venomous weed in her mind: vengeance. She buried the ambition—for now. On the third day, she ate and drank, and was alert and thinking when Wickliff brought her meal.

"Why is it only you and the captain wait on me?"

"Your pardon, miss, we don't wait on you exactly. We keep you among the living, is all."

"Well, why is it only you and the captain who keep me among the living, then?"

"I believe I'm the only one the captain trusts to...respect you."

The thought seemed strangely hilarious to her, and Miranda laughed despite herself. "Trusts you not to force me, you mean."

Wickliff blushed. The blush faded quickly and he said, gravely, "Yes, that's it exactly." The laugh died in Miranda's throat.

"Because you were in the Navy? And that makes you a gentleman?"

"More so than some others."

"Do you miss the Navy, Mr. Wickliff?"

"I'd have to be a fool to miss the Navy, Miss Davenport."

"Is it very bad there, then?"

"Is it very bad?" Wickliff snorted. "It's not enough food after the purser takes his cut. It's ten lashes if you're late to watch. Aye, it's not pleasant. In a lot of ways I'm better off now."

"But not in every way."

Wickliff said nothing for a while. "No, not in every way."

"In the Navy, you can anticipate a pension. Here..." She trailed off, fingering a loose lock of her dark brown hair.

Wickliff finished the sentence. "Nothing but a rope." Then he grinned morbidly and performed half a jig step. "But we're free of tyranny, at least! So says the captain, and his word is law. And a rope's a sight better than what you can anticipate, Miss Davenport."

"Why? What awaits me in Havana?" Miranda tried to remain casual, but urgency crept into the question.

"The grandest, finest slave market in the New World, miss. Oh, don't you worry. You'll get to be a plantation mistress yet, what with your fine skin, and your dark eyes—only a planter could afford you."

Revulsion seized her. To adorn the arm of some repugnant Don! "And that's why the captain has preserved me from the depredations of the crew."

"Aye. Unspoiled you'll fetch a higher price."

"I don't—I can't believe you. You deceive me! You slew Nona," Miranda hissed. "Serpent. Villain!"

Wickliff spoke quietly. "Orders are orders, miss. I was gentle as a lamb with her."

Miranda laughed, one harsh bitter laugh. "Gentle as a lamb? When you—what? When you cut her throat, and her blood poured. When you sliced her belly and her entrails tumbled out! When you hacked her skull open!" Miranda collapsed in the lone chair and held her hands palm upward, fingers curled like claws. "What did you do? Tell me what you did!"

Wickliff looked at the plates on the table, at the door to the cabin, at the lamp, at his boots. Finally he said, "The captain's getting a trifle impatient with you, miss. Sulking does you no good with him. I had a job of it convincing him to take you to Havana, and if you make it hard by not eating and not drinking, he may forget about the profit to be had. And you don't want that." After a while he added, "I don't want that." He left Miranda alone with her thoughts.

A shudder traveled the length of her spine, then another, and though she fought them tears leaked out, two by two. A single sob broke from her lips, and she wiped the tears away, sniffing. She would cry no more. She had more important things to do.

That night, when the captain brought her dinner, Miranda smiled blandly for him. She felt the smile might run away from her and widen until it split her head open, but she kept smiling and said "thank you" in a small and timid voice, startling Barclay momentarily. Then he laughed: "There's a good girl!" and stomped out. Miranda ate, swallowing each bite with solemn duty.

Barclay delivered her food again the following morning. He regarded her warily, expecting some new absurdity, and again Miranda smiled and thanked him, and again he laughed. "You'll get on fine here, sweeting."

"Tell me of your ship, captain," she said suddenly. Miranda didn't care a fig about Barclay's ship, but she knew Barclay did.

He coughed and scratched the back of his neck with one filthy hand. "What?"

"If I'm to be your passenger, captain, I want to know about the ship that carries me."

"Ah...very well." He massaged his nut brown scalp while he spoke. "The Ocean's Scourge. She's got forty-eight guns. Three masts, aftermost fore-and-aft rigged. Crew of twenty-nine. Fast! Doesn't draw much, either, so we ply the shoals. Took a Navy sloop once. How we got Wickliff. And a merchantman out of Barbados, with molasses by the ton." As he spoke, Barclay relaxed perceptibly. Soon he was sitting in the little wooden chair and telling Miranda of a raid on Panama, and then he spoke animatedly of outrunning Navy patrols in the Bahamas. He had a natural love of boasting, and Miranda encouraged it with occasional nods and impressed murmurs. Then four bells sounded and Barclay leapt to his feet. "You got me chattering on," he said, and dashed from the cabin. Miranda shook her head after he left, dispelling the memory of the loathsome man. The information she retained.

Wickliff came the next morning. "You occupied the captain for quite a while yesterday," he said.

Miranda demurred. "I remain unspoiled."

Wickliff laughed shortly. "I hardly meant that, miss." He studied her and Miranda could see the thoughts rolling ponderously in his head. "I don't understand, miss, why you'd care to talk to a man like that."

"A man like what? He's your captain, Mr. Wickliff."

"Aye. But he's a terror. He knows it. He wants the world to know it. Be damned if he gives or takes quarter, he says. He wants to shake the skies and boil the seas."

"And what does that mean?"

"It means blood, buckets and barrels of blood. Like your ship. No quarter, excepting you."

"He's treated me kindly."

Wickliff snorted. "Because he thinks he can make a pound or two from you. The instant he thinks otherwise, your life isn't worth a handful of sawdust. He'll kill you for the sport of it. He's mad."

"Mad? Is he truly insane?"

"Aye. He'd strike the sun from the sky if he could. You just haven't seen his madness yet."

"Then why serve him?" Miranda asked breathlessly. From across the cabin, she held her arms out to him in momentary compassion or appeal; then she blushed faintly and withdrew them.

Wickliff stared for a moment before replying. "Not my first choice, miss!"

"Not your choice?"

"I was impressed, Miss Davenport. I was Navy. They take our sloop, and line us up on the deck. Barclay scratches a line with the tip of his cutlass and bellows, 'All free men, cross! All others can perish!' What do I do then? I do what I must to survive. I cross, my captain cursing me for a traitor and a coward—but I'm drawing breath now, at least."

"And the captain?"

"He didn't cross. Barclay cut him down."

"And now you're an enemy of the Crown."

"Aye. To see my wife no more."

"You are married?"

"To a baker's daughter in Bristol. Sweet young thing, a humble lass, not educated and refined like yourself, madam, but goodhearted and kind. She looks—looked after this scoundrel well enough."

"And if you return to her—the rope."

"The rope," Wickliff echoed.

Miranda snapped her fingers as if she had received a brilliant inspiration. "You could obtain the King's Pardon. The governor is quite free with those, I understand. Mr. Fraser—my betrothed—has written to me of such things in the past. All but the worst ruffians can be pardoned for laying down their arms."

"I've heard of that. And there's the rub—'all but the worst'. As long as I sail under Barclay, I have no more hope of the King's Pardon than he."

"As long as you sail under Barclay. I judge that you are intelligent, Wickliff, from conversing with you. I can see that you are strong." Wickliff shrugged modestly. "And you're sane." She crossed the cabin and reached to touch his sleeve, but stopped. Wickliff stiffened. "You're sane," she whispered. "That's more than that animal has. He'll lead you into the jaws of hell, Wickliff. I know you for a good man. You've been so kind to me."

Wickliff shrugged, but Miranda could see her words working on him. "The crew..." he said.

"The crew will follow you. Tell them of the King's Pardon. They have to know that Barclay's mad. They have to fear him. They won't fear you; they'll respect you."

"And how do you know they'll respect me?"

Miranda clutched his sleeve in her delicate fingers. She fingered the rough fabric and stepped closer to him. His sunripe scent filled her nostrils. Miranda examined the dulled brass buttons of the coat, the worn stitching of the collar, and finally, looked Wickliff in the eye. "Because I do," she whispered.

Wickliff turned aside roughly and wrenched the door open. "I have a good many duties other than tending to you," he said as he left.

Miranda waited for Wickliff's return. She examined her little prison for the tenth time, going over every surface and object, searching for something, anything she could use. And, for the tenth time, she found nothing—except a rotted plank on the starboard wall. It ran horizontally, directly under her cot, and so she had missed it on previous inspections. Miranda scratched at it with her fingernails and little flakes of wood tumbled off. She took her tortoiseshell comb, one of the few possessions Barclay had left her, and scraped the wood. She wiggled under the cot and dug at the edge of the plank where it joined the other. The crack between the planks widened; she put her elbow to the rotten plank and it gave a little. She peered through the gap: a long table, two benches, and a large chair at the end, once grandly upholstered, now faded. The officers' mess. That explained the occasional laughter from next door. At the far end, light streamed through a pair of large windows at the very stern of the ship. She craned her neck and saw the rolling ocean beyond—vast freedom, just feet away! Footsteps echoed in the passage and she scrambled from beneath the cot. She swept the crumbs of wood away with her foot and rearranged her disheveled hair as well as possible.

Wickliff entered. "I departed in a temper," he said. "I apologize, Miss Davenport."

"No apology required," Miranda said. "Have you essayed the crew?"

Wickliff's red face darkened for a moment. "Some," he said. "The second mate, Jenkins, might prove agreeable. He's a Navy man, like me, and new, at that. Picked him in a public house in Tortuga six months ago, and he's still right sore about it.

"The first mate, Trent, may not be game. He's been with the captain a lot longer, and I think he came off a plantation—that maybe he escaped from bondage. So he's got nothing to go back to. But he's a powerful dog, quick as can be with a blade. He and the captain together—well, I couldn't stand before them."

"Then you won't," Miranda said. "See if Trent can be turned. If not—do what is necessary."

Wickliff furrowed his brow. "You don't mean murder, miss?" Miranda said nothing. "You do mean murder."

"And? Is it murder to murder a dead man? If Trent will not surrender his captain and seek the King's Pardon, he is a dead man. You would serve the King's purpose in this, and make possible the deliverance of all your fellow crew—your fellow prisoners." The color drained from Wickliff's face. "What?" Miranda was suddenly angry. "Are you a stranger to slaughter?"

"No...no, not at all, damn me for it!" Wickliff muttered violently. "But to hear such words—from a lady. How coldly you condemn him!"

Miranda lifted her pointed chin in a gesture of rebuke. "And? How they would condemn me! Or you—when they took you, they condemned you to death on the sea. I find it not cold but delicious indeed to turn their cannon upon them."

Wickliff stared, speechless. Miranda's anger grew. "Well? What do you have to say? Speak, if you have a tongue!" Fury overwhelmed her and she slapped at him. Her blow caught him across the face, and he reeled back, startled. "Excuse yourself! Tell me how you could slay my Nona, but not this wretch Trent! By what reasoning do you doff the executioner's hood now, when you wore it so well in the past?" She struck at him again and he raised his hands to defend himself. He advanced on her suddenly, fist shaking, and she drew back with a cry.

"Don't tell me my own mind," he said. "I know what has to be done. Do you think I don't know?" He ended in a shout.

"Shh, shh," she soothed. "I'm sorry, Wickliff, I'm sorry. You know. You're a strong man, more than able." Wickliff turned away, and Miranda wondered if he was ill. Then she saw that he wept, silently, wiping the tears away so she would not see. She put her arms around him from behind and leaned her cheek against his broad back.

"I was gentle as a lamb," he said in a thick voice. "I pinched her nose and mouth shut and sang 'Rock-a-bye' while I laid her down. And it soothed her, just like a wee babe. She drifted off with a smile, miss, I swear to you!"

"Shh, shh," Miranda said. "You did what you had to. You are forgiven. No need, no need."

Soon after Wickliff left, Miranda heard voices in the officers' mess. She slid beneath her cot and peered through the crack. Wickliff and another man, a shorter, older fellow, with a mass of curly grey hair and a missing eye uncovered by a patch or scarf. The void in his skull gaped blackly and seemed to rove over Miranda and her peephole. Wickliff stood before him, his voice strident and quick.

"Just hear me out, Trent," he was saying. "Hear me out. How old are you? How much older do you expect to get on an outlaw's ship? It's no life we live, Trent."

"Watch your words, Wickliff. Treason—"

"Treason? From a man of no country! From a convict—an exile!" Wickliff's voice grew louder, and Miranda saw Trent's hand go to his pocket.

"Do it!" she cried. Wickliff's pistol roared, and Trent fell dead, blood spouting from the wound in his chest.

"Oh, Christ…" Wickliff moaned. He didn't seem to know what to do. Blood flowed from Trent's chest in a widening pool. Wickliff stepped back from the pool.

"Wickliff! Listen to me!" Miranda whispered. He looked wildly about, his eyes searching the wall. "You must hide him! We aren't ready, and if they find the corpse, they will know you for a mutineer! Hide it! Wickliff!"

"Yes," he said. He replaced his pistol in its holster and regarded the body. Then his head jerked to the door—footsteps in the corridor. Someone had surely heard the gunshot.

"Hurry!" Miranda pleaded. Wickliff opened the port window. The salt breeze flowed in and Miranda breathed deeply of her first fresh air in days, mingled with the rusty scent of blood. Wickliff shouldered the burden of flesh and thrust it through the window; Miranda heard the distant splash. Wickliff watched for a moment.

"Sharks have him now," he said. The footsteps—closer, closer. The door to the mess creaked open, and Wickliff, covered in Trent's blood, whirled to face the intruder. Crimson soaked his shirt, his coat, his hands, his hair. Blood stained the floorboards.

"You cut yourself, then?" The voice was unfamiliar. "Or did you do for Trent?"

"Jenkins," Wickliff said, "It's not…it's not…" Miranda winced.

"I think it is, old boy. I think you did for Trent. I saw you call him below, and I thought—now what could he be wanting with old Trent? He's not enjoying his conversation, rosy and pleasant as it may be. Old Wickliff's known not to care for Old Trent. So what's he doing, then? And then I hear a shot."

"All right, then," Wickliff said. "Trent's feeding the sharks. I'll have you know I intend a mutiny. You can stand with me, or I can do for you, too. Stand with me, and the King's Pardon can be ours. Miss Davenport—"

"The harlot what Barclay nabbed?"

Wickliff bristled. "I'll not have her called that. You'll respect the lady."

"Aye." Jenkins moved into view, bowing elaborately as he walked.

"I suppose you'll be the new captain, so I'll respect you true enough." He was gaunt, his face thin and bony.

The sarcasm was lost on Wickliff. "And I'll respect you in turn. But I'll only be captain as long as it takes to reach the nearest British port. Then we surrender ourselves and take the King's Pardon."

Jenkins considered. "The King's Pardon? For us?"

"Miss Davenport says it's possible. Her fiancé is a captain in the Navy. You and I were Navy once, too. We bring them Barclay's head and it's beyond doubt."

"And if you're wrong, we'll swing."

"If I'm wrong, we'll swing sooner or later regardless. You know that's all we can hope for, right? A noose, a drum roll, and a short fall."

Jenkins nodded. "Right. I'm in."

"If you're in, and Trent's gone, the crew will follow. We've only to dispatch Barclay."

"And how do we do that?"

"At supper, during the dog watch. Have your pistols primed and ready. That's when Barclay will miss Trent. After us, only the quartermaster and the cookie'll be present. Can't count on any of them."

"Right you are, captain. I'll be ready."

Jenkins left and Wickliff leaned heavily against the wall. He wiped his brow, then stared at his bloody hand. "Oh, Christ," he said.

"Wickliff! There remains work to do!"

He snapped to attention. "Yes! So close now."

At her direction, Wickliff threw his bloody clothes through the window (Miranda averting her eyes), then fetched a change of clothes and a bag of sawdust. He soaked up the blood, scraped up the sodden dust, and disposed of that as well, leaving a dark stain on the floorboards. "Fetch a rug!" she ordered, and he returned with a moth-eaten scrap of carpet. It hid the stain admirably. "Now—until tonight!" she whispered. "And freedom!"

"And freedom," he echoed, not sounding convinced.

The minutes crawled unbearably. Miranda sat, in a careful frozen attitude. She could do little else. Everything depended on Wickliff now. She listened to the heave and sigh of the ocean. She trusted completely in her success. Never once did it occur to her to pray.

The door clattered open and shattered Miranda's trance. Barclay stood in the doorway, staggering a little. Miranda smelled rum as he approached her. That hideous fear reared in her mind and she fought it back. She was golden, she was charmed; things could not go awry when her plan was so close to fruition. Miranda knew for a fact that Barclay couldn't harm her; she would not allow it. She had no idea how she could prevent it, but it simply would not happen. Yet—she backed away as he fumbled across the cabin.

Barclay glared at her and collapsed sideways on the cot. He pulled at the bottle. "Pretty wench," he slurred. "Gad, so pretty." Miranda remained quiet. "Had a pretty wench once. Looked like you. But not so dark. And red hair, not brown. And freckles."

"What happened?"

"What happened?" Barclay laughed joylessly. "She lived in a place called Drogheda. Know you Drogheda?" Miranda shook her head.

"Course not, Gloucester wench. Daughter of a knight, not knowing what lives and dies—what mass of blood and bones you eat and drink and sleep upon."

"Strong talk, from a murderer!" Miranda said. Barclay didn't seem to hear her.

"Of course you wouldn't know Drogheda and my pretty wench. How English steel spilt Irish blood and made an apostate of Joshua Barclay. No country, no king. And you wouldn't know, either, the price of dying—how blood cries for blood and can't ever be sated. Drink, drink, and still thirst. What can you do?" Barclay put the bottle to his lips and tilted it until the bottom stuck in the air. He wiped his mouth with the back of his hand and wagged the bottle between thumb and forefinger, gazing madly at Miranda.

"Whosoever drinketh of me shall never thirst. But the water that I shall give him shall be in him a well of water springing up into everlasting life. Is that so?" Miranda only stared, horror-stricken. Her silence infuriated Barclay. He leapt to his feet and hurled the bottle at her; she ducked and it shattered on the bulkhead. His voice filled the room. "Drink of life and know everlasting life; I drank of death and know everlasting ruin! I can swallow the seven seas and not quench this thirst!"

Barclay fell upon Miranda. "But I can try!" he roared. His huge hands crushed her throat. She struck his boiled-egg skull with her fists and scratched at his eyes; death was at hand, death had her by the throat! Barclay's grin grew wide in her vision, vast, two feet, three feet across, filling her mind and obliterating all else. Only the grin—and death.

"God, Bridget," he moaned.

Suddenly she choked and spat on the floor of the cabin and he was gone, his lunatic assault broken off as quickly as it began. Miranda limped to the door and slammed it. She leaned against it, trembling; tears welled up and threatened to burst forth, but she would not let them. She collapsed against the door and shook with tearless sobs.

At length Miranda recovered. Her head stopped spinning and the pain dulled to a slow fire in her throat. She drew breath only with great agony, but still—she drew breath.

Supper could not come soon enough, and then it came too soon. Miranda went to her vantage point under the cot and watched as Wickliff and Jenkins entered. They kept their hands in their pockets and avoiding looking at each other. Wickliff's eyes darted to Miranda's peephole from time to time. Soon a short, round man—the quartermaster—joined them, and the cookie brought the plates and dishes. Neither Wickliff nor Jenkins touched the food, and the quartermaster, after a moment's befuddlement, helped himself.

"We may have to seek him out," Wickliff whispered.

"Aye, you may, or he'll miss his supper, and we'll all hear it then," said the quartermaster as he scooped potatoes from a steaming dish.

"You may not. He may come to you," said Barclay. Miranda craned her neck, but could not see the entrance to the mess. Barclay moved into the room, still quite drunk. He dropped into his big chair at the head of the table. "I see Trent has still not shown his face."

"He must be quite ill," Wickliff said. Miranda could see his hands shaking as he set down his fork with great concentration.

"He'd have to be dead in his grave to miss supper, if I know him!" said Barclay. "What think you, Wickliff? Is he dead in his grave?"

"Now!" Jenkins shouted. Three pistols fired and filled the mess with white smoke. The quartermaster screamed shrilly and Jenkins shouted, "I'm killed, Wickliff!" and there was a great crash of tin and wood as someone capsized the table. Through the thinning smoke Miranda saw Barclay and Wickliff locked in struggle, Barclay with a rusted dirk poised at Wickliff's cheek and Wickliff straining against the thrusting arm with all his might; Jenkins lay dying, eyes rolling heavenward. Dark blood pulsed from a puckered hole in his abdomen and his fingers worried at the wound. The quartermaster had vanished.

Wickliff deflected Barclay's thrust and the knife sank into the wood beside Wickliff's ear. Barclay drove his knee into Wickliff's stomach and Wickliff doubled over, empty of breath. Barclay rammed Wickliff's head into the sideways table and bloodied table and head alike. He dropped the swooning Wickliff.

The smoke reached Miranda and tickled her throat. She coughed, just a small cough, but Barclay heard it and his eyes darted to her peephole. "You," he said, and a pistol cracked and Barclay tumbled to the floor, his head burst by the ball. Wickliff slumped behind him, blood running from a diagonal gash on his forehead. The pistol dangled from his fingers and fell with a clatter.

"Wickliff! Mr. Wickliff, wake up!" Miranda pounded on the wall. "Wake up! Wake up! You've done it! The captain is slain, Wickliff! Wake up!"

Footsteps pounded down the stairs and the mess flooded with men and their shouts: "He's killed the captain!" "Barclay's dead!" The quartermaster returned and helped Wickliff to his feet.

"Boys," he said, his voice tremulous, "you're free men now, free in deed as well as word. An end to slavery to a madman. I've secured a King's Pardon for those who want it. All others will be set ashore with their portion to seek what fortune they may. What say you, boys?" A thunderous cheer went up from the sailors. Miranda stared, fascinated, at Barclay's corpse. The monster who ripped her from her world— slain. Yet relief did not come to her. Blood cried for blood, and would not be sated.

The Scourge raised a white flag and sailed for Kingston with Barclay's head swinging from the bowsprit. Wickliff unlocked Miranda's door and escorted her to the deck, where she blinked in the bright sunlight. She walked the deck, enjoying the fresh air and unbroken view, and Wickliff was always at her arm, glaring at the sailors who dared leer at her. She paid them no mind; Barclay was dead, dead, and she would be free!

The venomous weed persisted in her mind.

Two days later they spotted a sail. "Navy," Wickliff said, and handed her the spyglass. "Ship of the line."

"HMS Valor," Miranda read. Her heart leapt—Samuel's ship! "Bear for it, captain," she said. "They will escort us to port."

Wickliff looked from the white flag to the Valor and back to Miranda. He chewed his lip. "Forgive me, miss, for my reservations," he said, "but they are a warship, and we are—were brigands."

"Trust me," Miranda said. She took his big red hand in her small white one and squeezed it. "I trusted you to care for me, and you did. Now let me care for you." Miranda smiled without difficulty.

Wickliff exhaled. "Very well, miss. Full sail, boys—hard about!" The barque swept over the waves. Through the spyglass, Miranda watched as the blue-jacketed sailors of the Valor swarmed over the rigging; the starboard shutters opened and cannons rolled forth. "No worry, lads!" Wickliff shouted to his nervous crew. "Best behavior, boys!"

The Scourge drew near the Valor and an officer came on deck with a speaking-trumpet. His voice drifted across the gap. "Men of the barque: stand down!" Miranda scanned the ship with the spyglass. Marines lined the deck, dozens of muskets trained on the pirates. "By the power of His Royal Majesty, we seize your ship and all her crew. You are hereby prisoners of the Royal Navy. Resist and you will be fired upon." Miranda spied the officer—tall, bushy moustache, long black hair—Samuel!

"Samuel!" She waved her handkerchief. "Samuel!" The Navy officer produced his own spyglass. He lowered it and resumed the speaking-trumpet.

"You will surrender all prisoners immediately! We will send a boat. Do you agree to these terms?"

Wickliff cupped his hands and shouted his reply: "Aye, governor! Just the King's good subjects, returned from truancy!" He laughed in his relief.

A half-dozen sailors lowered a boat and rowed it across. Three of the sailors held muskets, which they kept on the pirates while Miranda descended. Wickliff squeezed her hand. "God grant you deliver us, love," he said, and released her.

The boat returned. The sailors handed her up and Samuel, her betrothed, her beloved, welcomed her. "My love!" He took her hands. "Tell me you have not been mistreated! Have they injured you?"

"Oh, Samuel!" she sobbed, collapsing to his chest. "I cannot tell you the horrors I have endured at the hands of these wicked, cruel men!"

Samuel's lip curled in disgust and rage, and he bellowed his command with all the breath in his lungs: "Fire!"

Twenty-nine cannons boomed and sixty-four muskets cracked. For a frozen instant Miranda saw Wickliff, tiny in the distance, whirl about, face red with shouting, his men dashing to battle stations. Then the sea exploded upward in mighty plumes of water, rending the sails and shredding the rigging, and the Ocean's Scourge, shattered by the bombardment, listed to starboard and sank beneath the waves. Some desperate members of the crew clung to barrels and burning wreckage, and the marines picked them off one by one. Miranda watched a redheaded sailor stroke frantically through the waves; a musket popped on the crow's nest, and the figure disappeared in a cloud of blood. Miranda watched the waves disperse the blood in a wash of red, then pink, then nothing but the clear Caribbean water.

Samuel was embracing her and muttering words of comfort, Miranda realized. "And Nona?" he asked. "Does she—rest in peace?"

"Yes," Miranda said. "I believe she does."

"Oh, I'm so sorry, my love." Samuel held her tight.

They were married two weeks later. Miranda slept late on the day of the ceremony. She slept extremely well. For a bridesmaid she had the governor's charming daughter. The two had become fast friends on her arrival, and under the daughter's care, Miranda recovered quite quickly from her ordeal. In fact, by the time of the wedding (which all agreed was perfectly beautiful), the daughter commented to her father that Miranda bore no ill effects at all. "She is the very portrait of charm and gaiety! Flowers fairly spring in her footsteps!" the daughter said, and the governor nodded assent.

Murder, Magic, and the Macabre

Leading off this edition of M—the horror magazine on the BIG PULP newsstand—are two poems by our second cemetery worker (following former groundskeeper Jason Rider in THE CHILL OF NIGHT). We think you'll enjoy John Davies' "The Annual Scarecrow Festival" and "The Lodger in the Ripper's Room."

But first, take a voyage into fear with Jennifer Povey "Aboard the Lady Maria." Then, witness a "Virgin Sacrifice," in Michael D. Turner's horror/adventure tale, and head to work with "Parker/Jesse" in Jonathan Golden's humerous, yet disturbing, office tale. Find out why Ed Kratz is "Paying For It" and witness the launch of an unlikely, unprecedented artistic career in Philip Roberts' "By Association".

Don't be scared – we're right beside you!

Jennifer Povey is in her mid thirties, and lives in Northern Virginia with her husband. She writes a variety of speculative fiction, whilst following current affairs and occasionally indulging in horse riding and role playing games. She has recent fiction in *Cosmos Online* and *Zombist: Undead Western Tales*.

ABOARD THE LADY MARIA

Ocean spread out as far as any eye could see. Only a strong telescope would have detected the land. It was calm, with not a breath of wind.

The yacht *Lady Maria* rested on the glassy surface. Her anchor had not been lowered, the wind and current not being enough to move her from the spot. On her foredeck lay a very young woman, dressed in a yellow bikini. She lay on her front, the straps of the bikini pulled off of her back to avoid tan lines, her breasts flattened against the deck itself. She seemed to be asleep.

At the wheel, an older man, old enough easily to be that woman's father, although there was no physical resemblance between the two. He had the boat heaved to and was reading a book.

They were, in fact, becalmed. Which in this day and age is no great terror...if all else failed, the *Maria* had an auxiliary, but they were determined not to use it until they had to. She had a radio. The fact that there was no wind was not a threat to life and limb, but rather an excuse to relax.

The young woman finally sat up, her brown aureoles visible for a moment before she re-secured her top. She did not seem to care if anyone saw her, and, for that matter, who would?

There was a third person on the yacht. That third person lay in the cabin, a pimply young man. The misery on his face indicated that severe seasickness had recently been experienced, although now he was stirring, starting to sit up, perhaps emboldened by the lack of motion the boat was currently displaying. He wore only a set of shorts, but the body thus shown had nothing special about it…it was scrawny and pale. He headed back, to the head, emerging a moment later with a befuddled expression before he started to climb up on deck, closer to the wheel than to where the woman now sat, rubbing on more sunscreen in a vain attempt to prevent the cancer she was courting.

"Dude. Where's the…" He trailed off, glancing off the back of the ship. At such an angle, only he could see the other boat coming towards them. "Watch out!"

The man at the wheel, who's name was Paul, turned…and then he kicked the auxiliary into action. Determined not to use it as he was, the other craft…somewhat larger…was coming in at speed, and coming right towards them.

The *Maria* leapt into motion, her narrow hull cutting through the waves.

"That's one lumbering whale of a boat. Who's not looking where he's going." Paul lifted his voice. "Ahoy!"

No response from the boat. It seemed to be ignoring them, but it, at least, kept on sailing past.

"I'm going to report him to the Coast Guard."

"Paul…"

"What is it, David?"

"Did you hear its engines?"

"No…" Paul trailed off, frowning after the boat. It had no sails and in any case there was no wind.

Then it was suddenly turning, within its own length. The *Maria* heeled away.

"It's a Dutchman."

The woman, moving into the wheelhouse, had turned pale under her tan. "Are they trying to run us down?"

"Yes," Paul said, shortly. "Hold on." He put on all speed, wishing for a wind. Any wind, even the breath of a wind. The *Maria* was far faster under sail than she ever could be on the auxiliary, and there were tricks he could do that he could not do with an outboard.

It missed them again, but so close they could feel the wind from its passing. Cold and chill it was, but it touched the yacht's sails not at all. It was as if it only had the reality it chose to have, here on the blue ocean.

The skies remained blue, the sun still beat down, as the boat chased the *Lady Maria*.

"We're all dead," David said, over and over again. "We're going to die, going to die, going to…"

The girl slapped him, hard, the red imprint of her hand on his cheek. "Stop that. We'll definitely die if you…"

The yacht heeled again, and David almost went overboard. "Maybe we should jump."

Paul was focusing on the wheel. "We're too far from shore. Who would pick us up? Them?"

The boat bore down on them, and then it struck…it struck aft, knocking the *Maria* sideways through the water. The three were flung into the ocean. The water was cool, chill after the heat of the sun, but not cold. The woman, not wearing a life jacket, flailed before she tread water. Paul had found his own water legs faster. He spun in the water. "Dammit."

David…there was no sign of, for he had been swept under the boat, down into the dark water, from which he would not rise until doomsday, should such an event occur.

The stream of curses that came from Paul were no more productive than David's earlier hysterics. As the boat turned again, the woman, Helen, treated him in the same way.

"Which direction is shore?"

"It'll follow us."

Helen shook her head. "You go." She had found something within herself most people possess to some degree, but few ever really learn to use. Courage.

Instead of swimming away from the boat, she swam towards it.

"Helen!" Paul screamed, not wanting to see the young woman pulled under. Or, worse, chewed up and spat out by it.

"Go!" It was still silent, it made no sound this boat, it was nothing but a shadow, as she got closer.

As she reached for the side of it, as she lunged for the ladder that so conveniently fell down the side, a chill ran through her. Her blood turned into ice, and she knew, knew with everything that was in her that if she did this she would never return to the world of the living.

What was it the Dutchman sought? A beautiful woman. Paul had said 'a Dutchman', though. A ghost ship, and...it was about to kill Paul.

That carried her up and onto the deck and into the wheelhouse. Her hands on the wheel, and she tried to turn it. Tried to. All of her strength, for a moment, could not budge it.

"You have me. You don't need him as well," she screamed to the air, to nothing, and it spun in her hands, swerving the boat away.

"I love you, Paul," she called, and then she looked again. It was solid to her now, the boat, the reality around it flowing away, becoming mist.

"Show yourself, Captain."

But there was no voice, and in truth, there was nobody on board. It was not a man who sought a beautiful women.

It was simply a boat, that sought a pilot. A boat from which Helen would never again step ashore...but which would claim no more victims, for she had done what she had done out of love, not a desire for revenge.

Yet, when the sea drew calm again, the boat could be seen once more, forming out of the mist. For just as the Dutchman could be freed by the love of a true woman...so could she be freed, by the love of a good man.

What of her Paul?

That was the real tragedy. He never loved her.

Michael D. Turner is a writer from Colorado Springs, Colorado. His writing has appeared multiple times in **Big Pulp**, and in *Aberrant Dreams, AlienSkin, Between Kisses, Flashing Swords, Every Day Fiction,* and *Tales of the Talisman.*

VIRGIN SACRIFICE

Flesh-eating zombies in Pomona, of all places. I don't mind regular zombies—not that you'll ever see many these days—they're strong but slow and the zombie-master's usually close by. Drop him and they all fall over dead. As opposed to standing around dead. Flesh eaters are another matter. They get everywhere, you're never sure exactly what's animating them, and it takes forever to ferret them all out.

Sometimes I wish George Romero had never made that movie.

At least we got the jump on them this time. It still took a dozen of us all weekend, but Pomona, and the rest of Southern California, was safe again tonight. Monster Fighters of America had things well in hand.

It's a dorky name, I know. I've been an active MFA member since high school. I guess that's when most of us join. It was kind of like a TV show, except instead of a bunch of brain-trust geeks and rich soc-types in designer clothes hanging in the library we were a bunch of stoners, rockers and car-geeks who hung out in auto-shop.

There could have been another group in the library, I guess. I wouldn't know, I never spent much time there.

Other than that, and the weapons—I mean, crossbows? Come on. Otherwise it was pretty much the same, a bunch of kids who went out and fought monsters nobody believes in. Most of the old gang drifted after graduation, but the bug bit me harder, I guess. I've been at it ever since.

I was looking forward to a shower and a long snooze when, ten minutes from home, my phone rang. I screwed the Bluetooth into my ear and answered. It was Gene, MFA's dispatcher for my area.

"Hey, kid. I got something for you."

"Gene, I haven't got home from the last one. I'm low on supplies, sleep and—"

"You're closer than anyone else by more than an hour. Relax, its just an observe and report. It won't take long and it's probably nothing. Reports of some sort of cult activity up in the hills, I've got an address. You still full up on recon gear?"

It wasn't like hunting zombies had used up the batteries in my night vision gear. "Yeah, I'm full up on recon gear, such as it is. I'm damn near out of standard ammunition and I haven't eaten since Friday, but I have my recon gear. Where is it?"

The address was close, at least on a Sunday night. Monday morning rush would be a different story, but that was at least eight hours away. Twenty minutes and I was pulling over to the side of the road in roughly the right neighborhood. Loading the zip full of topomaps for this area into my lap-top, I started planning my approach.

It looked like I could get closest working up a ravine running behind the strip of multimillion dollar homes that clung to the mesa's edge. You could almost assume any cult dabbling in the dark arts would be operating out of a big place with no close neighbors and this one had chosen an ideal place. Big house on a large lot well up on the mesa so it mostly looked down the ravine at the neighbors' backyards, rather than the other way round. I drove to where I could get into the canyon and got my gear out of the trunk.

Monster Fighters provided their own gear. We get together and swap some, and send out e-mail alerts on deals we run across, but mostly it comes out of our own pockets. There's one guy down in Burbank who has the whole James Bond/CIA covert ops set up—state-of-the-art night vision, boom mikes, infra-red cameras—all packed into the back of a hundred grand worth of Mercedes. He's a money-guy in Hollywood, arranging financing for movies and shit. Rolling in dough.

I work at a truck-stop as a diesel mechanic. I'm doing good to have a second-generation night vision monocle and a real classy pair of high-powered, low-light field glasses with an electric camera built in. Which I swapped some engine work on that guy's Mercedes for. Throw in a set of black mechanic's overalls and my web-harness and that's my recon gear.

After spending a minute considering my shotgun—too bulky for the job and I only had a partial box of ammo left after Pomona—I loaded up with my shock-baton and USP-45. They would have to do, and I still had two extra magazines for the pistol.

An arsenal wasn't really required for an O&R anyway. I was just twitchy after a weekend of zombie-slaughter. The first time I'd done an O&R in these hills, right after graduation, the 'cult activities' had turned out to be a professional porno-company making a movie in someone's backyard pool. The memory made me smile—I still had a few of the pictures I took. I even tracked down a copy of the movie, later.

Of course, the second time I'd come out here…

The house had a high wall around the back, stuccoed white. The place would be imposing in my neighborhood; it was bigger than the rec-center at my trailer park. Here it was just another house on the lane, a little larger than most. With the house set-up at the front of the lot and the back stepped down into the canyon behind it, the house wasn't likely to go mud-surfing down the canyon—as so many places do up here—though the pool-area might, someday. The layout meant you could just get a peek at the back from behind the up-mesa neighbor's place, though not from that neighbor's house itself.

I checked the ravine with my night-vision gear but didn't see anything resembling a sentry. That was a good thing in that I wasn't likely to get caught, but anyone up to real evil mojo activity would probably post some kind of guard, so the whole thing was probably going to be a wash. Of course, that'd be a good thing as well, so I huffed my way up the canyon to take a peek.

Before I'd gotten anywhere near the top I started to have suspicions of my own. The back of the house was reflecting an eerie glow, which isn't that unusual when you filter light through a swimming pool, but this glow was raising the hackles on the back of my neck. I was too far away, and too far below, to get much sound from the target but there was sound, that much I could tell.

I got up to the top of the incline, more of a climb than a hike, and crouched behind the neighbor's wall to get my wind back. There was sound, I could hear it even over my puffing—a sort of muffled bass chanting that set my spine on edge. I leaned around a corner and looked in. The light was low enough and the angle bad enough that I couldn't make out much by eye. That was why I'd lugged my field-glasses along. Sixty-X light gathering binoculars brought in more detail than I really needed.

It was an orgy alright. Not a bunch-of-high-school-kids-out-skinny-dipping-who-got-carried-away orgy or even a porno company letting off steam orgy. Porno people are mostly in shape, the girls anyway. Body-waxing, silicone implants and all that. This was more like a bunch of middle aged swingers gone horribly, horribly wrong. They were doing things in the writhing poolside pile that no sane human being could find pleasurable.

Look, I grew up in California, and like any healthy wide-band connected young man more often between girlfriends than not, I've surfed through a lot of porn-sites. I've seen a lot of sick, disgusting shit people get off on, but very little of it involved live fish, octopi and blood. In fact the blood alone set this apart—no one in these days of condoms in elementary schools engages in unbridled skin-breaking activities for recreation.

I took pictures. Once I got past the spectacle of the fish- and octopi-assisted orgy I got a better feel for the layout. The people were all on one side of the pool in a wide patio area, about forty of them. The pool itself was large and rectangular—maybe fifty feet by twenty. I couldn't see where the light was coming from, other than somewhere in the water. The water was scummy green. The far side of the pool was obscured by a massive form of some sort—an idol of their fish-god, I supposed. From the back, in the dark, it didn't look like much.

I switched to the IR monocle. The poolside pile stood out clear, no other people that I could see, none beyond the pool, none patrolling beyond the wall or on the canyon slope. This was real cult activity, so I turned on my cell phone to call in for back up.

No signal.

As much as I'd like to curse my service provider, the signal might have been blocked by the mystic ceremony. Maybe. I've heard about it happening, in bull-sessions after a mission. It didn't matter why. I could either press on alone or go back down the ravine until I got a signal. It was seventy feet down and another sixty or so back up to the back wall of the place. I had no actual supernatural manifestation to deal with, the mission was still observe and report. I decided to get closer.

Scrambling around a scrub-filled ravine is a romp for a twenty-year-old. I know, it's how I spent my days when I was a twenty-year-old. A dozen years later and on the tail end of a long, hard weekend, it felt more like a day trip on the Bataan death march, but I got up to the wall behind the place without breaking anything, or making enough noise to get noticed.

Up close brought details I could have done without. The patio area was set off from the house by a wall of screens painted garishly, as if by children. Disturbed children, with an unwholesome fascination with sea-life. The chanting came from men with painted faces. They were seated right down with the orgy but took no part in the orgy, instead controlling its tempo with the rhythm of their chant.

The festivities had stepped up in tempo while I repositioned myself, taking on a frantic air. The light pulsed in time with the chanting, and the scum on the top of the water stirred. I started working around the wall, trying to get a view of the idol. That would give me a better idea of what I was dealing with.

The wall wasn't uniform in height, at least not on this side, but the ground rose up nearer the house. That put me closer to the ceremony than I liked, almost too close for the binoculars to focus for my camera but I made the move.

The idol was hideous, but I've seen worse. Fins, scales and tentacles over a form only vaguely man-like, carved as if seated on the edge of the pool, its lower half obscured by the scummy water. It's back sported two sets of overlapping, bat-like wings that had obscured the rest of it from behind. The image sent alarm bells chiming in my hind-brain.

Images from the MFA's bulletin—I downloaded the PDF every quarter—I tried to recall everything I'd ever read about dark rituals, diabolic summoning, I couldn't put a name to the idol but I knew it was bad news, and the ceremony itself...this wasn't some ongoing, weekly fish orgy. This was the cumulative ritual of a major working.

Which meant I was going to have to try to disrupt it.

One of the orgists wormed her way out of the pile and stood on the edge of the pool. My field glasses brought her into focus in time for a picture—she looked seventy but was probably a hard-used fifty, her body awash with fish-slime, blood and other bodily fluids, her eyes rolled back in ritual-induced madness—then she stepped into the water and slid under the slime with hardly a splash.

She never came up, but the water started to boil with motion. From behind the screen there was motion, two of the cultists were pushing a large object across the concrete to the edge of the pool. It was an anchor—not a boat anchor but a large ship's anchor, four or five feet long and maybe a couple of hundred pounds.

They brought it right to the edge of the pool—the surface of which trembled with movement below the scum, now. The cultists withdrew, the orgy spread out into a semi-circle facing the pool. The chanting increased in both tempo and volume. I put aside my field glasses and rolled over the wall.

I landed behind a low bush of some sort, unseen or at least unremarked on. I drew my pistol. I had ten rounds in the magazine, two more magazines on my hip—but how to use them to stop this and, hopefully, cover my escape?

The huskies who'd dragged in the anchor returned. This time they had a girl between them. She was woman-sized, with a woman's shape, but she hadn't had it long. She was naked and scared, they had to drag her, stiff legged, to the anchor. She wasn't resisting so much as she was just paralyzed. Perfect skin, no droop in her full breasts—if she was in high school she was a freshman, probably a virgin. A virgin sacrifice.

They stood her astride the anchor's shaft and began fixing her hands to the cross-piece with cable ties, and I got up and moved. I reached the far corner of the pool area, next to the idol and across the roiling, scummy water from the cultists.

I'd drop the huskies when they went to push her into the water, and then unload into the crowd. I wished I'd brought a grenade, I wished I'd brought a tac-team. She was just a kid, California gorgeous with white-blonde hair and coppery skin showing white with tan-lines—junior high jail bait. The girl I'd wished I was dating in eighth grade.

The huskies drew the ties tight and faded back into the crowd. Maybe they weren't going to push her in after all...

Tentacles slid up out of the pool, purple shafts with yellow suckers like a Harryhousen movie on acid. Trailing scum over the pool's edge, uncurling in a graceful semi-circle that mirrored the cultist's perches. They weren't going to push her in...

The gun in my hand barked twice. From sixty feet away a two-hundred-forty grain copper-jacketed slug intersected the tan line that bisected her cleavage, another found her mouth open in its silent scream, bypassing her pink tongue and perfect pearly teeth to spray her brains across the gibbering filth that ringed the obscene tableau.

Instead of an unblemished virgin sacrifice, their God would eat a hundred pounds of dead flesh. I sprinted for the back wall, certain the thing in the pool would not appreciate the meal. I'd disrupted the ceremony.

Belly-flopping across the top of the wall, I tumbled over it and down the nearly vertical slope of the ravine. Behind me voices screamed. I lost my gun on the first roll, and then my arm broke. White noise drowned out the screams, and the sky lit green.

Two-hundred fifty—maybe three hundred feet before the ravine slope leveled from the steep climb of fill below the houses to the normal, Manzanita covered ancient run-off cut. My neck should have broke a dozen times, my ribs practically did by the time I came to a stop in the middle of a bush. My monoscope and my pistol somewhere on the slope above, my field glasses smashed as flat as I was.

I saw the house go. The whole place, house, wall, idol and cultists as well as six feet of California hardpan, into what was described by the TV news that evening as a "freak sink-hole". A sink-hole to the nether reaches of hell, and good riddance to bad rubbish.

Gene's follow-up team found me, got me to a hospital. They even got my car and most of my gear out, nothing left to connect me to the place at all. I have medical coverage through work, and a good thing, too. I was in the hospital for three days and off work for two months. Hard to turn a wrench with busted ribs.

Story is I got clipped while standing by the roadside, a hit and run. The MFA had a fund-raiser to replace my gear—they recovered the pictures from the remains of my field glasses, and they found my pistol. Not that I'll ever use that gun again. I'll probably trade it for another.

Nightmares are par for the course for a Monster Fighter. I never see the tentacles, or that awful idol. Just a flash of white-blonde hair, a white–and-copper tan line. She's probably on a milk carton somewhere; I could find her on the internet. They have databases for missing children; I could put a name to her.

Instead I'll light a candle Sunday mornings, and pray for understanding, if not forgiveness. I don't take solo O&R's anymore, and never, ever take a job in those hills. Not if I can help it.

Jonathan Golden lives in Boston. His work has previously appeared in *Hulltown 360* and *NiteBlade Fantasy and Horror Magazine*. He has a cat named "The Bandamager."

PARKER/JESSE

Parker slumped into the office, crept past the receptionist that reminded him, for some reason, of Gossamer from those old Bugs Bunny cartoons, and quietly sat down at his desk. The rain had wet his shirt and it stuck uncomfortably to his chest and back. He shook out his hair, spraying a fine mist on his keyboard and monitor. He sneezed.

"Bless you," came a timid voice over the cubicle wall.

"Thanks," he answered.

"You sick?" the timid voice asked again.

"Nah, just allergies," Parker lied.

He turned his computer on and stared at the monitor, waiting for it to come to life. He was motionless for almost a minute before he realized that the monitor hadn't yet been turned on. He reached forw—

"Packer!" A voice boomed from behind him.

Parker jumped. His hand moved forward violently and knocked his monitor, making it teeter on the edge of its base. He immediately launched for it with too much enthusiasm and caught it before it fell. He paused for a moment, hugging the computer screen.

"Heh heh! *Just checking!*" his boss bellowed, putting extra emphasis on "checking." Parker never understood this little catchphrase that he used all the time.

Parker let go of his monitor, sat back in his chair, and took a few moments to calm himself down. After his heart rate returned to normal, he pressed the "ON" button on his monitor, and the screen lit up. He stared blankly at the desktop background, a picture of Mondrian's 1927 *Composition with red, yellow, and blue,* and waited.

"Parker?" It was the timid voice again.

"Mmm?"

"Why do you let him talk to you like that?"

Parker paused, then, "I don't know, Jesse. I couldn't tell you."

There was silence, punctuated almost imperceptibly by the tiny clicking noise that never quite went away. Parker stared at the Mondrian, studying it. He appreciated the crispness of it, the subtle difference between the whites, the slight fade in the yellow, the sharpness of the red. He leaned closer, staring more intently. He could make out the brushstrokes in the black for Christ's sake! He inhaled, convinced that he would be able to smell the stale smoke of Mondrian's cigarette as it hung loosely from his mouth.

"Parker?"

"Yes, Jesse?"

"I could kill him for you, if you wanted?"

"Yes Jesse, I know you could, but I don't think so."

"Well, just let me know, okay?

"Okay, Jesse."

Parker leaned back in his chair and closed his eyes. He tried to imagine what Mondrian looked like. He had seen images of him, but he wanted to know what it was like be near him, in the same room. What were his mannerisms? How did he carry himself? What did his voice sound like? Parker decided that he'd like it if his voice were high pitched and nasal. Not too high pitched, but just enough to cause people to think "Hmm, I didn't imagine his voice to sound like that."

"I was late this morning."

"Is that right?"

"Yeah. I cut my dog open and I had to clean it up, that's why I was late. I snuck right past Jackie. She didn't even see me."

"That's great, Jesse."

Parker opened his internet browser and did a search for "Piet Mondrian." The first link was to Mondrian's Wikipedia page. He clicked it. He had read this article, every word, over 100 times, yet he began to read it again. He went slowly, absorbing every word, every minute fact. He was born Pieter Cornelis Mondriaan on 7 March, 1872, but changed the spelling to "Mondrian" in 1912. He was an important contributor to the De Stijl art movement. He died on 1 February, 1944.

Parker wished that he had been alive back then so he could have met him. He imagined what it would have been like to shake his hand, to look into his eyes. He—

"What did you bring for lunch today?"

"I don't know, um, peanut butter and jelly."

"That's it?"

"And a bag of chips."

"I brought some gazpacho I made this morning. It's in the fridge, cooling down."

"Nice. I don't like gazpacho."

Parker finished the article and closed it. He'd read it again later, he told himself. He took his notebook and a pencil, and, turning to a blank page, began to draw. He drew a square first, then some crisscrossing lines, then started to lightly shade in some of the smaller squares the lines had formed. He worked on this piece for perhaps a minute, then turned to a new page and began another. He completed four in this manner and was about to begin a fifth, but he stopped drawing and put away his notebook. He sat motionless for a few moments, staring at the image on his desktop background. He reopened the internet browser and searched for "Piet Mondrian" again. He clicked on the Wikipedia article and began to read it again, from the beginning.

It's warm and delicious, isn't it? Yes, warm and delicious. Blood is getting everywhere. I'll need to clean this up before I leave. I don't want it seeping in between the floorboards, dripping down through the crevices and leaving a red stain on my neighbors ceiling, although, on second thought, maybe he deserves it, the way he's always complaining that my bass is too loud. He came up—when was it?—two or three days ago and asked, not very politely I remember, for me to turn my FUCKING music down. I looked him dead in the eye, with deserved aplomb, and told him that I wasn't playing any music. He looked like he wanted to punch me. I would have liked that if he did.

Okay, okay, I need a bowl or a pot or something to put all this in. It's too goopey for a bag, although, I do have…nah, it'll have to be a bowl. Here, here's a decent sized one. I should cover it with Saran Wrap or something. It's too warm still! It's fogging up the Saran Wrap and making it bulge. I should poke holes in it.

I have my warm gazpacho, my briefcase, my bag of potato chips, my coat hanger, and my pens. I'm ready for work. But, I forgot about that damn receptionist! I have to walk right past her! She's going to know I was late and she'll tell Mr. Doyle, and he'll call me in his office and rip me a new asshole. Mr. Doyle is such a dick. He uses his speakerphone all the time and forgets people's names. I think he called me Jerry for the first year I was with the company. I hope today's the day I have an excuse to ram my coathanger down his dickhole and twist it around. I hope.

Luckily—luckily!—I'm able to sneak past that she-beast of a receptionist. My friend Parker said she reminded him of Gossamer from those old Bugs Bunny cartoons, the guy that's all red hair but he has two eyes and two white sneakers. Actually, I'm assuming it's a guy, there's really no telling what Gossamer is. That's an odd situation, not being able to tell someone's sex. I can't imagine that ever happening to me.

I can hear Parker getting in. He's my best friend in the office. I wonder if he likes gazpacho. I'd share it with him if he wanted. I might not tell him that it's my dog, but he's smart, I'm sure he could figure it out if I drop enough hints. He just sneezed. He's so cute when he sneezes. He reminds me of a little dog. He's such a big guy and he sneezes like a little girl, it's funny.

"Bless you," I tell him.

He says, "Thanks."

I read somewhere that people get colds more in the winter not because it's cold, but because in the winter people are inside more often, in closer quarters with each other.

"You sick?" I ask him. I'm polite to Parker, but for some reason I think he doesn't like me very much. I have a feeling that our best-friendship is one-sided.

He tells me, "Nah, just allergies."

He still sounds sick, but no matter. Parker doesn't seem like a liar to me, a little strange perhaps, but not a liar. He has some weird obsession with this painter from the '50s. Pete something. I don't know, I don't really get it, all the paintings he's shown me are just red and yellow squares. It seems foolish.

Shit, I can hear Mr. Doyle coming. He rumbles when he walks. It's like when you're listening to a song and the levels have been mixed all wrong, the bass and the treble are too low and the mids are too high. Something's just off about the way he moves.

"PACKER!"

That's him, the dumb shit. He probably scared Parker, too. I don't know why Parker doesn't correct him. I corrected him every time he called me the wrong name and it took him almost two years to finally get it right. Parker doesn't even try. That's something that bothers me about him; Parker, I mean. He's just too apathetic. Someone like Mr. Doyle deserves to, I don't know, have his balls smashed with an apple corer or his ears sliced off, but Parker just lets him walk all over him. One day he's gonna snap. It's not normal for people to act like that.

"Hehe, just *checking!*"

That idiotic line he uses all the time. Checking what? He never has a reason, or even a *thing* to check. He should just do nothing but sit at his huge desk, then on Fridays cash his huge paychecks. God, he makes me sick. My resolve to shove my coathanger down his dickhole strengthens.

"Parker?" I'm always careful when I talk to him. He's fragile, like a flower, or like a—what are those things?—a Jing Vase. It's funny, I think to pronounce it "vaahhz." It gives it an air of sophistication.

"Mmm?" He must be looking at one of his paintings. I think he's sexually attracted to that artist. I don't know why, it's just the way he looks at him. Like he *longs* for him.

"Why do you let him talk to you like that?" I ask him.

"I don't know, Jesse, I couldn't tell you." Parker's really good at deflecting my questions.

He defends Mr. Doyle's arrogance sometimes. I forget when it was, maybe last year sometime, Parker and I were talking about it during lunch. Parker had a peanut butter and jelly sandwich and I had a thermos full of some hobo's vomit that I gotten the night before. I asked, off handedly, if he ever thought about killing Mr. Doyle. He

175

said to me, "I don't know, Jesse, some people are just like that." I couldn't believe it! How could he justify something like that? It was inexcusable. I remember having some bad thoughts about Parker, the only time I ever did. I imagined that he and Mr. Doyle were actually in cahoots, and their sole mission was to fuck with me. That night I bought a cat at a pet store down the street from my house and I fucked it then killed it and ate it, imagining it was Parker.

The next morning, I realized I had been acting silly.

I like being sophisticated. Parker inspired me to get involved in art. One time, when I asked him what was so special about the paintings he looked at all day, he said, "They're simple and they don't change. I need something like that." I was kind of offended, I mean, I'm simple and I don't change. Of all the people I know, I'm probably the most normal. Why didn't Parker think of me like that? I decided to try it out. I went to an art store in the mall that sold replicas of famous paintings, and the kid behind the counter, this pretentious little shit, asked me what I was interested in, so I told him, "I want something simple that doesn't change," and he immediately pointed me to this painting of a kid blowing flames in a backyard while his dad barbeques and his mom and sister are in a pool, naked and smiling. I didn't really get it, but for some reason I wanted this kid to think I "got" it, so I said "It's perfect!" with feigned enthusiasm. I bought it and took it home and hung it over my bed. It's still there, despite almost being torn down numerous times.

I hear Mr. Doyle rumbling again, and my first thought is what I want to do to him. I ask Parker all the time if he wants me to kill him, but he always declines. One day, I'll wear him down, and he and I can go out back by the dumpster and Parker can watch me cut him up. I'll have gazpacho for a week!

"Parker?" I ask.

"Yes, Jesse?"

"I could kill him for you, if you wanted?" Maybe today was the day. I hope.

"Yes, Jesse, I know you could, but I don't think so." Looks like I'll have to try again tomorrow.

Parker doesn't think I'm weird. I know this because he told me.

Some people are taken aback if I tell them how I mutilate animals and eat them, and then they go and have a cheeseburger. If you ask me, they're the strange ones. I just cut out the middle man. And I save money. Sounds sensible. But tell someone you eat dog liver or you like to fuck ferrets, and they look at you like you have ten heads. People are fucked.

But it's the way of the world, I suppose. People would rather live with their heads up their asses, so I only kill animals in my house and I call my food gazpacho.

Parker knows though. He came over my house one time and saw a dead cat in my sink. He didn't mention it, but I know he saw it. And I'm pretty sure when I opened my refrigerator, he peeked and saw the parrots I had put on skewers for dinner that night.

"I was late this morning," I tell him.

"Is that right?" He has that detached tone, like he does when he's looking at his paintings, which is pretty much all the time.

"Yeah. I cut my dog open and I had to clean it up, that's why I was late. I snuck right past Jackie. She didn't even see me."

"That's great, Jesse." He's definitely into one of his paintings. No matter.

It's only 9:30, but I'm already bored. Whenever I get bored, I start to think about lunch. It really is the only high point of my day, and I usually bring my gazpacho. I'm not even really sure what gazpacho is supposed to be really. I think it's tomato soup served cold. If that's all it is, then "gazpacho" is a pretty fancy name. I'd just call it "cold tomato soup," but then, that's why I'm not a famous food critic.

Parker usually brings a peanut butter and jelly sandwich because he's boring. Plus, I think he's a vegetarian.

"What did you bring for lunch today?" I ask him, knowing full well the answer.

"I don't know, um, peanut butter and jelly." Surprise, surprise.

"That's it?" I don't really know why I'm continuing this conversation; we have it everyday.

"And a bag of chips."

"I brought some gazpacho I made this morning. It's in the fridge, cooling down."

"Nice. I don't like gazpacho."

That's probably all the conversation I'll get out of him all day. He's too involved with that artist. I'll just sit and wait until lunch, then sit and wait until I can go home and be with my animals.

Lunch time is almost here. It's going to be cold and delicious, yes, cold and delicious.

Ed Kratz is a career civil servant resuming writing after a long hiatus. He's an affiliate member of the HWA based upon his short story, "Poppa," being published in the Space and Time Anthology, "Bringing Down The Moon" many years ago. He has recently had stories published in OG's *Speculative Fiction* #12. *Every Day Fiction*, and *The Shine Journal.*

PAYING FOR IT

He spots his prey as soon he enters the bar. He stands beside her and she smiles at him. She will soon be another victim of his superior power. After all these years, he is still eager, and he's not sure if his anticipation is due to his hunger or how he's looking forward to the thrill of seeing her trembling before him when she discovers he is a terrifying monster.

It isn't long before she says she wants to leave, and she takes his offered arm. They walk to her house. He knows it is close. He knows she lives alone. He is a skilled stalker, a bright wolf among these inferior sheep.

She pauses at her door. "I don't usually do this," she says.

Of course, she must invite him. He loves that tiny tease, the highly remote possibility that he might fail, when he must once again rely on his finely honed skills.

"I don't usually do this either. What kind of man do you think I am?"

She laughs. His charm has won another one. Still smiling, she says, "Come in."

In a flash, she's lying beneath him on her bed, and he's looking at the white expanse of flesh revealed by her low-cut blouse, especially her neck.

"Eager, aren't you? Well, so am I," she says.

As he leans forward he reveals his fangs.

"You're a vampire! No! Help!" she screams.

He rises as though he'd seen that ancient enemy, Van Helsing. "You call that frightened? Actress? I can see why you're driven to prostitution."

"Wait!" she says, "Let me try again."

"Don't worry. I'm not going to stiff you." He throws the bills on her bed with disdain and starts toward the door.

"Hey! Times change. Just give me a quick bite. I'll give the money back. Your kind is so in now."

"In?" He shakes his head. He never thought he'd live to see a world so twisted that ancient evil was attractive. "In?" he says, continuing out.

"How about I scream? I can scream good. Listen. Help! Help!"

He leaves, her horribly false, so not bone-chilling scream sounding like the grating of fingernails on a blackboard to his acutely sensitive ears.

Philip Roberts lives in Nashua, New Hampshire and holds a degree in Creative Writing with a minor in Film from the University of Kansas. A beginner in the publishing world, he's a member of the Horror Writer's Association, and has had numerous short stories published in a variety of publications, such as the *Beneath the Surface* anthology, *Midnight Echo*, and *The Absent Willow Review*. More information on his works can be found at www.philipmroberts.com.

BY ASSOCIATION

A boy of eighteen once proclaimed to his friends and family that he would one day be a famous artist. A man of thirty-seven opened his eyes to the clouds floating peacefully through a dark blue sky.

He still had in his clenched right hand the neck of an empty bottle marked Bourbon. Ted Moore knew well the pain of bad hangovers. Before he could pull himself up from the ground he heard the humming, along with a person moving about just a few feet away.

A grunt shook from him as he pulled himself up, and put an immediate end to the joyful humming. It took only a few seconds for Ted's vision to clear enough to see the forest filled with colorful green, and the man no more than ten feet away at the edge of the grassy patch, standing near the base of a tree.

But what Ted stared at were the two, five foot tall stakes that had been hammered into the ground, and the barbed wire strung densely up in-between them. In the middle of that barbed wire a body had been hung, the wiring wrapped around it over and over again, holding the arms up, the legs out, the head tilted back. Even the eyes had been pulled open, tiny needles piercing through the skin to ensure they didn't close. A smile was pulled back on the dead man's face. He wore a necklace of silvery wire, his body nude and muscular and long since dead.

Beside this masterpiece the man watched Ted with a look of shock, his features much different than the beauty of the dead youth. He was certainly nearing forty, dressed in a gray, pin stripe suit unbecoming of the surroundings he stood in, the glasses atop his nose thin wires holding equally thin glass.

Ted couldn't honestly say what he saw in the man's expression, and Ted found himself staring more at the strung-up boy than the man who had done the work. He was only vaguely aware of the man's arm rising up to bring the hammer above his head, or the step the man took towards Ted.

"It's beautiful," Ted finally whispered.

The arm dropped down. Ted's eyes shifted back to the artist, and the smile spread across his face.

◊◊◊◊◊

"You can imagine my surprise," Russell laughed as he held out the cup of coffee to Ted, "seeing a man actually rise up from the grass. Who would've thought someone would actually be sleeping out there?"

"I end up all sorts of odd places after the long ones," Ted said, took his coffee. They sat in Russell's meticulously kept office. On the walls he saw replicas of most well-known paintings. All of them were upbeat in nature, nothing malevolent or violent in any of the images.

"And you say you're an artist," Russell asked, leaning forward with interest.

"I...I try to be, but I've never really had any success. I can do things, paint things really well, but not my things. I don't think I have anything in my mind *too* paint, it seems like."

"And you truly enjoyed my work?" Russell leaned in even more; his eyes were alit behind his glasses.

"It was amazing." Ted couldn't honestly say why he felt no revulsion for the violence that had created the work, and didn't find a single part of him recoiling in disgust. He meant every word of it. Perhaps the alcohol had dulled his senses too much for him to care anymore, or maybe his string of rejections had removed any sense of empathy from him, not that he'd ever had much to begin with.

"I can't tell you how wonderful it feels to have someone validate my work. I mean, I've seen various articles over my work after people discover them, but they so rarely focus on the artistic side of it, too preoccupied with the death."

"How long have you been doing this?"

"Oh, a few years, but it isn't easy deciding what the next piece will be, and I rarely create more than two larger works a year. These are delicate matters to plan out, after all."

"I'd imagine it would be. Not exactly like buying another canvas at the store."

"Yes, exactly. Buying another canvas. I'll remember that one," Russell said, smiled with a short laugh. "I've taken a liking to you, and would like to help you if I can. A private lesson, perhaps." He tore out a piece of paper and handed it to Ted. "My address."

"I'll be there," Ted answered, and he intended to follow through. For the first time in far too many years Ted felt a sense of purpose flowing through him, and prayed he would finally be able to transfer it into art.

◊ ◊ ◊ ◊ ◊

Ted brought his aging, near dead pick-up truck to a halt in Russell's driveway. The truck didn't look right sitting in the driveway of such a lovely home, the lawn well kept, lush bushes and flowers surrounding the front yard.

Only after Ted got out of his car did he notice that the bushes surrounding Russell's front door were tall enough, and thick enough to obscure any view of the path leading up to the front door, and no one would see if the man dragged something into his home.

Russell opened on the first ring, smiling, motioning for Ted to enter. They proceeded through a nicely decorated home, the carpets white, the furniture deep brown mahogany. Through another door and the lavish surroundings changed into bare, gray bricks and a wooden staircase leading down.

Only briefly, with Russell behind him, and Ted descending down those steps, did Ted question whether or not he was to be the next work of Russell's art, but even then he felt no fear. To be honored by having the privilege of being worked on by someone he had already developed such respect for seemed almost welcoming.

Their journey took them across a cement floor to another room, and then down a much narrower stone hallway ending in the final door, and the small, square room.

In the middle of it, a boy of no more than twenty years old sat tied in a chair, his head slumped, the bloody gash that had rendered him unconscious visible on the back of his head full of blond hair.

Ted stopped before him, while Russell moved around to the back of the chair and placed a hand on the unconscious boy's shoulder.

"Why did you like my work?" Russell asked. "Or better put, why were you not revolted by the brutality of a life strung up in such a horrific fashion?"

"I couldn't tell you exactly what it is that appealed to me so much, but seeing what you had created, the violence that had led to it didn't seem to be particularly relevant. All I could see was the effort and emotions you had placed into the finished product."

A quick jerk brought the boy's head back to reveal his throat, and as Ted watched Russell ran the blade swiftly across it, spraying a fountain of blood down the boy's exposed chest. And within those last few seconds the boy's eyes fluttered open, his mouth grimacing, a low, painful moan echoing through him. But almost as soon as the eyes had managed to open they were closing again.

Ted found his gaze shifting away from the grisly scene, found his stomach turning in on itself, his mouth suddenly frowning.

Russell let the head fall back down until the boy's chin was against his bloody chest. The breathing had stopped. When Ted looked back up he could see Russell staring at him, and understood the man had been staring at him the whole time.

"The death itself disturbs you?" he asked.

"I guess. It...it isn't art yet. I'm not detached enough from the act itself."

"But what about now? Seeing this boy sitting before you, are you seeing a corpse, or a blank canvas waiting for your touch?"

Having those words spoken to him, Ted did see the blank canvas opening up, the possibilities, so endless it seemed, just waiting to be realized. Russell stepped away from the boy's corpse towards a cabinet in the back corner. He opened the metal doors to reveal the blades of all shapes and sizes hanging there, waiting to be used, and Ted's gaze shifted back to the boy.

It was time for his first lesson to begin.

◊◊◊◊◊

But the lesson proved lacking. As soon as it came time to start, all of those doors began slamming shut. Ted could almost see them in his mind, one after another, the boom so loud Ted couldn't concentrate on anything.

Three hours had passed away at some point. The mutilated corpse Ted found himself standing in front of had no artistic merit within it. He saw only a stomach torn open, the organs pulled loose, like an animal had ravaged the corpse at some point.

From somewhere an image came to him, perhaps a photo he had seen of the very same, a corpse after a pack of wolves had had their way with it. This wasn't unique, nor was it his own. All he had down was what he always did: recreated someone else's art.

Ted stared down at himself, his clothing splattered in red, small chunks of severed flesh sticking to him. When the door opened behind him he glanced back at Russell walking in.

Russell took in the monstrosity Ted had created, a young boy's face torn to bloody shreds, his muscles covered in congealed blood visible through the ragged remains of his skin, his eyes punctured into wet sockets.

This boy had not died to become a work of art. Ted had taken who he was and turned him into nothing more than a piece of trash waiting to be thrown away, never to be viewed or cared about by anyone.

Russell said something to him, but Ted couldn't hear the words. The small, cement room with its single bulb hanging from the ceiling was closing in on him, sealing him away from the world of true creativity. He could see empty sockets staring up at him, a ruined mouth frowning, and Ted found the tears begin to pour down his cheeks.

Some part of him registered Russell's soothing tone as he guided Ted away from the meaningless corpse. The dim basement rippled through the streaming tears. Ted had never wanted a drink so badly, the wasted canvases he had left strewn across his floor at home nothing like the overwhelming emotional breakdown he suddenly felt.

And deep within the pain a single impulse pulled at him, one he'd felt before, but never so overpowering.

Ted *had* known something about Russell, about the articles on the murders, and Ted had deep down felt a sense of envy towards whoever the person had been, the same sense of envy he felt every time he walked into a museum and saw what he would never be.

The need to be known, to be famous, was what had driven Ted since the day that eighteen year old boy had first stood before his family and proclaimed his future success.

◊◊◊◊◊

Russell handed Ted a drink in the study, a room quite similar in elegance to the office Ted had seen before. He let the whiskey warm his stomach as he listened to Russell's subdued voice.

"I feel I should apologize. Having found someone to share this craft with...it overwhelmed me. I hadn't considered the prospect that you, well..."

"Would be such a failure?" Ted asked with a cruel smile.

"You're being too harsh. This isn't about whether or not you failed, but whether you were ready for such an advanced step so soon. I must confess, the first time I actually took a life for my art the mere presence of the body sent a charge through me like nothing I had felt before. A part of me had assumed the same would be true for you as well."

"Who was he?" Ted asked. Tears were building in his eyes again. The whiskey's warmth couldn't stop them.

"Please, you're in no position to deal with such information right now," Russell said. "Who the boy was doesn't matter anymore. He's gone and you still have a chance to build upon this experience."

Ted leaned closer to the desk Russell sat behind. "Then you'll continue to teach me?"

Before Russell could even shake his head his eyes gave away his answer. "This isn't like the classes I teach. If you're going to actually end a life for your art you have to be certain that you're prepared to give that person a truly unique, if macabre, work of art. What happened tonight simply can't occur again. You can't use live creatures to train yourself. Your training needs to have already been taken as far as it can go, and only you can figure out what your creative voice should be."

Ted felt the mental snap. Perhaps the alcohol had done it, or perhaps all he had needed to do was see that morbid face he had left down in the basement. "What if I don't have a fucking creative voice?" Ted screamed, face red, eyes livid.

"Then you shouldn't be wasting life on your failed endeavors." Russell's face settled into a light, tense frown. "I'm afraid this is final. I won't reconsider. This doesn't mean you have to give up completely."

Ted stood up from the seat without another word. Russell had nothing else to offer him. Both men knew it.

He felt Russell's gaze follow him out the door, felt Russell's presence behind him up until he stepped out onto the porch, and heard a soft apology before the door clicked shut behind him.

In his hand he stared down at the rectangular piece of plastic with Russell's name and picture in the middle of it. Russell hadn't seen Ted grab it off the desk. Ted slipped the driver's license into his pocket before getting into his car.

◊◊◊◊◊

His only light came from what the moon could provide and the small beam of his flashlight wedged into a tree, illuminating his nude body glistening with sweat. The supplies were simple. Ted had gathered two stakes, which he hammered in the ground. Neither was as large as the ones Russell had hung his last work of art on, and Ted accepted his knees would be on the ground, but that was something he could live with.

The razor wire Ted had purchased was similar, yet uniquely different from the barbed wire Russell had used.

Alone in the dark woods, Ted found himself smiling for the first time since he had stared down at the butchery he had committed. He couldn't recall how many years it had been since the last time he had felt such a strong sense of purpose and commitment.

He strung up the wire, arranging it carefully, his eyes giving him a level of precision he wasn't acquainted with but gladly accepted. The bladed wires lapped over each other again and again, and in the glow of his flashlight Ted could see the true image taking shape, and knew what he would look like when the time finally came to pull himself into the cold metal's embrace.

A light, upbeat tune whistled through him as he lay out the knives he would use. Even though he knew he was merely copying the basic elements that Russell had already established, Ted also knew something only Russell would be able to appreciate: what Ted prepared to do was so much greater than Russell's crowning achievements, because every bit of passion from each cut would be reflected in Ted in a way Russell could never attain.

Ted picked up the first knife, the largest one he had, the paintbrush meant to do the broad strokes, to define the image. The cut was swift and powerful. He felt the force of the blade run through him like a force of nature, felt his entire body alive, joyful, and aware of what he prepared to do.

The blade dug through the flesh, sent an entire strip of wet, bloody skin to the dirt ground. With precision unlike any he had been capable of before he cut through his own body, formed a design with loops of dripping red, dipping here and spiraling there.

He didn't even feel the fatigue he knew was coming over him as more and more of his blood trickled down his body. The large knife stained in red fell into the grass. He grabbed quickly for the next one, forming smaller marks in the skin, adding new depth to the violence.

As the second knife struck the ground and the next one began its work, the notion came over Ted that these markings were like those one would paint on themselves to give celebration to a deity. It felt as if an outside power filled his body, gave him the strength to never falter.

Everything was coming together. Was this the way Russell felt as he made those last incisions? Perhaps something similar, but Russell would never be able to throw himself into his work the way Ted was accomplishing. He would never know the joy Ted felt as he stared at the slick muscles and intricately cut designs in the harsh glow. Russell could only give others the glory of being turned into something so magnificent.

In that way Ted surpassed him, but he felt no hesitation to give Russell the credit he deserved.

Ted dropped the final knife onto the ground. The effort it took to turn off the flashlight and throw it into the woods was almost too much for him. The blood loss made him stagger, nearly fall, as he turned towards the wiring.

But that was fine. Everything had been prepared. Ted opened his left hand for the first time since the cutting began, and let Russell's bloody driver's license fall to the ground.

There was nothing left. Ted felt his eyes close as his body fell forward. The design was perfect. Almost immediately he could feel the wire cut into his raw muscles, dig deeply. All he needed was a simple jerk to properly wedge his arms and legs into the sharp blades, to feel them dig deeply into his throat, two meticulously placed blades cutting into his closed eyelids.

Whether he wanted it or not, Russell was about to become famous. Ted had a feeling people would be talking about the man for years to come, analyzing everything he had done, and marveling at the artistry he had accomplished. And Ted would be the pinnacle of that work, and a secret he knew Russell would keep until the day he died.

All artists eventually died. It wasn't the artists that people cared about, but the art they were capable of creating. Ted found a smile creeping onto his face as the end reached him. He finally understood how creative he had always been.

John Davies is from Liverpool, England and a member of the Poised Pen Writers, a fortnightly poetry/prose workshop. His work has appeared in *Smoke, The Interpreter's House, Fire*, and *Nerve*, amongst other magazines. John is also an apprentice gravedigger at St. James' Cemetery.

THE ANNUAL SCARECROW FESTIVAL

The Annual Scarecrow Festival
was cancelled this year—
in the fields as you enter the village,
in the strawberries,
there is one left over,
like a sign warning last chance for a hundred miles.

Unofficially, they made them anyway,
fleshing cast-offs with fistfuls of straw, stalks
poxing the backs of hands, wrists.
Either gouging out their eyes with peeler, scissor,
or scoring their face on sack-cloth, pillow-case.
Back-boned them on garden rakes, or on rough wood
that fused broom, spade;
belted their waists round avenue trees.

In detached streets
they appeared in net-curtained windows, waving.
Stood in the post office queue and it did not dwindle.
In The Landlord's Daughter, pint pots glooming,
no one serving the no one drinking.
In a stalled tractor, in a quiet lane,
one found slumped over the wheel,
thick of its head torn,
protest of orange pulp on the screen.

In class they sat in rows and stared
at yesterday's blackboard,
oozing through the backs of wooden chairs
made for children. Hay fever came late this year
and Mrs McIver missed her first day—
lying in a sweat in a dream
where their autumn breath filled the room,
sweet and near spoiling,
others crowding the window, looking in.

And in The Wyndham, the amateur dramatics theatre,
the scarecrows took their seats,
rustled their applause
as the stage described the scarecrow players;
the more clamorous hands thinning
from the Circle to the Stalls.
Nothing hit them yet, no smell
of orchards burning, of summer failing,
as tiny flame from the footlights
sniffed out the nearest actors,
the bundles of their ankles,
then fed upward, inside,
in their clothes, moving.

And the fire ran for the grinning rows
like a whisper through string between two tin cans.

Through dark country fields,
passing one left over
like a mast in a storm,
they entered the village and found
cars and houses stalled,

(continued)

no one in the pub or school.

In the cemetery, in the rows,
heads in the mud, heads in a hole,
they splintered the first box and saw,
where the body should have been,
only a broken hat, black slumps of clothes.
Straw.

LODGER IN THE RIPPER'S ROOM

Open his door. The shock the mind lives
and lives in freeze-frame, stop/start, is more
than this long and narrow room can show;
too long and too narrow
to fit your understanding
of the shape of a room.

Church bell comes disfigured through the window—
the rooftops, the other windows. Glass bears
a layer of old words he smeared,
that only when held up to the moon
make themselves known;
are otherwise, as in a lemon juice trick, nowhere.

Room drips with small superstition-
shivered face of a stopped clock
he never replaced.
And here where he tucked in the chair to his desk,
taking care it did not scrape, refilling
the inkwell with enough words to last long letters.

Mirror above the sink hoards the man shaving,
all routine, how he ordered his flesh,
soap as death-mask telling his face.
Razor-blade moves in swipes you do not see
but for the jaw that shows gradually,
like a dawn's winter road clearing of snow.

Under shawl for it's night now,
blue and green bird in a small silver cage;
macaw, he said, from Rio De Janeiro
or Mozambique. Eyes bruised as cobbles
address you only from the feet up.

Hole in the drip of its beak

as if a nail driven through.
Keeping in its feathers,
denying knowledge of its songs from home—
saw his eyes in the dangling glass go black
and a thousand thoughts died; the lamplight flinched,
the room picked up and set down again.

Big Pulp Submission Guidelines

Before submitting, please check for any changes to our guidelines online @ **www.bigpulp.com**

Big Pulp publishes all types of genre fiction including fantasy, mystery, science fiction, horror, romance, as well as western, pirate, super-hero, and just about everything in between. Please read our magazine, read some of our fiction or poetry online, and visit our website for more information on the types of stories we like to see.

- ➢ Big Pulp accepts submissions twice annually in March and September, and we read and respond during April and October.

- ➢ We publish both fiction and poetry. Please see our website for our current needs (length, genre, etc.) as well as payment rates and additional details.

- ➢ During each submission period, please limit your submissions to ONE story or up to THREE poems. Multiple submissions beyond that will not be read.

- ➢ Previously published works are acceptable, provided the author has the rights to reprint the work. However, preference is given to unpublished material. Simultaneous submissions are okay.

- ➢ Submissions must be sent electronically in MS Word or RTF format *as an attachment to your e-mail.* Please format your document as you would if you were sending a hard copy (ie: double-spaced, indented, one paragraph break, etc.). Also, please pick a legible font for your submission. Times New Roman is easy on our eyes, but is not required. DO NOT embed your submissions in the body of your e-mail. These will be rejected without being read.

- ➢ In your subject line, enter your name and the title of your story or poem. Cover letters are not required, but a polite greeting is appreciated.

- ➢ Big Pulp is open to new and previously unpublished authors.

www.ingramcontent.com/pod-product-compliance
Lightning Source LLC
Chambersburg PA
CBHW072111170626
46813CB00004B/1508